His Other Child

By
Dawn Martin

WORDS MATTER
P U B L I S H I N G
OUR WORDS CHANGE THE WORLD

© 2019 by Dawn Martin. All rights reserved.
Words Matter Publishing
P.O. Box 531
Salem, Il 62881
www.wordsmatterpublishing.com

ISBN 13: 978-1-949809-50-3

Library of Congress Catalog Card Number: 2019954629

For all my friends and family who still believed in me when I stopped believing in myself

CHLOE

Chloe sighed deeply. She didn't know how long she had been sitting at her desk, but it must have been a long time because her elbows were beginning to burn as they rested heavily on the hard-wooden surface while she stared wearily at the blank computer screen in front of her. Apart from the low-pitched drone of a vacuum cleaner in the waiting area and the usual chitchat from the cleaners, the surgery was silent, and she treasured these rare moments of peace. The white noise from the vacuum cleaner usually helped her to focus, but today it did nothing to soothe her troubled mind, and she knew she should probably go home.

She glanced at her watch and was alarmed to see it was already 7.30 pm. It was Friday, and her shift had finished two hours ago, but even though the patients were long gone, she always found an excuse not to go home on time. She told Grant it wasn't uncommon for nurses to run late because patients had an annoying habit of being needy, and even though she rarely ran late herself, there was no need for him to know any different. There were always things that needed doing of course like ordering more stock or tidying up the doctor's rooms because she liked to leave every room spick and span ready for her colleagues to start work again on Monday morning. She grabbed her coat and headed for the door but couldn't resist taking one final glance around the room just in case she'd missed something. It was cold outside, and the car windscreen was frozen solid which meant she would have another ten valuable minutes of time to herself to allow it to defrost before driving off. She turned the fan on full and cursed under her breath as a rush of cold air blew at her face causing her eyes to smart. For a brief moment, she felt like she might cry, and she inwardly scolded herself for being so feeble. She vigorously rubbed her cold hands together under the freezing fan in a futile attempt to thaw them out and practised her well-rehearsed excuses out loud until they were pitch perfect to avoid arousing Grant's suspicions. She had done this so many times now she was almost starting to believe them herself, but Grant was gullible, and for that she was grateful. As she grabbed the ice cold steering wheel, her entire body shivered. She had been adamant that she wanted a car with leather seats and a leather steering wheel, but on days like this, she wished she had been able to afford to upgrade to the newer model that came with the luxury of heated seats and a heated front screen. The car was always too hot in the summer and too cold in the winter, but it was still her pride and joy and no one, not even Grant could convince her to trade it in for something more comfortable.

She could feel her phone vibrating in her pocket. It wasn't the first time it had rung, but she was deliberately ignoring it. She always kept her phone on silent mode at work anyway, and that was her excuse for not responding to his calls. She knew he would be angry, and she didn't blame him, but every extra minute alone was precious, and she wasn't ready to face him or the rest of the world just yet.

It was only a ten-minute drive home, but with the poor weather conditions, she reckoned she could get away with stretching it to twenty. Things were difficult at home right now, but she knew he would never forgive himself if she were to rush and have an accident and with a bit of luck by the time she got in that brat of his would be in bed. As she turned into the small cul-de-sac where they lived, she could see the curtains were still open, and the lights from the living room illuminated the outline of her husband pacing anxiously up and down in front of the window holding their small daughter in his arms. She could see the television was on, and as she pulled the car onto the drive, another smaller figure joined him at the window, and she was disappointed to see she was still up. She had promised Grant that she would try to make more of an effort to bond with his daughter, but that promise didn't come with a guarantee of success, and it was at times like this that she wished she had a superpower, so she could fast forward the time to Sunday evening because that was when Crystal went back to her mother.

She met Grant after being introduced by a work colleague who was keen to remove her from the internet dating scene for her own safety. She had pretty much given up on internet dating anyway after three years of disastrous dates involving several run-ins with the police and finally the heartbreak of a lost unrequited love. Grant had come along at a time when she was vulnerable, and although it wasn't love at first sight for either of them, they formed a natural friendship which gradually turned into love. At least she thought it was love, but she wasn't entirely sure. After their first date, she had left it almost two weeks before contacting him again despite constant reminders from the well-meaning work colleague who had introduced them. Eventually, she contacted him because she needed his opinion on a car she wanted to buy, and she knew he shared her love of cars. He loved the shiny, red low-mileage Ford Puma almost as much as she did and even though it was a bit small she couldn't resist buying it, and she was still the proud owner of it now even though with only two doors and a one-year-old daughter at home it was totally impractical. After Phoebe was born Grant nagged her to find something more suitable but she was adamant she could manage, and besides it gave her the perfect excuse not to travel in the same vehicle as that kid of his. She had known about his daughter from the day they met because Grant, who was clearly besotted with the child, hadn't stopped talking about her. She wasn't surprised to learn he had a child, after all, he was in his late forties when they met, but she had expected her to be a bit older like her own children were. As it turned out, Grant had been something of a late starter, but she was thankful there was only the one, and at the time she hadn't anticipated there being any major problems.

At the age of forty-eight, she hadn't expected to become a mother again, but Grant was thrilled at the news and keen to seal their family unit with a gold band and a mutual exchange of wedding vows. Her dreams of a romantic wedding on the Italian coast were replaced by a quickie at the local registry office kitted out like an overdressed Heffalump from the outsize shop a mere four weeks before giving birth to their precious baby daughter. Initially she thought her lethargy, weight gain and scanty periods were part of the menopause, after all, she was knocking on the door of fifty but when her modest breasts grew to an enormous double H and her bra started to resemble a hammock she knew she must either be pregnant or have a grossly underactive thyroid gland, the latter of which was ruled out by a quick blood test.

When Phoebe was born, she was perfect in every way with a mop of fair curly hair, and a delicate slightly turned up nose. People automatically assumed she was her grandmother, but she ignored their remarks because she was proud to be a member of the more experienced geriatric mum brigade, and she was determined that she and Grant would be good parents and always put her first, regardless of any unresolved differences they may have had.

As she put her key in the door, Grant opened it forcefully, and for a moment she was taken aback. She was nearly always late on a Friday night, and he knew the score by now but the sight of Phoebe sobbing uncontrollably holding out her arms for a 'huggle' as she liked to call it was enough to tear at her heartstrings. As she took the sobbing child from her husband's arms she almost tripped over a pile of carelessly placed bags at the bottom of the stairs, and assuming they belonged to Crystal she shot Grant a critical look. Phoebe was fretful and overtired, and Chloe knew she hated going to bed if her mummy wasn't home and although Grant had tried his best to pacify her, she was inconsolable. For a moment, she felt guilty, after all this was preventable, but the sudden appearance of Crystal standing at the doorway grinning like a possessed cat changed her mood in an instant. Grant saw the hatred in his wife's eyes and told Crystal to go upstairs and get ready for bed, and for once she did as she was told without kicking up too much of a fuss. As she climbed the stairs, she didn't bother looking back, after all, Chloe rarely spoke to her anymore, not even on good days and by the looks of it, today hadn't been a good day for her. She was disappointed, but that was nothing new because weekends with her dad were not the same now that he was with Chloe, but she remained hopeful because tomorrow was another day, and she was excited because her daddy had told her they were going on an adventure together.

CRYSTAL

Crystal was only four years old when her dad first met Chloe, but she didn't get to meet her until she was six and the day hadn't gone to plan. Her parents had divorced soon after she was born, so she was too young to remember them ever being together, and she was used to the perks of having a weekend dad all to herself. Before Chloe came into his life, she looked forward to spending weekends with him because he always took her to places where they could do fun things together. Her mother always made a point of reminding him that the time they spent together should be quality time and as a result, he did spoil her a little bit, but he said it was okay because that's what daddies do. When Chloe came on the scene, things seemed to change, and whenever they argued, which seemed to be whenever she was around, Chloe referred to her as a spoiled brat. Initially, she only said it when she thought she was out of earshot, but now she said it all the time, and it hurt knowing just how much her stepmother hated her. At first, she had pretended not to care, but she quickly learned to manipulate the situation, and she knew that if she cried her daddy would leap straight to her defence and any attention from him was better than no attention at all, and better still it caused conflict between him and Chloe. Deep down though she was desperately unhappy, she was still only eight years old, and according to her grandfather, she was getting to that awkward age where she needed an understanding female in her life. She wasn't entirely sure what he meant by that because whenever she asked, her grandma always told him to stop fussing and be quiet. Her grandparents were getting on a bit in years, and there were times when she exhausted them with her constant barrage of questions, and recently she'd overheard her grandad tell her grandma that she had become worse than ever since her dad met Chloe. She had her mother of course, who she loved dearly, but there was no denying her mother was different to the other mums at school, and just because she wasn't interested in joining them for coffee mornings or yoga classes the other kids said she was weird. It had never occurred to her that her mother was different until she went to school, but her gaudy outfits frequently drew attention and made people stare. She often wished her daddy was there to take her to school instead, because drop off time was always the worse, because that was when the other kids laughed and pointed at her mother's multicoloured hair and outrageous outfits. The parents who were always huddled together in groups, would turn around briefly before quickly turning back and sniggering childishly among themselves, but her mum just smiled and ignored them and said she was pleased she was able to give them something interesting to talk about.

Crystal was glad she had to wear a uniform at school because she didn't have any clothes in her wardrobe like the other kids wore on mufti days and on one occasion her teacher had tried sending her home to change because he thought her mother had mistaken a non-uniform day for a world books fancy dress day instead. When her mother explained to him, that she wasn't deliberately dressed as a child war evacuee, he blushed with embarrassment, and after that, a letter got sent out to all the parents saying that for practical reasons there would be fewer non-uniform days scheduled throughout the year. On one occasion she had tried pleading with her mum to buy her some normal clothes, but her pleas fell on deaf ears because according to her mum her clothes were normal, and it was the other kids' clothes that were different. Recently she'd learnt to embrace what her grandparents called her *'alternative dress sense'* and her mum was visibly delighted by her choices. She told her they were just like *"two peas in a pod"* and although she didn't know exactly what that meant, she assumed it must be a good thing because it made her mum happy. However, not everyone was so accepting of her choices and the teachers were forced to intervene when the kids started to call her *'stinky'* just because someone's mum had spotted her mum in town holding up a placard about excessive use of detergents destroying the ozone layer. Her strict policy on what items should be washed and when was no secret, and she was proud of the fact that she only washed her own clothes as and when they started to smell. Underwear she agreed was an exception which she said must be washed every other day for hygiene purposes, but when she innocently told Chloe about wearing her knickers inside out on the second day she seemed horrified and immediately told her dad to have words with her mother because otherwise she would seriously have to consider reporting her to the social services for neglect.

She had been desperate to meet Chloe as soon as

she knew her daddy had a girlfriend, but he told her he wanted to be certain Chloe was fully committed to him before introducing them, but two years was a very long time for a little girl, and she knew her grandparents thought so to because she had overheard them talking about it to her mum. When the day finally came to meet her, she was literally bursting with excitement especially as she knew Chloe had older children because she had always wanted a brother or a sister of her own. However, the day didn't go as planned because Chloe spent the entire day vomiting and she had ended up spending the day with her grandparents instead. Her mother was furious and angrily accused her father of taking unfair advantage of his aged parents and her father retaliated by shouting at Chloe for being sick in the car which caused her to throw up even more violently. As it turned out, she was in the early stages of pregnancy with her half-sister Phoebe, so it wasn't entirely her fault, but no one knew that at the time, not even Chloe.

Her mother was called Amberina named by her parents after their favourite two-toned American glassware which was something of an acquired taste but could be found in abundance in their modest but somewhat dilapidated bungalow. After they died, some of the more sentimental ornaments found their way into her own home, but her mum told her there had been far too many to keep so the remainder were divided between the various charity shops in the town. She didn't remember her mum's parents because they had died when she was a baby, but her mum told her she was named Crystal to follow the family tradition. Her name hadn't bothered her too much until she went to school when the other kids giggled every time the morning register was called and even though her mother told her there was nothing wrong with being different she wanted a normal name like Amy or Sarah. Eventually, the teacher agreed to remove her hyphenated middle name from the register, and the other kids soon got bored as Crystal Leere didn't sound as funny as Crystal -Shanda Leere. Her daddy told her that when she was older, she could change her name by something called deed poll and that day couldn't come soon enough especially after hearing Chloe tell her dad her name was 'cheap' and 'chavvy" and best suited to a child from a council estate. She found out later it was her mum who chose her name because she was born a girl, but if she had been a boy her dad would have chosen a name, and there were times when she thought it might have been better if she been born a boy. She wasn't the delicate little baby her parents were expecting; indeed she was a whopping 11 lb. bruiser with chubby legs and feet and a mop of bright red hair exactly like her mothers. To this day, everyone still told her she was her mother's daughter, but she didn't want to hear it, she wanted them to say she was her father's daughter because he was tall and dark with piercing blue eyes and she was short, fat and ginger with a face full of freckles. Her mum told her she was beautiful as she was, but she didn't feel very beautiful, and it was never the pretty girls that were made to throw the shot put on school sports days.

When Phoebe was born, she was perfect. At just under 7 lbs., she looked like a fragile doll with her soft, delicate features and fair wavy hair. She reminded Crystal of one of those dolls her mother used to buy for her at Christmas with her clear, fair skin and pretty blue eyes with long dark lashes, and when her dad proudly showed her off, he told everyone that one day she would be a heartbreaker. He had never said that to her, but then again, Phoebe was everything she wasn't. She didn't have a fat ginger-headed mum, and she was lucky enough to have inherited the best physical features from both parents. She would never be called a *'ginger minger'* at school and she was glad of that because she was the little sister she had always dreamt of having and even though she knew she would have to share her daddy with this other little girl she didn't mind too much because for some reason she already felt fiercely protective of her.

Chloe was also protective of her new baby daughter. It didn't matter that she was already a mum of four because they were all grown up now and leading their own lives and she didn't feel needed by them anymore. This tiny bundle was helpless and vulnerable and relied on her for survival, and that was a huge responsibility, her responsibility, and her desire to nurture and protect her daughter was overwhelming. Crystal tried to get close to Phoebe, but Chloe always made excuses and pushed her away. She wanted her baby sister to love her, and despite her stepmother constantly pointing out she was only a half-sister, she hid her feelings of rejection well. She hoped as Phoebe grew older things would change, but they didn't because Chloe watched her every move and restricted her access to her dad and her sister even more. Weekend visits changed from weekly to fortnightly and then eventually it was reduced to once a month providing, of course, she could prove she wasn't carrying any germs that could be passed on to Phoebe. It had got to the point where she was afraid to sneeze on a Friday just in case Chloe, who her mum said was a bit of a know- it- all nurse, insisted on something called a fit note from the doctor prior to her monthly access visit. She didn't know what a fit note actually was but her mum said it was something a doctor could give to grownups to prove they were fit to go to work and she wanted to know why the doctor couldn't give her one to say she could visit her daddy. Her mum said it didn't work like that which caused a massive meltdown and she was sent to bed. She missed her dad, and she missed her little sister, and Phoebe was growing up fast without her, and she was afraid that now her daddy had a new family he would forget about her.

As Phoebe changed from a baby to a lively toddler, her character truly reflected the meaning of her name *"radiant, shining one."* Her impish mischievous smile was contagious, and she knew her dad was totally smitten with her. She felt left out, and it wasn't long before she was overwhelmed by feelings of jealousy because she could feel her daddy slowly slipping away from her and she didn't know what she had to do to make him love her as much as he loved her little sister.

GRANT

G rant met Chloe through his best friend's wife Maria who he knew was also a work colleague of hers. She'd put him on the spot by arranging a double date at the bowling alley, and he'd agreed to go along for something to do. He didn't have any real expectations, but he'd heard a lot about her and was intrigued to find out more. He couldn't help but admire her courage for persevering with the online dating despite all the setbacks she'd had, especially as he never had the nerve to try it himself. He wasn't privy to all the details, but he had been told she'd had some *'near misses'* and needed some stability in her life. He wondered what was meant by *'near misses,'* but Maria hadn't been keen to elaborate, so he decided to let it go.

He knew he was considered a safe option, but he came with baggage and from what he'd heard about Chloe she wasn't all that keen on other people's children despite having four of her own. His daughter Crystal was still young and impressionable, and with a mother like Amberina, she needed some normality in her life. Crystal was desperate for him to meet someone new and although he'd been on a few dates, they fizzled out within weeks which he put down to lack of effort on his part. He often wondered if he was too safe an option for most women but from what he'd heard about Chloe she didn't sound like the sort of woman who was attracted to the safe guys, so he didn't rate his chances of a long-term relationship with her being all that high.

He had met Crystal's mother Amberina by chance while out shopping in town one chilly Saturday afternoon. She was standing outside a shop that sold real fur coats with a group of other people holding up a placard campaigning for animal rights. As an animal lover, he stopped briefly, and before he knew it, he was standing with them waving banners and demanding a ban on animal hunting and of course the fur trade. Afterwards, they ended up going to a local cafe for coffee and cake, and before he knew it, he'd asked her out on a date.

She wasn't really his type, but he still didn't actually know what his type was and considering he was knocking on the door of forty and still single, he decided to take a chance on her.

Amberina was short and decidedly plumper than the ladies he usually dated but with the shock of bright red head curling around her chubby cheekbones and her prominent thick but shapely eyebrows he thought she looked rather cute. She didn't look like the type of high maintenance woman who spent hours in the bathroom getting ready for a date either and he liked that about her. As it turned out his first impressions of her were spot on because she had no interest in makeup whatsoever although she did wear the occasional bright red lippy for special occasions providing, of course, it hadn't been tested on animals. She was also a vegetarian which didn't surprise him too much given her strong ethics about animal welfare, but he couldn't help wondering which vegetables contained enough calories to make a person so fat. It wasn't long before he found the answer, her passion for creamy dairy products, especially cheese which she ate in abundance because according to her it was a good source of calcium and would help stop her from getting osteoporosis later on in life. He briefly thought about mentioning some of the other calcium-rich foods such as spinach, broccoli, watercress or sardines with bones but thought better of it because something was telling him this was an argument he was never going to win.

They had been dating for about six months when Amberina suddenly announced she was pregnant. They had been using protection, so the news came as a shock to both of them, but Grant was deliriously happy at the prospect of becoming a father and couldn't wait to tell his parents they had a long-awaited grandchild on the way. Amberina wasn't so enthusiastic about the prospect of motherhood, after all, she still had the entire planet to save, and a baby wasn't a part of her agenda but as a devoted pro-life campaigner, abortion was totally out of the question. They decided to get married because according to their old-fashioned parents, under the circumstances, it was the right thing to do and because Amberina didn't want a big wedding they settled on a simple ceremony at the registry office and invited only a handful of family and friends to join them.

Amberina was only about three months pregnant when they married, but pregnancy seemed to emphasise her already ample frame, and the shocking, hippie-style, peach dress that she chose with yellow tassels hanging from the hem and sleeves clashed outrageously with her auburn hair. After the wedding, she changed the colour of her hair every week after discovering products that she could wash in and out. Unfortunately, the different combinations of products and bleaches eventually reacted, and her hair turned a luminous shade of green, but Amberina embraced the colour and laughed it off saying it symbolised the extreme nausea she was experiencing as a result of her pregnancy.

He had been present at the birth and was thrilled when the midwife announced they had a healthy, baby daughter. Amberina was almost two weeks overdue when Crystal was born, and the pregnancy coupled with a long labour, took its toll on her. They had already agreed if it was a boy Grant would name him, but if it were a girl, Amberina would choose the name. Grant knew given her family history their daughter would never have a normal name, but he hoped she would choose a name that other kids wouldn't make fun of at a later date. He struggled to conceal his dismay when she announced their daughter was to be called Crystal - Shanda Leere knowing full well in years to come their little girl would despise them for it but predictably the ever-stubborn Amberina refused to foresee any problems. In some ways he wished they hadn't bothered getting married because then he might have suggested giving her a double-barrelled surname and even though Crystal -Shanda Livingstone-Leere was a bit of a mouthful it had to be better than kids chanting Crystal Shanda-Leere every time they saw her. He already feared she would have a tough time at school because it was evident from the outset she was going to be a redhead like her mother and her mother wasn't exactly the typical playground mum who would blend in and go unnoticed in the crowd. Once upon a time, he had been that same child desperate to fit in, but thanks to his parents, he had zero chance of achieving acceptance from his peers. He was singled out because his mum and dad had him later on in life, and despite his protests they still insisted on collecting him from school at the age of eleven years in their beloved three-wheeler Reliant Robin which they claimed would now be a sought-after collectors' item had they not traded it in in favour of a Ford Fiesta. He pleaded with them to let him walk home with the other kids, but they were so overprotective of him they even insisted he wore shin pads and a helmet to protect him from injury in a conker match. He knew it could have been worse, they could have bought an entire suit of body armour for him to wear and even now in their eighties they still treated him like a child, but at least they could no longer dictate what clothes he should wear. He still cringed at the memory of the day they insisted he wore the shortest of shorts complete with long socks and sandals on his first day at secondary school when all the other boys were in long trousers and proper shoes with laces. He was the laughingstock of the class, and although he loved his parent's dearly, he was grateful times had changed even though his parents clearly hadn't. He wanted better things for his daughter, but most of all, he wanted what he never had as a child, and that was acceptance for her.

He knew his parents weren't Amberina's number one fan, but they were old school and politely welcomed her into the family without passing judgement. His friends, especially his best mate Tom, were less forgiving and couldn't understand what he ever saw in her and deep down he knew they were right. They were poles apart, and clearly, opposites don't always attract, so that was another theory out the window. The marriage wasn't working so they agreed to part amicably when Crystal was only three months old. They agreed to joint access so Grant could still run his accountancy business during the week, allowing Amberina time to eliminate world poverty and plant more trees to save the planet at the weekends.

The only problem with having Crystal every weekend was he didn't get the opportunity to *'get himself back out there'* as his mates aptly put it and find a new love interest. Lad's nights out and stag parties were a no go because he had Crystal to consider and in some ways, he was relieved to have her as an excuse. Now Crystal was a bit older his parents didn't mind having her overnight occasionally, so that was where she was heading this weekend so he could go out and double date with his best friend Tom and his long-suffering wife, Maria.

AMBERINA

E ven as a child, Amberina never really wanted to get married. While other little girls were busy dressing up in bridal clothes and marrying off their Barbie dolls to the super trendy Ken, she was preoccupied with the encyclopaedia Britannica and preaching to her confused parents about the importance of keeping the environment green.

Her parents thought it was just a phase that she would eventually grow out of, but by the time she reached her teens she was already an active member of Greenpeace and the World-Wide Fund for Nature, and they came to the conclusion that their daughter was born to be different. She never showed any interest in boys, or girls for that matter, and was happy to be a loner at school, preferring to spend lunchtimes in the library so she could keep up to date with the latest developments on world conservation issues. She knew she was a bit of a geek compared with most other kids of her age but fitting in wasn't a priority when there was an entire planet to save. With her tangled mass of wild red locks and frumpy thick-framed glasses the other kids often teased her, but she had better things to do than worry about them, and eventually, they got the message and left her alone.

Having a baby certainly wasn't part of her agenda which was just as well because up until now no man had ever looked twice at her before. She decided if she ever got broody enough to want a baby of her own, she would probably have to resort to the sperm donor route and artificially inseminate herself with a syringe full of baby batter. In some ways, she rather liked the idea of selecting her baby's genes by browsing through a catalogue of attractive looking men with all the right physical and intellectual attributes but seeing as the baby would inherit half of her genes to the chances were it would turn out to be a ginger nut like her anyway.

Her parents were disappointed that she never made any effort to meet anyone, but bars and nightclubs weren't her sort of thing, and the local library wasn't exactly brimming with eligible bachelors either. They were desperate for a grandchild, but she had made it clear to them from an early age that she wasn't interested in children. As a child, they bought her dolls to encourage her to develop her maternal instincts and play like normal little girls, but she quickly lost interest in them preferring books or chemistry kits to conduct experiments with instead. She remembered asking her parents why the dolls never looked like her; they were always so pretty with their fair skin, piercing blue eyes and long flowing tresses, not chubby and ginger like she was. They told her that she was beautiful as she was, but now that she was a parent herself she knew all parents were naturally biased when it came to their offspring.

She knew lots of people, mainly from her campaigning and protest marches, but they were all like-minded people with a singe goal, to defend the natural world and promote peace. Meeting Grant that day in town was a pure fluke, and she couldn't believe her luck when he joined their protest and came and stood next to her. When he asked her if she fancied going for a coffee afterwards, she thought he must have been talking to someone else as guys didn't generally notice her but when she looked around the crowds had dispersed and there was only the two of them left standing together.

She ordered a large hot chocolate with extra cream, marshmallows and chocolate sprinkles and an iced bun while he settled for a skinny latte. As she squeezed her heavy frame into the compact booth, she noticed for the first time how attractive he was. As he leaned forward to brush his dark wavy hair away from his magnetic blue eyes, their hands briefly touched, and she noticed how his long soft fingers complimented his impeccably manicured nails. His hands were far too soft for manual work, so she assumed he must be a white-collar worker of some kind, and it was only then that it dawned on her that she had forgotten to ask his name. She must have sat staring at him in a semi-hypnotic state for a while because by the time she realised he was speaking to her; he was starting to look quite apprehensive. After reassuring him she was absolutely fine they made their introductions and chatted comfortably together for the rest of the afternoon before going their separate ways. It was his idea to exchange mobile numbers, but she didn't believe she would ever hear from him again, but it didn't really matter because she'd had a lovely afternoon in the company of an extremely attractive gentleman and that in itself was not only a miracle but also an enormous morale booster.

Grant had enjoyed the afternoon to a lot more than he had expected. He wasn't sure why he'd invited her for a coffee, and he had blurted it out without thinking by which time it was too late to question his motives. She certainly had a good appetite although he couldn't help noticing it wasn't exactly a healthy one which accounted for her curvy figure. He didn't usually go for big girls, but it made a pleasant change to be able to hold an intelligent conversation with a girl whose priority wasn't all about running to the lavvy every five minutes to re-apply her lippy. He noticed she wasn't wearing any makeup, but she seemed totally comfortable with herself, and he liked that. He'd asked for her mobile number because he wanted to see her again, but he still wasn't sure if she was interested in him. At one stage, she spent a long time just staring at him across the table in a trance-like state, and he wasn't sure if it was his conversation that was boring her or whether she suffered from an underlying condition like narcolepsy. She was unique and a bit quirky, and he liked that in a woman, so he decided he would take the plunge and text her. After all, it was the only way he was going to find out if she wanted to see him again.

Amberina was thrilled to get the text thanking her for a pleasant afternoon just a few hours after they'd parted company. She thought he was just being polite when he asked for her number, and she really didn't expect to hear from him again so she couldn't believe her luck. She wasn't used to dates or men for that matter, so she decided to do some reading up on some of the do's and don'ts of a first date before discarding it as complete and utter nonsense. She always did what came naturally, and she had no plans to change now, not even for a handsome guy like Grant.

Grant suggested they go for a meal for their first date which met with her approval because she adored food providing it was vegetarian. There were plenty of local restaurants with good vegetarian options, but she had her eye on a particular one that served delicious cocktails as she was partial to a Pina Colada and luckily Grant was more than happy to oblige. She ordered a large pizza with chillies and mozzarella with a cheesy stuffed crust and garlic bread while Grant stuck with a more traditional thin crust pizza. Much to her dismay, her order came with a pile of green rocket which she thought looked completely indigestible and without thinking she liberally scooped it all on to Grant's plate without bothering to ask whether he even liked the stuff. He looked somewhat surprised by the gesture but rather than waste it, he happily tucked in, and Amberina nodded her approval.

After that, they started to see each other regularly, and it was soon time to move their relationship on to the next level. She had never had sex before and after taking a sneaky peek at the Kama Sutra book in her local library when no one was looking she decided she would need to be a contortionist to have sex and she wasn't nearly flexible enough to bend her body in that way. She never dreamt there could be so many different sexual positions and she couldn't help wondering what type of people invented them in the first place. If she was forced to choose then the one with the female on top looked to be the most comfortable but she feared she would crush Grant under the pressure of her hefty frame, so to avoid breaking his bones she opted for the boring but safe missionary position at least until she managed to lose some weight which she knew was unlikely to be anytime soon. She made an appointment to see her doctor to discuss contraception, but he told her she was too fat to go on the combined pill, so she could either have the progestogen-only pill which she would have to take every day or try the 3-monthly injection which was likely to make her even fatter in the long term. She opted for the daily pill and followed the doctor's verbal instructions as well as the written instructions inside the box down to the very last word but still managed to get pregnant. She didn't think she was good enough at sex to become pregnant and even though Grant told her she was fine; she was certain he was just being nice and telling her what she wanted to hear. She certainly didn't want to hear she was pregnant, and she must have bought at least a dozen home tests before acknowledging the second blue line on the stick was not going to go away on its own accord. Grant was thrilled at the prospect of becoming a dad, and because both sets of future grandparents were old-fashioned and keen for the child not to be born out of wedlock, they forged ahead with a wedding that neither of them really wanted and unsurprisingly just over a year later they joined the country's divorce statistics.

The divorce was amicable, and they both agreed that Crystal's well-being had to be their main priority. She was only three months old when they parted, so she wasn't old enough to know the meaning of a normal family unit where both parents raised a child together which made it easier for her to adjust. To their credit she seemed to be growing up all right despite her mother's eccentricity, but she had got to an age where she wanted more, not in the way of material possessions, even though they were nice to have, she wanted a brother or a sister or if she was really lucky one of each but to her disappointment it looked as if both of her parents were destined to remain single forever.

THE DOUBLE DATE

It had been quite some time since Grant had been out with an attractive lady and he was looking forward to it. He knew Chloe was pretty because Tom said so and Tom knew because his wife Maria who worked with her, told him she was without a doubt, good on the eye. She hadn't said anything about her personality, but he assumed she must be a good person because otherwise, they wouldn't have set him up on a date with her.

Tom and Maria had been inseparable since they were at primary school together, and despite moving on to different secondary schools at the age of eleven, their bond was undeniable. It was no surprise to anyone when they announced they were going to be married at the tender age of eighteen years and thirty years later they were still happily married and managed to prove all their doubters wrong. Like all couples, they'd had their ups and downs, but they'd got through them and had come out the other side united and stronger than ever before.

Grant met Tom at secondary school and had the honour of being best man at his wedding, which at just eighteen years old seemed an overwhelming responsibility at the time. It was a bit of a cliché, but Tom and Maria were made for each other and Grant hoped that one day he would find the kind of love they shared. He'd met a few girls but none of them were what he considered to be marriage material, and he didn't want to rush down the aisle with the wrong woman. Thirty years later he still hadn't found the right woman, and although his marriage to Amberina hadn't worked out, he'd been fortunate enough to have a child with her. Crystal was four years old and desperate to be a big sister, so she was really excited when Grant told her he was going on a date. She didn't seem to grasp the idea that it was only a date or that babies weren't produced in an instant like cups of tea or coffee, but he promised her he would try and luckily, she seemed happy with that.

After dropping Crystal off at his parent's house, Grant headed back home to get himself ready. He'd bought new jeans and a shirt for the occasion not because he needed them but because Tom would be critical if he hadn't. According to Tom, first impressions were important, and Grant was keen not to let him down. He spent longer than average in the shower and made sure he was clean shaven before applying some moisturiser that Amberina had bought for Crystal to give to him as a Christmas present two years earlier. It was some body shop balm in a bright orange jar which he thought was the sort of stuff only poofters used, but he was pleasantly surprised at the soft and smooth texture and applied it liberally to his fresh clean-shaven face. He took a brief look at himself in the mirror before heading out and was impressed at the image staring back at him, he scrubbed up pretty well for a bloke in his mid-forties, Tom would be impressed, and he hoped Chloe would be to.

They arranged to meet at a popular bar at a picturesque local marina. The bowling alley was only a ten-minute walk from the bar but seeing as they had already decided to keep the date informal and eat burgers at the bowling alley there was no need to worry about booking a table at one of the marina's exclusive restaurants. Grant enjoyed eating out at restaurants, and whenever he went out with a lady he usually preferred to go somewhere where they could enjoy a more intimate dinner together, but Tom insisted burgers would be fine and he knew better than to argue with him. It was only 7 pm, but the bar was already starting to get busy and even now it was standing room only. There was music blaring from a jukebox, and a band was busy setting up in the far corner. Grant was pleased he was tall because otherwise he would have had difficulty spotting Tom who he could see standing at the bar with Maria and another lady who he hoped was Chloe because she was, indeed very pretty. Tom waved cheerfully when he caught a glimpse of Grant anxiously scanning the room with his eyes, and he nudged Maria playfully. He had seen the glint in Grant's eye when he saw Chloe standing with them, and he had high hopes for the two of them. Maria, on the other hand, wasn't so convinced because despite working with Chloe for over three years she wasn't an easy person to get close to and although they got on together okay as work colleagues she didn't feel comfortable calling her a friend. If it wasn't for her husband Tom being Grant's best mate, they would never have arranged this evening out, and although she didn't mention it to Tom, she had reservations about it from the outset. Tom had been trying to set Grant up on a date for as long as Maria could remember. The only respite was when he married Amberina, but as Tom had predicted that relationship was short-lived, and Tom was delighted to be proved right on this occasion. Tom found it hard to keep his opinions to himself at the best of times, and he made his feelings about Amberina very clear. He described her as a freak and although Maria agreed she was odd she thought it unfair of Tom to judge her so harshly. Poor Grant was caught up in the middle of the rift, and consequently, they lost contact for a while. They weren't even invited to the wedding which she knew Tom was miffed about, but in hindsight, it was probably a good thing because if Tom had done a speech, their marriage most probably would have ended before the first dance.

Maria was one of only a handful of colleagues who Chloe had opened up to about some of her internet dating experiences. She wasn't convinced she knew everything, but she knew enough to be sufficiently concerned to confide in Tom about her. In hindsight, she wished she'd kept quiet because Tom had instantly decided that Chloe would be the perfect match for Grant, and he didn't stop going on about it until she gave in and agreed to drop a few hints during a casual conversation at work one day.

At five foot ten, Chloe was tall for a woman, and Maria knew she had a major hang-up about dating any guy shorter than herself, so she wasn't surprised when her first question was about his height. When she said he was about 6'4" her eyes registered immediate interest, but when she mentioned he had a kid, she said she would have to have a think about it. She didn't elaborate about Crystal because she didn't want Tom to accuse her of sabotage and if it worked out between them, which frankly she didn't believe it would, Grant would tell her all about it when the time was right for him.

Despite having four kids of her own Chloe made it clear to just about everyone that she wasn't fond of other people's children, especially girls. Realistically she knew her chances of meeting a forty or fifty-something-year-old guy without baggage as she not so affectionately called it was unlikely, but she assumed they would be the grown-up type of self-supporting baggage that wasn't constantly attached to anyone's hip or purse strings.

Chloe briefly glanced up to see who Tom was waving at and caught her first glimpse of Grant. He was more attractive than she'd expected, and she wondered what Maria's motives were for not mentioning him before now. Like most women, she liked a bit of eye candy, and she couldn't help wondering why he hadn't already been snapped up by some other lonely soul, but people often said the same thing about her so perhaps they were two of a kind, damaged discarded goods that no one wanted any more.

When the online love of her life Mel eventually left her life forever she felt completely deflated and without thinking she deleted her online dating profile at the same time as his phone number although she had since found a way of retrieving his number. At the time, it had seemed the right thing to do, but she had been naïve in thinking that getting rid of everything connected to him would help her to forget him. Sweeping her feelings under the carpet was nothing more than a temporary solution to a long-term illness and a fruitless attempt to conceal the shattered fragments of her broken heart from both herself and the outside world. Invariably there were people who could see through her protective barriers, and Maria was one of them, which is why she had opened up to her about her dating disasters. She often worried in case she'd told her too much, but Maria was the epitome of discretion and not the sort of colleague to indulge in office gossip, and she was fairly certain she could trust her. There were days when she wished she could wrap herself up in a protective bubble so she could stop herself from getting hurt again, but if that were possible, which of course it wasn't, her heart would remain broken forever and more than anything else in the world she wanted to find love again.

Grant fought his way through the crowds and made his way over to where Tom and Maria were standing. Chloe smiled shyly at him and felt herself blush. She wasn't usually the shy sort, but she could feel her cheeks burning so she made a quick excuse about being hot so she could get to the door to cool down for a few moments outside. Maria decided to join her. She was a couple of years older than Chloe, and by now Tom was used to her menopausal flushes, so she didn't have to explain herself. She wasn't actually all that hot, but she had never seen Chloe react in that way before, and it seemed only polite to go and check up on her to see if she was okay. By the time she reached the door, Chloe was standing outside taking slow deep breaths to compose herself and before either of them had the chance to speak they both fell about laughing at the absurdity of it all. If nothing else, it broke the ice between the two women, but it had been a long time coming, and for the first time ever Chloe thought of Maria as someone who she might actually be able to one day call a friend.

By the time they got back to the bar to join the boys, they were chatting and giggling like old friends, and Tom was delighted to see them getting on so well together. He had been worried about the atmosphere feeling strained, but now he was hopeful that going out as a foursome might become a regular thing. He wanted to make up for lost time because he and Grant had temporarily lost touch for a while after Grant married Amberina and he was feeling a bit guilty about it. He had never liked her, and he made that blatantly clear to poor Grant who he'd unashamedly put in the impossible position of choosing between his wife and him.

Tom was in a celebratory mood and offered to buy

the first round of drinks and seeing as it was a cocktail bar Chloe opted for her favourite Pina colada giving Grant an uneasy feeling of déjà vu. Pina colada was Amberina's favourite tipple to, and he sincerely hoped that was the only similarity between the two women. Tom had been right about her to a certain extent, but he was basing his judgement solely on her physical attributes and quirky eccentricity, and he was still too stubborn to admit that looks alone weren't enough to make her a bad person. Eventually, they'd agreed to disagree because they were going round and round in circles and they both decided it wasn't worth losing years of friendship over. He hoped Tom would mellow when Crystal was born and struggled to hide his disappointment when he failed to congratulate him on the birth of his first child, but Tom started out as he meant to go on and much to Grant's dismay he deliberately ignored Crystal. Grant knew most guys wouldn't tolerate such ignorant behaviour from a so-called friend towards a child, but he and Tom went back a long way, and as Tom kept reminding him he couldn't afford to be choosy. With that in mind he took another glance at Chloe and smiled to himself, she was indeed very pretty, and she wasn't exactly looking disappointed either, so perhaps Tom was wrong, or perhaps he could afford to be choosy after all.

After two Pina colada's Chloe was starting to feel a bit tipsy, and the conversation was flowing almost as freely as the alcohol. She was beginning to wish she had eaten something beforehand though because alcohol on an empty stomach never agreed with her and she didn't want to make a show of herself on a first date.

The biggest surprise of the evening was Maria's husband Tom who was getting louder by the minute and laughing at his own jokes which he unashamedly directed at Grant's ex-wife and daughter. Maria looked extremely uncomfortable, and Grant was trying hard to ignore him, but Chloe could see the hurt behind the smile in his piercing blue eyes, and for a moment her heart went out to him. Fortunately, Maria came to the rescue and broke the awkwardness of the situation by glancing at her watch and announcing it was time they were on their way to the bowling alley. This wasn't the first time Tom had embarrassed her in public, and she knew it wouldn't be the last, but she would have words with him later and remind him why setting Grant up with Chloe hadn't been a good idea. She knew how much Tom hated Amberina and poor Crystal for that matter to and Chloe was definitely not the type of woman who needed any ammunition because she suspected she wouldn't think twice before firing the gun.

The fresh air had a sobering effect on all of them, and Tom temporarily fell silent. It was only a ten-minute walk, but the night air was crisp, and a frost was already beginning to form on the roofs of the nearby houses. Chloe shivered and pulled her jacket tighter to her body and simultaneously stumbled over in her ridiculously high heels only to be caught by the strong arms of a worried looking Grant. She lingered in his arms for slightly longer than necessary before apologising for her poor choice of shoes, and they both giggled. Grant noticed how slight she was although he only really had Amberina to compare her with and anyone would be small in comparison with her. He was pleased now he had agreed to come out tonight despite Tom's unnecessary insults, and he hoped Chloe was enjoying the evening as much as he was. He liked her and judging by the way she looked at him he was fairly certain she liked him too, but he didn't want to get too ahead of himself just in case he had misread the signals and got it all wrong again. He hoped there would be another date with just the two of them, but he would have to wait and see because Tom had already made him out to be a complete moron and as he well knew first impressions were important.

When they arrived at the bowling alley, they had to change their shoes to the unflattering two-tone flats that Chloe thought looked like something her gran might have worn. She usually loathed them, but today she was relieved to be rid of her toe pinching painful high heels, if only for a short time. They had two games booked, and the plan was to stop and have a bite to eat between games. Chloe was already hungry, and her tummy was making all kinds of gurgling noises which thankfully were disguised by the dreadful racket coming from the speakers. With a smug grin on his face and quietly confident that the boys would win, Tom decided they should play in teams of boys against girls, but Chloe had other ideas. She was a competitive sportswoman, and at one time she had bowled for the county team, but Tom had no need to know that. After repeatedly bowling one strike after another and collecting special bonuses along the way she and Maria were soon way ahead of the boys and Tom was looking perplexed. He wasn't used to losing, and he was annoyed that Maria hadn't told him Chloe was a pro at bowling. As it turned out, Maria was just as astonished as her husband having had no idea that Chloe was so good, but she was secretly delighted because for once, Tom was getting his comeuppance.

After the first game, they stopped as planned for some food. By now, Chloe was ravenous, especially after putting so much energy and determination into winning the game, but after seeing Tom's face, she knew it had been worth the effort.

For food there was a choice of burgers but little else, so she opted for a chicken burger with chips which was served in a plastic carton. As a general rule, she avoided fast food restaurants simply because she disapproved of eating out of boxes of any kind and she also had concerns about the welfare of the animals used by the fast food industry. At the age of thirteen, she and a group of friends decided they wanted to become vegetarians, but her mum didn't support her decision and refused to cook separate meals so after living off nothing but cereals for six weeks she changed her mind and decided some meats were okay providing animal welfare protection standards were maintained. These days she referred to herself as a lapsed vegetarian because despite avoiding red meats she still enjoyed chicken and couldn't imagine eating anything other than the traditional turkey at Christmas time.

Before starting the second game, Tom decided he wanted to swap the teams around. He wasn't used to losing and thought it might be fun if he and Chloe played against Maria and Grant, but Chloe was having none of his nonsense and Maria admired her resolve. Predictably Tom sulked like a spoiled child after losing the second game and made a mental note never to go bowling again. In the meantime, Chloe and Maria were rubbing salt in his wounds by doing a humiliating victory dance around him and Grant, and he decided there and then that there would be payback for this, he didn't yet know how or when, but he had a few ideas up his sleeve, and he was pretty certain he still held the trump card when it came to Chloe.

When the games were over, they decided to go home. It was getting late and although Grant didn't have work the following day his parents would expect him to pick up Crystal bright and early, so they could go to church. Much to Tom's dismay Grant offered to drop Chloe home and she accepted, so it was a lost opportunity to find out more about her. Maria never elaborated when he asked questions, but she had made one or two comments in the past about her being a serial internet dater with an intolerance of other people's children, and this was enough for him to work on for the time being at least.

Grant dropped Chloe off at the door and gave her a quick peck on the cheek. He was disappointed that they hadn't had more of an opportunity to talk during the evening, so he hoped his small gesture of affection wouldn't be misinterpreted. He was out of practice when it came to dating women, and he wasn't sure if there was a protocol he should follow. In the end, he went with his gut instinct, and she was happy enough to exchange phone numbers, which he hoped was a good sign. He wanted to see her again, but she was playing her cards close to her chest and didn't give anything away, so he thanked her for a lovely entertaining evening before driving home.

During the drive home, he chuckled to himself. It certainly had been entertaining, and she had given Tom a run for his money, but Tom hadn't seemed so happy and that unsettled him because Tom had a nasty streak in him and he was afraid he could spoil what could be a new chapter in his life before it even got started. He decided not to dwell on it. After all, what would be would be and if nothing else he was a firm believer in fate.

Tom

M aria was unusually quiet on the journey home and Tom knew he was in the doghouse again. He had never truly forgiven Grant for not inviting him to his wedding, and he couldn't resist making insulting remarks about his ex-wife and daughter at every opportunity. He knew he was being unfair, but he couldn't help himself, and by the looks of it, Maria was about to give him a major ear bashing for it.

Maria's obvious disapproval was never enough to deter him. They had been together for so long he knew she would never leave him, and by tomorrow it would all be forgotten. He glanced over to where she was sitting in the passenger seat, but she didn't turn to look at him. Instead, she sat staring blankly at the road ahead of them, and he knew he might have to work a bit harder this time to win her round. Usually a box of chocolates or surprise bouquet of flowers delivered to her workplace was enough to do the trick, but judging by the look on her face this time he was going to have to step up the ante and agree to the long weekend away in a country hotel that she had been harping on about for ages. He didn't really want to go, but if they were to invite Grant and Chloe to join them it would make it a lot more interesting, and he was certain Maria would jump at the opportunity.

Maria was still in pretty good shape for her age, but she wasn't as pretty as Chloe. She'd had an early menopause which caused her to gain weight which made her moody and resulted in her libido hitting an all-time low. There was a time when they'd had an adventurous sex life, but he couldn't remember the last time they'd made love, and lately, this had become a constant source of arguments between them. Unfortunately, they'd never been able to have any children of their own and Maria seemed to accept this better than him. They'd discussed adoption, but Maria decided she'd prefer a cat and before long they had ten of them in the house and Maria became known as the mad cat woman by the neighbours. It hadn't been easy for him when Grant had a daughter but looks wise she took after her mother, and he couldn't resist telling poor Grant that their ginger Tom cat was more attractive than Crystal. According to Maria, he was jealous because Grant had the one thing he couldn't have, but he didn't agree and regularly joked that if they'd had a child that ugly he would have put it straight up for adoption. It saddened her when he said things like that because a child was a precious gift that had sadly been denied to them, but she believed everything happened for a reason although she had no idea what that reason was. Despite everything she believed Tom would have been a good father if they had been lucky enough to be blessed with a family of their own and as they had married so young there was every chance they would be grandparents by now too. Deep down, she knew he felt cheated, which is why she had let him get away with so much, but enough was enough, and it was time he learned that his behaviour had consequences.

Tom almost felt sorry for Grant, after all a failed marriage and a kid to support was enough to take its toll on anyone, but Grant was besotted with his daughter and took his responsibilities as a father seriously which interfered with their longstanding bromance which Tom openly begrudged.

Now Chloe was on the scene he hoped there would be more evening's out. She was good on the eye and he fancied his chances. He wasn't opposed to a bit of flirting, and after what Maria had told him about Chloe's online dating antics, she sounded like the sort of girl who would be up for a good time. He had it all planned out in his head and was confident his idea would work, and in a few days, Maria would forgive him because she always did.

MARIA

Maria knew what Tom was thinking. In some ways, she blamed herself for being such a walk over and always giving in to him but tonight he had gone too far, and he needed to know he couldn't simply buy his way out of every difficult situation. The trouble with Tom was he said things without thinking, and as a result, he made things awkward for himself. At least she assumed he said it without thinking because if it was deliberate that would make him a monster and she sincerely hoped she hadn't been married to a monster for all these years. She had seen the haunted look in Grant's eyes on more than one occasion, and she felt ashamed even if her husband didn't. She wished Grant would retaliate because deep down she knew Tom was a coward and only did it because he knew he could get away with it, but Grant was a pussy cat, a male version of her and that meant he would do anything for an easy life.

The silence between them was starting to make Tom feel uncomfortable, and he was secretly willing her to say anything just to get the inevitable row out of the way. He knew it was coming and although he was tired he didn't like going to bed on an argument despite the fact she was unlikely to give him the chance to kiss and make up. He blamed Maria for a great deal of his behaviour, after all, she was never in the mood for sex anymore, and he had to take out his frustrations on someone, and Grant was an easy target.

When Maria eventually spoke, she chose her words carefully, she'd had enough of his bully boy tactics, and it was time for her to take a stand. She was sick of his excuses, and now it was apparently all her fault because she didn't respond to his advances in the bedroom. Despite everything she still loved him, after all, they'd been together since primary school, and he was all she'd ever known, but there were days when she wondered if she had missed out by not having other boyfriends. Other lads had shown an interest in her at secondary school, but at the tender age of eleven years she and Tom had made a pact to be *together forever,'* and she had remained loyal to that promise. It all seemed a bit crazy now but in those days Tom was a true gentleman with impeccable manners, and she believed she was the luckiest girl in the world to have him by her side. She couldn't remember exactly when he'd changed, but she seemed to remember it being around the time they discovered they couldn't have children and he went from a man who rarely uttered a swear word to a man with newly diagnosed Tourette's and frankly that's not what she signed up for when they made their childhood pact together.

Maria was angry and she hoped her anger would give her the strength to say the things that needed saying. Only a bully would mock a small defenceless child, and she was anxious that Crystal should never hear his cruel words which almost certainly would be enough to traumatise her for life. Crystal was a sensitive soul who loved animals, and as the cats were partial to a chin rub and a comfy lap to sit on she would have loved to be able to have her over for tea from time to time, but she couldn't because she had a duty of care to protect her from her own husband and that truly disgusted her. She briefly wondered what would happen if it were the other way around and Grant spoke badly of their child, but it was all hypothetical because they didn't have any children of their own and Grant would never do that because he wasn't that type of man.

Tom was relieved when Maria eventually broke the silence, he was starting to panic in case he'd gone too far but he was confident he'd be able to talk her round after all he always could, and he didn't see why this time things should be any different. Although he was listening, he wasn't really hearing what she was saying, but he heard the words *"counselling"* and *"anger management"* and then finally *"trial separation"* before it finally dawned on him that his wife was actually talking about leaving him.

THE DAY JOBS

Chloe and Maria only worked on the same days a couple of times a week, so they didn't get an opportunity to catch up very often although Chloe was considering increasing her hours now her kids were older. Up until now, she'd only been able to work part-time because her ex-husband Pete ran off with another woman and left her to bring up their four children on her own but against the odds she'd coped admirably, and they'd all grown up to be well adjusted young adults. There wasn't much of an age gap between the four of them, so they'd always been close, and now the eldest two were working their way up the career ladder while the younger two were still enjoying all the benefits of university life. Chloe always thought once her children were grown up she would be able to stop worrying about them so much but if anything, the reverse had happened, and she worried about them more now than she did when they were younger. She put it all down to the loss of control because she still liked to know what they were doing and who they were with, but these days they didn't tell her, and that fed her overactive imagination and made her believe they were up to no good. Her eldest daughter Imogen had recently met a divorced man fifteen years her senior at work with a young child, and she was concerned she was seeking a father figure. She briefly thought back to Pete who was far too busy enjoying exotic holidays with his Brazilian bimbo and his new family to give any of them a second thought and despite not bothering to turn up for Imogen's graduation ceremony for some inexplicable reason she still worshipped the ground he walked on. To her dismay, Imogen seemed blissfully happy with this man who didn't appear to have two pennies to rub together due to the hefty monthly maintenance payments for his daughter and frankly Chloe thought she could do better. She also believed her daughter was far too young to consider taking on another man's child, although now aged twenty-three Imogen didn't agree. She hadn't yet met him, and she knew very little about him apart from the fact his parents were clearly going through some sort of crisis when they chose the ridiculous name, Quentin, and he hated tomatoes, but she had already made up her mind that she didn't like him, and she secretly hoped their relationship would fizzle out before her daughter got too involved.

A full working week went by before Chloe and Maria got some valuable catch up time together. Chloe thought Maria had been a bit quiet but dismissed it because Maria generally kept herself to herself at work anyway. It was Friday afternoon, and it was unusually quiet at the surgery, but no one ever mentioned it because the 'Q' word was banned as it usually led to a last-minute surge of patients all requesting so-called urgent appointments before the weekend. Of course, the appointments were never really urgent, they were either disorganised people who had run out of their medication or neurotic mothers worried because little Johnny had a sniffle and it was his birthday weekend, and he needed antibiotics to stop him getting a chest infection because apparently these things *"always went to his chest"*. It didn't matter how many times she tried to explain to parents that antibiotics were not the answer to poor little Johnny's viral illness and quite frankly she was getting fed up with having to repeat the same speech over and over again only to be threatened with a lawsuit if little Johnny happened to end up in hospital with pneumonia.

There was only the two of them in the staff room and although Maria seemed comfortable making small talk she said little else, and Chloe immediately knew something was wrong. Maria had been there for her when she'd fallen victim to a bunch of psychopaths on the dating site and by the looks of it now was the time for her to return the favour. It all seemed a bit strange because as far as Chloe was concerned they'd had a good time bowling and she'd enjoyed getting even with Tom and watching him cringe, but Maria hadn't even asked if she planned to see Grant again and Chloe assumed she'd be itching to know all the details by now.

Although they had swapped numbers at the end of the evening she hadn't got round to texting Grant yet, but he hadn't contacted her either, and she was still a bit old-fashioned about courting as her late mother would have called it and preferred the man to make the first move. Her kids joked that she was living in the dark ages, and as it was the twenty-first century, no one would think she was a loose woman if she dared to make the first move.

She had been thinking about contacting him because she needed to change her car and she'd seen a shiny red Ford Puma advertised locally that she wanted a second opinion on. She no longer needed the bright orange people carrier that her kids said resembled a rotting tangerine, but it had been a godsend to her when they were little, and although she no longer needed it she felt getting rid of it would mean letting the last of their childhood memories go. She knew it was unusual for a woman to get so attached to a car, but it was full of memories like the home she and Pete once shared together, and it wasn't an easy decision to put your memories up for sale. She knew the Ford Puma was totally impractical, but she no longer had practicalities to worry about, and because of its low mileage, she was certain that one day it would become a classic. When Pete left, she had a stunning black BMW which had been her pride and joy, but as a single parent, it had become too expensive for her to run. Pete told her she would never be able to afford it long term, but she had been too stubborn to listen and her main priority at the time was to stop him getting his grubby little hands on it. When she finally gave in and sold it, she cried for weeks on end, but there was no such thing as a support group for mourning the loss of a car, so she joined a bereavement group instead and pretended to everyone that her beloved BMW was her lost online dating love, Mel.

She didn't know whether to laugh or cry when she was eventually forced to replace her cherished car with the orange box on wheels and even though the kids said it was an embarrassment and asked her to drop them off a good four hundred metres away from their respective schools to avoid being seen, it had served its purpose as a taxi service for them, and for that she was grateful and she thought they should be to.

After years of being a nurse, she was seldom surprised by anything anyone told her anymore and pretty much thought she'd heard it all so she was taken aback when Maria blurted out that she and Tom were having marriage difficulties. Like everyone else because they'd been together so long she thought they were one of the few *together forever* type couples who would be able to work through their problems, so this news came as a complete shock to her. She had picked up on the tension between them on their night out, but she put that down to Tom's inappropriateness and hadn't really thought anything of it. After all, no relationship was perfect, and it wouldn't be normal for a couple to not argue from time to time.

Poor Maria was close to tears, and Chloe sat and listened not really knowing what to say. She was glad Maria felt able to confide in her, but she didn't know her well enough to give advice, and after her own failed marriage and online dating catastrophes she wasn't convinced she was equipped to provide any form of relationship guidance. As it happened, Maria didn't seem bothered whether she spoke or not because by all accounts she wasn't looking for advice. She just wanted to offload because she had already made up her mind what she was going to do.

Chloe was shocked by some of Maria's revelations about Tom. He had seemed a bit cocky and sure of himself, but at the time she thought it was probably all been a show for her benefit. She had no idea he hated Grant's ex-wife and daughter so much, but she agreed with Maria that it was almost certainly because he was jealous because why else would anyone hate a young child. She thought back to her own experiences with other people's children and her intolerance of most of them. She and Tom were different because she had children of her own, but in other ways, they were so similar it was uncanny, and it unnerved her. It was almost too shameful to admit, but she knew she had a jealous streak in her, and she didn't like the attention children craved especially if it meant they took the focus off her and her thoughts immediately turned to Grant and what might happen if one day they were to become an item.

Maria apologised for going on so much, and Chloe reassured her that it was okay because as a nurse it was her job to listen, but she wanted to help because she hoped Maria was now someone she could comfortably call a friend and not just a work colleague.

According to Maria Tom had agreed to get help for his behaviour, but she said she had been the victim of his broken promises too many times before and even though she wanted to believe him, she didn't think he was committed enough to see it through. Tom had pleaded with her to give him another chance, and he even offered to take her away to the lovely country hotel that she'd spotted in a brochure a few months back, but it was too little too late, and she'd packed a few bags of essential items and taken herself off to her sister's house for some much-needed time away from him. Maria's theory was it would give them both some thinking time, and if Tom could prove he was serious by getting the help he needed, then there might be some room for negotiation. She also wondered if they would actually miss each other because if they didn't that would be mean the end of their marriage for good and she wasn't sure if she was ready to accept that possibility that yet.

After talking with Maria, Chloe made up her mind to send Grant a message straight away. She hadn't wanted to make the first move, but realistically she knew she was just being stubborn, and she needed his opinion on the car she was hoping to buy because if she didn't hurry up the trader might sell it to someone else and then she'd be disappointed.

Maria said Grant was shy but she'd seen a spark between them which she suspected would take very little to ignite and despite her reservations about Chloe and Crystal she thought it would be a pity if they didn't at least try. She hoped she wouldn't live to regret her role in bringing them together because she couldn't help being protective of Grant and little Crystal, and she was relying on the somewhat improbable theory that Chloe might have grown up enough to learn from her past mistakes.

Tom

Somewhat predictably, Tom had retreated into his man cave to sulk. He and Maria had argued before, but he'd always found a way round it, and he was convinced she would jump at the opportunity of the weekend away at the expensive country hotel. He felt insulted when she told him that she wasn't prepared to be bought anymore and apart from anything else he thought it was downright unappreciative of her.

She insisted on working full time although he earned more than enough in his job as a city banker for them both to live comfortably. As they didn't have children, she said she would be lonely on her own at home all day and besides *those damned cats of hers* as he always called them cost a small fortune in food and pet insurance. He was also fed up with having cat litter trays everywhere, but she insisted they were indoor cats, so their home stank like a public toilet the majority of the time. Initially, the litter trays were confined to the utility room, but now that there were more cats, they were scattered all over the house which was not only unsightly but unhealthy too.

It had been over a week since they'd argued, and he

thought she'd be back by now, but he'd heard nothing which was unsettling. It was odd not having her around, and he thought he missed her, but he wasn't sure if it was for the right reasons. She was a good wife and always made sure he came home to a decent home cooked hot meal, and she cleaned up after the cats too, but if he wanted he could hire a housekeeper to do all those things which made him wonder whether he would actually miss having her around at all.

She'd told him she was going to her sister's house which was only a few miles away, but he'd never been fond of Maria's high-flying spinster sister Thelma, so he kept his distance and presumed she'd come back when she was ready. Maria said he was jealous of Thelma which he staunchly denied but deep down he was intimidated by her stern business-like approach which Maria said was just something that came with the job. She was a senior manager in the NHS and a bit of a financial genius, and against all the odds, she managed to make sure her department never overspent. She was the first to admit she ran a tight ship, but that was how she'd got to where she was today, and she intended to stay there. She wasn't interested in marriage or children and lived extremely comfortably on her own in a large double fronted four-bedroom house in a quaint village on the outskirts of town. Tom thought it both extravagant and unnecessary for a single person to live in such a large property, but as far as Thelma was concerned, she had earned it, and she could afford it, and it was no one else's business how she chose to spend her money. Apart from the two girls Maria's parents had no other children and made no secret of the fact they were disappointed not to have any grandchildren. Maria was a private person and chose not to discuss their fertility problems with her parents, but he knew they had an inkling that something was wrong because Thelma had told them to stop dropping hints about grandchildren and after that, they miraculously stopped pestering them.

Although all the tests had been inconclusive, Tom was certain Maria was the reason they couldn't have children. It had been fifteen years since he first met the pretty French au pair girl Arielle on the train on the tedious daily commute to work and they'd had a brief fling which resulted in her getting pregnant. He panicked and shamefully told her to get rid of it but had later heard on the grapevine that she'd gone back to France and had a healthy baby boy who she opted to have adopted. He hoped the lad had a happy upbringing wherever he was, and his heart ached for the son he would never know. It had been his dream to have a son of his own to carry on the family name and play footie with, and the irony of it was he did have one somewhere who would be a teenager by now but in all probability, would never know or even want to know him. He knew now that he had been selfish, but like a lot of blokes, he wanted the best of both worlds, and a baby would have complicated things. He often wondered if Maria would have understood if he'd been man enough to tell her but knowing how much she wanted a baby of her own he couldn't risk losing her over it so when Arielle fled the country he was able to breathe a huge sigh of relief. The baby was confirmation that he wasn't firing blanks, but Maria could never know about him because Tom was convinced she would never be able to forgive his infidelity and it would almost certainly cost him his marriage if it wasn't already over that was.

In an attempt to save his marriage and appease Maria, Tom reluctantly explored counselling options. He wasn't convinced he was the one who needed help. After all, he didn't choose to have ten cats, but if it kept her quiet and got their marriage back on track, he was willing to give it a go. The waiting time for counselling on the NHS was six to eight weeks unless you were suicidal or at crisis point, and he sincerely hoped he would never be unlucky enough to reach that level of desperation. He thought it was a pity that it wasn't Thelma's department because she would have made sure that funding was in place without a lengthy wait, but it wasn't, so he had no choice but to scroll through the endless list of private practitioners until he found one that sounded okay.

At first, he wasn't sure whether to select a male or female therapist. He thought a man might be more sympathetic to his needs especially if he got as far as talking about his affair with Arielle and his son who was presumably still living somewhere in France oblivious to his existence. On the other hand, a woman might be more sensitive and sympathise with him about his childless marriage, but then he thought about Thelma and changed his mind as she was living proof that not all women had a sensitive side.

The names were listed in alphabetical order, and there was a link to a webpage under each one. He decided to start at A and work his way down the list until he found one he liked the look of. The first name on the list was Abigail who frankly looked about twelve in her photograph followed by Abraham who looked distinctly camp and according to the first line on his webpage believed only God could heal 'broken souls', and as he was neither broken or religious, he ignored the rest of the gumpf on the page. He carried on scrolling past more names Adam, Aiden, Alicia which he thought was an incredibly beautiful name but sadly her picture didn't match his expectations, Alison and then Amberina. He stared at the name for several minutes before clicking on her profile, surely it couldn't be her or could it. To the best of his knowledge, she was a tree hugger, not a therapist, although in his opinion both were a bit peculiar. He drummed his fingers impatiently on the desk while waiting for the page to load and then found himself staring in disbelief at a picture of a chubby redhead with an awkward grin that looked more like a grimace and his suspicions were confirmed. Under normal circumstances, he would have closed the page and skipped to the next name on the list, but curiosity got the better of him, and he felt compelled to read on. According to her profile, she'd completed an open university degree only two years earlier and now specialised in helping female victims of bullying, especially those struggling with low self-confidence or poor self-esteem. She offered one to one counselling sessions which Tom thought would be worse than a prison sentence or group therapy for those who felt strong enough to cope with a group environment. He couldn't help grinning as he imagined Amberina reeling them in and then brainwashing them all about the dangers of aerosols and plastics to the ozone layer as part of her singlehanded mission to save the planet. There was strength in numbers, and before long she could be the leader of her very own cult with a whole army of female converts with hairy armpits and body odour. He couldn't understand why Grant hadn't told him about this, after all, they were supposed to be best mates, but then again, he hadn't exactly been very kind to Grant about Amberina so there was no real reason why he should. All the same, he felt a bit put out about it and made a mental note to mention it next time he saw him.

Eventually, he decided on a therapist called Cain as he thought the name sounded manly and seeing as Maria was obsessed with some rugged-looking bloke called Cain in one of the TV soaps, he hoped it might be a good omen. On the other hand, there was some geezer called Cain in the Bible who allegedly killed his brother Abel in a fit of jealousy, so for all Tom knew he could be an axe murderer but he wasn't religious and didn't believe in all that stuff anyway, so it didn't matter, the most important thing was for him to win Maria back because despite everything he couldn't imagine a life without her.

GRANT

It had been almost two weeks since the double date, and Grant had resigned himself to the fact he was unlikely to hear from Chloe now. He was disappointed because apart from the gobby Tom he thought the date had gone well and when he held her in his arms for that brief moment when she tripped over her own feet he felt certain there was a connection between them.

He'd thought about ringing her several times, but he'd chickened out after Tom told him she was out of his league. When he first saw her standing at the bar, he couldn't believe his luck, and he loved the way she blushed shyly like a teenager with a crush before rushing outside making some daft excuse about being hot. He really thought he had been in with a chance with her, but unfortunately, it looked as if Tom was right yet again and he really was punching above his weight this time.

Tom liked to be right, and most of the time Grant let him get away with it, not because he was always right, but because it was easier than arguing with him about it. He had been right about Amberina to a certain extent, and he took great delight in reminding Grant about it on a regular basis. With Tom he always seemed to be in a no-win situation. Amberina was too ugly for him yet apparently Chloe was too pretty for him, but so far he hadn't had any luck finding an in-between version of either of them, and even if he did Tom would undoubtedly find fault with something because he always did. He often wondered if Tom was jealous because he could be obstructive when he wanted to be, but according to Maria, he'd been the one that instigated the double date so that wouldn't really make any sense.

He was overjoyed when a text came through from Chloe asking if he'd mind giving her a second opinion on a car she was interested in buying. It was only a little step, and he didn't want to read too much into it, but it was a step in the right direction, and he hoped they would be able to carry on moving forwards from there.

He didn't tell Tom about the text because he didn't want him putting a downer on it again and just for once he wanted to be able to prove him wrong. Over the past week he'd had to put up with Tom whinging and moaning more than usual but under the circumstances he was doing his best to be supportive because he had been brought up to believe that's what friends do during times of crisis even though he knew Tom would be unlikely to do the same for him if it were the other way around. He was also pushing 'the friend in need' cliché to its upper limits right now, and Grant wished he had the courage to tell him he was nothing but a self-centred pain in the arse because at the end of the day he had more than enough of his own problems to deal with.

Tom and Maria had been the perfect couple once, but they'd married young and grown apart. At one time they would have pulled together but nowadays it looked like they were on opposite teams with different goals and Grant wondered whether they would get through it. He hoped they would because divorce was unpleasant and generally bought out the worst in people, and Tom's attitude was bad enough now. Nevertheless, he was surprised it had taken Maria this long to leave him. Lately, she had started to look tired, and everyone except Tom could see she was struggling to cope with the psychological impact of the menopause which had brutally shattered her dreams of ever becoming a mother. Grant thought the arrangement was unlikely to be permanent because despite everything Maria was the hinge that still held strong while Tom was falling apart, and Maria was far too compassionate a person to allow that to happen. He was certain she was just teaching him a lesson and in his opinion not before time, but Tom played his cards close to his chest and Grant was certain there was something he hadn't told him, something very important that he didn't want anyone to find out about but now wasn't the time to pry because although Tom would never admit it he was vulnerable, and Grant wasn't the type of man to use that to his advantage.

FIRST DATE

Chloe arranged for them to view the car on Saturday morning, and Grant was rather hoping she would be agreeable to a spot of lunch afterwards. She had already been to see it on her own, but she was keen for someone else to give it the once over before committing to buying it. He didn't know why she had chosen him because although he had an interest in cars he knew very little about them mechanically and he'd already told her that. He secretly hoped it was her way of saying she wanted to see him again, but Tom's words still echoed at the back of his mind, and he was beginning to believe that he was right, and she was out of his league after all.

He wasn't sure if it was a proper date as such, after all they had only arranged to go and look at a car together, but he hadn't been out on a proper one to one date with a lady since the breakup of his marriage, and he was determined to make the most of some female company. According to Tom Amberina was no lady and wouldn't have looked out of place in the New Zealand rugby team but for Grant beauty was more than just skin deep and despite everything he knew she had a good heart, and he was grateful to her for giving him the opportunity to appreciate her emotional, intellectual and spiritual qualities.

He was careful not to overdress for the occasion, but he still wanted her to notice he'd made an effort because as Tom kept reminding him first impressions were important. He usually preferred to blend in but there was a lot at stake today, and he was mindful that this might be his last chance to impress her. He pulled on a pair of dark blue jeans and then spent a ridiculous length of time trying to decide what top to wear with them. Eventually, he decided to keep it simple with a black polo shirt and modern tailored tweed jacket which he'd bought on impulse a few months previously simply because it was in the sale but was still outrageously expensive and almost certainly an unnecessary, extravagance. He nearly took it back, but as Tom pointed out, he rarely treated himself these days and somehow that helped to justify the expense. He also knew how much Tom disapproved of the amount of money he spent on Crystal and said he was turning her into a *"spoiled little brat"* but it would have been cruel to remind him that he couldn't possibly understand because he wasn't a father and deep down he knew that was part of the problem.

As he pulled up outside Chloe's house, he felt his tummy turn somersaults in anticipation of seeing her again. He assumed it was first date nerves, but it was not something he'd ever experienced with Amberina so he couldn't be sure but whatever it was it made him feel all boyish again, and as a man on the wrong side of forty it felt good to feel young again. Having been raised by elderly parents, there hadn't been many occasions when he'd felt youthful. On parent evenings his teachers always said he had an old head on young shoulders which at the time he took as a compliment but now realised they probably meant he was a weird geriatric kid who'd grown old before his time thanks to his old-fashioned parents.

Chloe was keeping watch from an upstairs window while surreptitiously hiding behind a curtain waiting for Grant to arrive. She'd deliberately kept herself hidden from view as her neighbours had a tendency to be nosey and she didn't want Grant to see her as he drove down the road in case it made her look too keen. She was looking forward to seeing him again, and although she hadn't yet told him, the car was a bit of a ruse because she had already informally agreed to buy it and had even put down a small deposit to secure the sale. She planned to pay the outstanding balance today and then hopefully drive it away, but she needed a lift to the garage because unsurprisingly the man had refused to take the ancient tangerine orange box in part exchange.

She had deliberately dressed a little bit flirtatiously for the occasion in a figure-flattering skater dress that emphasised her long legs before pulling on her favourite ankle boots with small wedge heels that she hoped she wouldn't trip up in. She blushed at the memory of that trip, but her body still tingled from his touch, and she hoped he wouldn't need an excuse like that to hold her in his arms again. As he stepped out of his top of the range company car her eyes were drawn to the jeans that accentuated his toned body and tight buttocks and without warning, her heart started to beat so fast she momentarily felt giddy and faint. She forced herself to take some slow deep breaths, so she could compose herself before answering the door. Up until this moment, only Mel had ever had that effect on her, and she wasn't ready to allow another man to have that sort of power over her, at least not yet.

By the time she reached the door, her breathing had almost returned to normal, and she managed to greet him with a cheery hello which she hoped would be enough to hide her inner turmoil, but she needn't have worried because Grant was far too busy concentrating on his own behaviour to notice. He had been rehearsing what to say all morning, but now she was standing in front of him she might as well have been naked because he was temporarily lost for words.

She was even prettier than he remembered, and Chloe wasn't disappointed either. She liked a guy who wasn't afraid to experiment with different dress styles and admired the mix and match smart jacket with the jeans. There was a time when she thought tweed was for farmers and country bumpkins, but it'd had made a comeback, and this guy could definitely carry it off. Her mum used to joke tweed was for Hooray Henrys, a disparaging term used to describe loud- mouth arrogant public schoolboys but when Chloe joked she must be the female equivalent of a Hooray Henrietta because of her own private school education her mum quickly changed her mind about it and decided it was evidence of good breeding.

Grant hadn't yet spoken, but by the look on his face, she assumed he approved, and she was glad she'd made the effort. Impulsively she took him by the arm and light-heartedly asked him to escort her to his car, after all, they made a good-looking couple, so they may as well step out in style.

Like a perfect gentleman, Grant opened the passenger door for her and Chloe smiled as she climbed in lifting her dress just a little higher than necessary to expose a glimpse of thigh before pulling it back down again. He hadn't commented, but she could tell he had noticed because his cheeks had coloured ever so slightly, and she couldn't help but admire his natural innocence. As usual, the neighbours' curtains were twitching but she no longer cared what they thought. In recent months she had given them all free tickets to see the circus clowns, but today it was showtime.

When they arrived at the garage Grant was expecting them to spend time together inspecting the car, but Chloe seemed happy to just point to where it was parked while she disappeared inside the portacabin to chat to the car salesman. He wandered over feeling a bit confused but also a bit relieved because he didn't really know enough about cars to advise her and he didn't want her buying something that was not up to scratch mechanically. He had seen the orange box as she called it parked on the drive in front of her garage and it reminded him of something a new age hippie like Amberina would drive about in. It wasn't the sort of vehicle that would earn you much street cred, and although he didn't like to think of himself as a snob it wasn't exactly compatible with the neighbourhood, and he imagined Chloe's neighbours would be glad to see the back of it too. He wandered slowly around the car, admiring the shiny red metallic paintwork and alloy wheels. It was stylish and sporty although a bit on the small side he thought for a tall lady like Chloe, but he could already picture her driving it and she obviously could too because when he got to the front windscreen, there was a very clear sold sign displayed in the window. He smiled when he realised he had been nothing more than a chauffeur, and she had got him there under false pretences, but secretly he was delighted because it had to mean she liked him and despite Tom's morbid negativity perhaps she wasn't out of his league after all.

Chloe came skipping back excitedly jangling the keys to her shiny new set of wheels, and he impulsively swept her off her feet and spun her around until she pleaded with him to stop before she was sick. He didn't know exactly what made him do it, but he couldn't help himself because she reminded him of an excited schoolgirl and it was something that always made Crystal squeal with delight whenever she came running to him. Tom said she took after her mother and squealed like a pig, but he turned a blind eye to the hurtful comments because Crystal was his little girl and although it would've been nice to have support from the guy who was supposed to be his best mate he didn't actually need it, and he certainly didn't need his approval to carry on being a good dad to her.

Now was his chance to ask her out to lunch but he was worried she might turn him down in favour of her new car, but she beat him to it and boldly suggested they take the shiny red Ford Puma out for a run and stop for a spot of lunch somewhere along the way. As it happened, Grant knew of a lovely country hotel that offered superb afternoon cream teas with thick clotted cream and strawberry jam on a choice of tasty fruit scones. He wanted to get away from all the hustle and bustle of the town centre and with Crystal at her grandparents for the day it was the perfect opportunity to relax undisturbed and get to know the new lady in his life a little better. As it was a hotel he hoped she wouldn't think he was being presumptuous, but he had been there a couple of times in the past with Amberina who on both occasions managed to eat an entire afternoon tea for two all by herself, but he knew Chloe was different and would be more likely to appreciate the classy regency style conservatory with its comfy chairs, and far reaching views over the rolling English countryside before stumbling across the glistening sea and rugged coastline far beyond.

The salesman was happy for him to leave his car at the garage and as they headed south away from the city towards the coast in the surprisingly powerful little car

Grant finally felt able to relax. After working hard all week it made a change not to be trailing around some zoo or theme park somewhere with Crystal on a Saturday, but he had no doubt she'd make sure he made up for it tomorrow. He wondered if Tom was right because deep down he knew he did spoil her, and he didn't want her turning in to a brat, but like most part-time dads he felt guilty for not being there for her and giving her what she wanted seemed a small price to pay to compensate for his absence as a full-time parent. He made up his mind it would be sensible and also much kinder on his pocket if he were to gradually cut back on the treats and reduce her expectations. He knew Amberina didn't indulge her and she needed to learn to appreciate there were other ways of spending quality time together like doing puzzles or playing board games or simply just going to the play park. The park would be good because it would encourage her to be more active and hopefully run around with other kids because although he'd tried to ignore it and put it down to puppy fat it was beginning to look like she'd inherited her mother's genes and appetite and at only four years of age she was already starting to look a bit podgy. He didn't want a fat kid because he didn't want her picked on at school and he knew it would be partially his fault for giving her too many sweets and despite Amberina's excuses about having a slow metabolism he knew the reason she was fat was because she ate far too much food.

The hotel car park was busy and full of luxury cars and limousines because it seemed the hotel was hosting a wedding fair that day. Grant suggested they move on to somewhere quieter, but Chloe said it might be fun to wander around pretending to be the next Mr and Mrs and although he wasn't entirely convinced by the idea he went along with it because as she pointed out, it was something different to do.

Luckily the car was small, and Grant was impressed as she expertly reversed it into a small gap between a vintage Bentley and a Volkswagen camper van with ribbons on. They got a few funny looks from people, but Chloe didn't flinch and much to his embarrassment she wound down her window, and apologised for being late before announcing that the Puma looked great with ribbons on and was available for bookings.

At the other end of the car park near the hotel entrance, Grant thought he saw a car he recognised, but there were so many people milling around he couldn't be sure. It was an Atlantic blue Volkswagen Golf and a car that would usually stand out in the crowd but today parked among all the luxury vehicles it almost looked insignificant. There was only one person he knew with a car like that, but to the best of his knowledge he would have no reason to be here today, so he put it down to coincidence and forgot all about it.

Outside it was warm and sunny so Grant slipped the tweed jacket off and then raised his arms up above his head to stretch them out after the journey. Chloe couldn't help noticing his strong rippling biceps and toned chest muscles and wondered why he was still single. He looked more like a male model, but he was far too modest to know it, and that was one of the things she liked best about him. He was so unpretentious unlike the majority of the guys on the dating site, and she wondered if one day they would come to a wedding fair like this for real. Today was all about having some fun in the sun, and she giggled as she looked back and saw a couple staring bewildered at her modest little car.

Grant loved seeing her so relaxed and playful, and before he could stop her, she made a beeline for a classic open-top vintage American Ford before loudly announcing *"this car is a must-have darling don't you think"* after which Grant had difficulty shaking off the owner who was desperate to get them booked in.

They continued to wander around outside watching the soon to be married couples laughing and holding hands as they posed together in posh cars with a glass of bubbly in their hands and Grant wondered how long it would be before they became divorce statistics. Since his divorce, he was cynical about marriage and couldn't understand why couples spent thousands of pounds trying to impress ungrateful guests for one single day when that money could be put to better use like buying a home. After they'd exhausted all the outdoor exhibits, they decided to make their way inside for a much-needed cup of tea and a slice of cake. Chloe said there would be cake designers inside and she reckoned there would be free samples to taste, but Grant had set his heart on a cream tea and providing there was room in the conservatory that was where he intended to go.

As they reached the hotel entrance, Chloe stopped to admire the blue car. It looked familiar but she couldn't remember where from, but Grant had already spotted the personalised number plate V007 TOM and he knew exactly who the wannabe James Bond car belonged to, but he couldn't for the life of him think what the hell someone like Tom would be doing here.

He didn't want to bump into Tom today of all days, and he hoped Tom might have lent his car to someone for the day, but he knew that was unlikely because Tom was a poser and his car was his most prized possession, and predictably just as they opened the door Tom was making his way out. Tom looked just as surprised to see them as they were to see him, and he stared accusingly at Grant as if to say why didn't you tell me you were meeting Chloe today. Tom had an annoying habit of making Grant feel guilty even when he had nothing to feel guilty about and at forty-something Grant didn't see why he should report his every move to Tom who in the absence of having anything better to do was becoming more like his parents every day. As far as Grant was concerned, Tom was the one who had the explaining to do and he was still waiting to hear what he was doing at a wedding fair.

As usual, Tom took over, and before Grant could stop him, he had managed to invite himself to afternoon tea with them. Grant flashed him a look of annoyance, but Tom chose to ignore it and led the way to the conservatory to find a table for three. Grant hoped there wouldn't be one, but a family was just leaving, and Tom rushed over before anyone else could get there. Grant was fuming, but Chloe was intrigued because she could sense the tension between the two men, and as far as she was aware they were supposed to be best friends, even though she couldn't help thinking their friendship seemed a bit one-sided.

It had been dark when Tom and Maria picked her up to go bowling that night which is why she hadn't recognised the car straight away, but she knew there was something familiar about it, and now Tom had solved the mystery. Considering his wife had recently left him Tom seemed to be in good spirits, almost too good and it wasn't long before he was laughing at his own jokes again and as usual poor Grant was playing the role of the easy victim. She willed Grant to stand up for himself after all everyone had baggage of some kind and surely his ex-wife and kid couldn't be as bad as Tom made them out to be. Maria had told her they couldn't have children and she agreed Tom sounded jealous and immature, but it almost seemed more than that, like he was holding a grudge against something or someone and whatever it was it was eating away at him.

Eventually, Tom ran out of insults, and for a brief moment, they were all quiet. Grant was still wondering why he was there, and up until now, Tom hadn't willingly volunteered any information. Finally, he blurted out rather sheepishly that he was looking at venues to renew his wedding vows as a surprise for Maria and seeing as this particular hotel was a favourite of hers he thought it might be a welcome gesture and a way to mend their broken marriage. As usual, Tom had managed to make it all about himself, and it took a good two hours for Grant and Chloe to persuade him he was getting a bit ahead of himself and to convince him to cancel the reservation.

By the time Tom left, Chloe was feeling mentally exhausted. Tom pleaded with her not to tell Maria about his plans, and she reluctantly agreed providing he promised to keep up the counselling sessions and not come up with any more stupid ideas.

Tom was grateful to Grant and Chloe for being there to talk him out of what he now realised was an impulsive and stupid idea. It must have been fate them all being at the hotel at the same time but seeing them together had helped him to realise that being part of a couple was important to him and now he was more impatient than ever to win Maria back. He could tell by the look on Grant's face that he wasn't welcome there, but he didn't feel wanted by anyone anymore, and he was lonely. He missed the companionship and seeing the two of them together made him feel redundant and even though Cain said some things couldn't be rushed the whole counselling thing was starting to feel like a very long-winded way of winning his wife back.

Grant and Chloe made the decision to leave shortly after Tom. Grant's plans for a nice relaxing afternoon had been turned upside-down, and they were both emotionally exhausted from it all. He knew Tom hadn't deliberately gate-crashed his date although under normal circumstances he wouldn't put it past him to do something like that but in his mind, it was a missed opportunity, and now he was worried it might have ruined his chances with Chloe forever.

CHLOE

G rant appeared preoccupied on the journey back to the garage to pick up his car, and Chloe stayed silent as it seemed rude to interrupt his thoughts. He clearly had something on his mind, and although the day hadn't quite panned out the way she thought it would it hadn't been all bad. She knew it had been a bit mean of her to tease Grant about the wedding car, and although she wasn't entirely convinced he appreciated the joke, he had still behaved like a perfect gentleman and gone along with it to humour her.

She knew she could be impulsive but to leap into a wedding car on a first date was probably a bit wild even by her standards. Of course, Grant could never know that the striking vintage American car was the car of her dreams should she ever get married again. She had come close once with Mel and had even got as far as choosing her dress, but it had all been hypothetical because although they'd talked about marriage a few times, he had never actually got around to proposing to her. She knew now that he had never really been hers to have, he had been like a book on loan from the library, the only difference being it didn't hurt to give a book back, and if she had really wanted to keep the book there was always the option to buy it, but sadly for her Mel hadn't been for sale, except perhaps in her dreams.

When they reached the garage, Grant turned to her and apologised about Tom interrupting their plans. Chloe laughed and brushed it off before telling him not to be so silly, after all it wasn't his fault Tom was there, before jokingly adding in they would have to make sure he wasn't there the next time they went out together. She said it without thinking, and blushed with humiliation when she realised she was being presumptuous in assuming Grant wanted another date with her, and she was relieved when he ignored her obvious embarrassment and responded by giving her an appreciative hug instead. As he released her she met his gaze and once again she was drawn to his warm, hypnotic eyes, and she knew that given time she could fall in love with him, but she also knew he was part of a package and that worried her, because what if Tom was right about his ex-wife and kid and they really were as shocking as he made them out to be.

MARIA

At work the following week, Maria was convinced that Chloe was ignoring her, and she intended to find out why. She knew she'd arranged to see Grant at the weekend, and she had been looking forward to an update, but Chloe was suspiciously quiet, and it seemed to her like she was deliberately avoiding making eye contact with her. She was disappointed because after their night out she thought of Chloe as a friend now and in view of the fact she had been there for her during some very dark moments she assumed Chloe would be happy to return the favour.

She didn't mind staying with Thelma, but it wasn't the same as being in her own home or sleeping in her own bed, and despite Thelma's insistence that she treat the place as her own she couldn't help feeling like a guest staying in a luxury hotel somewhere.

Thelma's house exuded elegance and grandeur both inside and out and with its impeccably maintained interior it could easily have passed as a show home, but Maria wasn't used to living in a show home and like every holiday she knew it would have to end at some point. She still wasn't sure if she was missing Tom, but she missed her cats and Thelma didn't have any animals because like children they made a mess and she couldn't abide mess under any circumstances.

She wanted to miss Tom, and if she thought about it long and hard enough she could almost convince herself that she did miss him, but deep down she knew it was the routine she was missing, and Tom was a bit like a comfy pair of slippers only they weren't quite so comfortable anymore. Whatever the outcome she certainly wasn't going to do a Chloe and rush down the internet dating route. Staying single like Thelma had its benefits and providing she had her cats for company she thought it might actually suit her.

When they were kids, she and Tom spent many happy hours discussing what type of house they were going to buy and how many children they were going to have but the kids never came along and the only thing that made the house feel like a home now were her beloved cats. She knew that if they'd had children they would probably be grandparents by now and there would be memories to treasure in every room, but it wasn't to be and if it weren't for the cats the house would be nothing more than four walls supporting an empty shell.

Tom had sent her a text message over the weekend and despite her telling him not to contact her until he'd sorted himself out she was surprised it had taken him so long. She knew he didn't like his own company and he wasn't good at entertaining himself, and she imagined poor Grant had probably had enough of him by now especially if he and Chloe were an item. She thought Chloe might have told her if they were, but for some reason, she was acting strange, and Maria was certain she could see guilt written all over her face.

Tom said he was missing her, but she was sceptical

about his reasons. He was the typical arrogant male who still believed the woman should be the chief cook and bottle washer in the house and he wasn't used to looking after himself and up until now he had never had to. Despite going to work herself, she had always been the dutiful wife making sure he came home to a hot dinner and laying out his clean neatly pressed clothes ready for work the next day. As a city Banker, he had to dress smartly for work, and she knew that if she didn't keep up with the washing on a daily basis, the basket would be overflowing with his dirty shirts and ironing wasn't her favourite hobby. These days it wasn't so bad because he was happy to wear non-crease cotton shirts, but he had gone through a stage some years back where he insisted on wearing silk shirts, and they had been a bugger to iron especially if they had accidentally found their way into the tumble drier beforehand. He no longer bothered with the expensive bottles of aftershave either that he used to splash on almost as liberally as the vinegar on his chips and she was relieved to be rid of the stale smell that lingered in the washing basket for days on end even when the basket was empty. She'd had her doubts then, and there were days when she playfully teased him about trying to impress another woman, but he would always laugh and tell her she was the only woman he needed and because it had ended almost as quickly as it started she decided not to pursue it any further. At the time she thought she might be able to forgive a minor indiscretion and she acted on the basis of what she didn't know couldn't hurt her, but deep down she knew it had been eating away at her for years and she could no longer afford to ignore it. She wanted to ask him but at the same time she was afraid of the answer because she was no longer convinced she would be able to forgive him and if she couldn't forgive him their marriage would definitely be over, and she wasn't ready to make that decision just yet.

She wasn't really worried about Tom, after all, he was a fully-grown man who was more than capable of looking after himself, but she was worried about the cats because they couldn't fend for themselves and she knew that if Tom had his way they would all be put up for rehoming at the local rescue centre. She decided to put her mind at rest and sneak home one day in the week while Tom was at work just to check up on them and make sure they were okay, and Tom would be none the wiser about it.

He told her he was attending counselling sessions with some bloke called Cain and Chloe had confirmed this, so she knew it was true. She wouldn't have put it past him to fib just to get her off his back but for once it looked like he had kept to his word and she was proud of him for that because she knew he found it difficult to accept blame when things went wrong. She almost felt sorry for the counsellor but if this Cain was anything like the rugged bad boy in her favourite soap he would not be intimidated by a guy like Tom and the image of a standoff between her husband and her sexy soap hero bought a temporary smile to her face.

Meanwhile, Chloe was hiding in her office trying to look busy. It had been a quiet morning, and although no one ever mentioned the 'Q' word because it was considered to be bad luck, she would normally have wandered out to reception to have a chat with the girls by now. Although she couldn't bring herself to look at her, she could feel Maria's eyes chiselling through her back, and she felt guilty because Maria was a friend, and because of her dumbass husband and his stupid ideas her loyalties were now divided. She had promised him she wouldn't tell her about the wedding thing, but after seeing the hurt in Maria's eyes, she was no longer sure if she would be able to keep that promise.

In a roundabout way Mel had taught her about integrity, and the importance of doing the right thing even when doing the right thing was the last thing she really wanted to do, but now she was confused, and her brain was too mixed up to know what the right thing was, and she was afraid of getting it wrong. A loud knock at her door brought her to her senses but the caller didn't wait for a response and before she had a chance to speak Maria flung the door open, and it was a relief to know her dilemma was over.

THELMA

Although Thelma enjoyed having Maria to stay she had anticipated it being a short-term arrangement but seeing as she was showing no signs of going home anytime soon she decided she was going to have to make some ground rules.

Maria was untidy, and her cleaner who usually had very little to do because Thelma couldn't resist tidying up before she arrived was already making hints about a pay rise. According to Thelma, a disorganised house meant a disorganised mind, and there was no room on her agenda for inefficiency.

She could cope with minor inconsistencies like the toilet roll being hung from the holder the wrong way around, but lately, she had been tempting birds into the garden by hanging trays of wild bird seed from the trees, and now her shiny triple glazed windows were covered in pigeon droppings. To make things worse, she was also encouraging the neighbourhood cats into the garden, and her neatly dug borders were quickly turning in to the local cat toilet.

She wasn't keen on animals or children although she

was starting to mellow with age, and it had been her personal choice not to have either. She knew her parents were disappointed they didn't have any grandchildren, but she wasn't prepared to compromise on her lifestyle and have children just to please them. She knew Tom thought she was a frigid spinster who had never even had a boyfriend let alone sex, but that wasn't entirely true. She had never been short of admirers, and she'd had a few flings in her time but as soon as the guy started to want more she had ended it because she didn't have time in her busy itinerary for long term relationships.

She was happy with her lifestyle choices, but for Maria, it was different because the one thing she desperately wanted in life was cruelly denied to her. Even as a little girl Maria was the maternal one always nurturing her dolls whereas Thelma preferred to read books. At school, Thelma was the brainy one whereas Maria managed to scrape by with basic grades, but they both wanted different things from life, and everyone knew from the first grade that one day Maria was going to marry Tom. She vividly remembered the day when Maria found out that she and Tom were going to different secondary schools and the hysteria that followed for what seemed like months afterwards. Their parents believed they were doing the right thing by sending her to an all-girls school, but Maria kicked up such a fuss they instantly regretted it and to make things worse places had already been allocated, and it was too late to change.

While Thelma went to university to study business and economics, Maria went to secretarial school to learn shorthand and typing. She only went to keep their parents happy because getting a job was never part of her plan and everyone knew she was counting down the days until she and Tom got married so she could settle down and become a full-time wife and mother.

As the eldest daughter, their parents automatically assumed Thelma would be the first to get married, but Thelma had no desire to get married and joked she would always be the bridesmaid and never the bride. Maria insisted she was her maid of honour because as she wasn't married, she couldn't be a matron of honour, and she reluctantly agreed to wear a big purple dress with outrageously puffy sleeves and follow her sister who was wearing a gigantic stiff white meringue down the aisle. She could still picture the image of Grant standing nervously next to the very self-assured Tom, and for some reason, she had winked at him impulsively which made him blush a deep shade of crimson which much to her amusement continued throughout the entire service. Secretly she had always found him attractive, but he was shy, and even though she'd had her fair share of toy boys she was no cougar, and she knew he'd probably run a mile if she came on to him in that way.

She'd graduated from university with a first-class honours degree and secured an immediate job within the NHS. She knew she would be able to work her way up the ladder, and if she stayed put, there would be a nice, little pension pot for her to enjoy at the end of it.

When she'd first started work at the eye department, she secretly thought it was the most depressing place she had ever seen, and she made up her mind she was going to be the person to turn it around. The staff were despondent and lacked motivation as an increasing aged and disgruntled population flooded the already cramped and overcrowded waiting areas. Staff sickness levels were unusually high in comparison with other hospital departments, and waiting times often exceeded two hours. From the outset, she made a mental note of ways that she thought could improve the service before going on to develop her very own failsafe plan to show senior management how making a few subtle changes could be effective. She had done her homework on the subject of change management, and she knew from personal experience that change of any kind couldn't and shouldn't be rushed, and luckily, her efforts paid off.

After only six months, the department was exceeding all targets, and a glowing report by the Care Quality Commission followed which at the age of just twenty-six accelerated her promotion to the administrative head of ophthalmology. At the time she was the youngest senior manager in the entire hospital, and now almost thirty years later she was one of the hospital's longest serving members of staff. She could easily afford to retire after all her mortgage was paid, but she wasn't ready to retire just yet especially as Maria claimed to have read somewhere that most senior NHS staff dropped dead within a year of retirement and having had no children of her own she still hadn't decided who she was going to leave her estate to.

After leaving secretarial college, Maria struggled to find a permanent job, so she thought she would do the sisterly thing and offer her a clerical job in the department. She always knew it would be a bit of a gamble because Maria wasn't exactly enthusiastic about the offer and only accepted on the basis that it would be a short-term solution until she and Tom had a baby. As it happened Maria didn't bond with her colleagues or the patients and resigned on her own accord in favour of a job at the doctors' surgery where she was working now, but she still held a grudge and referred to the clinic as the *'waiting for god'* department because of the high proportion of visually impaired mostly elderly patients who she said had a higher than average chance of getting hit by a bus. Thelma ignored her sarcastic comments because deep down Maria had done her a huge favour by resigning as it had spared her the humiliation of having to fire her own sister. Afterwards, she made a promise to herself not to do favours for family ever again, but once again it looked as if another goodwill gesture might have backfired only this time she was stuck with a permanent lodger.

CRYSTAL

Although Crystal enjoyed spending time with her grandparents at the weekend, she was desperate to meet her daddy's new girlfriend, and she was becoming increasingly frustrated by his reluctance to introduce her to the family. She was five years old now, and her daddy had been dating Chloe for more than a year, and even her rather old-fashioned grandparents were making hints about meeting her. She was like her mum and naturally curious about everything, and she loved nothing more than listening to her dad talking about Chloe because she could feel the softness in his voice when he spoke, and she could tell she made him happy.

She knew Chloe was pretty because she had a pretty name, and she had overheard her daddy tell her grandparents that she had *"a cracking pair of legs on her"* which had made her grandad chuckle. Thanks to her mum, she was fast becoming a good reader, and she was already in the top group in the class for English at school. They had looked up the meaning of the name Chloe together and even though she didn't understand the meaning of a fertility goddess she thought it sounded rather grand and certainly a whole lot better than being named after a type of light fitting like she was. Her mum told her a crystal chandelier was a rather majestic looking decorative light fitting used in posh hotels and country houses and even though she liked the sound of that she still wished she had a normal name like most of the other kids in her class had. When her mum told her that a fertility goddess was a term associated with pregnancy and childbirth she jumped up and down and became super excited because she was convinced she was finally going to get the gift she had always wanted her very own baby brother or sister.

Her dad had laughed at her when she pointed to the book and asked if they were going to have a baby soon, but he hadn't actually said no which she thought had to be a good thing.

She didn't get to spend quite as much time with her dad as she did before he met Chloe, but she didn't really mind because he explained about some of the different ways they could spend quality time together and even though she was only five he said he thought she was becoming a bit of a pro at monopoly now which made her feel important. It was a game that could easily go on for hours which meant she had a good argument for delaying bedtime, and she got to stay up later than usual. The only downside was the lack of sleep made her grumpy the next day, and it wasn't long before her mum put two and two together and gave her dad a good ticking off for not sticking to the agreed bedtime.

Whenever she asked her dad when she was going to meet Chloe, he would always say *"soon"* but soon was beginning to seem a very long time and she was starting to get impatient. Her mum had tried to explain to her the importance of taking things slowly especially introductions of new partners to children, and she wanted to be sure Grant was fully committed to Chloe and vice versa before introducing her to their daughter, but deep down she was as surprised as anyone that it was taking him so long.

There had been no other men in her life since Grant left although there was a guy at the holistic therapies trade fair she'd recently attended who'd briefly caught her eye. It seemed they had a mutual interest in reflexology and they managed to waste an entire afternoon discussing their personal foot fetishes much to the amusement of the stall holder who was surprised it took her so long to work out he was, in fact, a podophiliac who was mentally undressing her scruffy trainers as they talked. When she wasn't with her daughter, she was either busy building up her clientele for her counselling service which she was working hard to establish or working alongside a growing conservation group called 'Buglife' to help save the planet's invertebrates, so she had very little time left for dating anyway. She was pleased Grant had found someone though because despite everything he was a good man and a good father, and she knew she could rely on him to put Crystal's needs first and so far, he had never let her down.

GRANT

Although his relationship with Chloe had blossomed, there was something missing, and even though he knew what it was, he was finding it difficult to resolve. It wouldn't have been difficult if Chloe hadn't been so adamant that they were fine as they were which in a way was true, but he was becoming increasingly concerned by her indifference towards Crystal. Maria had warned him that Chloe wasn't fond of other people's children, but he had made a point of being involved with her family, and he expected her to do the same for him. He knew it was different with her children being that much older than Crystal, but so far it had all been one-way traffic, and now it seemed like they were stuck at the end of a one-way street. To make things worse, Crystal had been going on and on at him about meeting her, and now his own parents and Amberina had joined in, and he was fast running out of excuses.

Chloe said she wasn't ready to meet her because it could complicate things between them and so far, he'd let the matter go but he wasn't prepared to label his daughter as an unnecessary complication any longer and if Chloe wasn't happy to accept the complete package then maybe she wasn't the right woman for him after all.

He didn't expect Chloe to love Crystal like a parent, but he did expect her to want to be a part of her life and the occasional day out at the zoo surely wasn't too much to ask of the woman he hoped might one day be his future wife. They hadn't discussed marriage, but he wasn't ready to rule it out despite Tom's sarcastic comments about it being nothing but a worthless piece of a paper. He no longer worried about what Tom thought because at the end of the day Tom was jealous because it was he who got to share his bed with a beautiful woman while Tom got to share his with Maria's menagerie of cats. Much to everyone's amusement Maria insisted he had to demonstrate his commitment to all the cats before she would even consider returning home to him and they had laughed together about it because they both knew she was only doing it to get her own back on him for trying to organise another wedding behind her back. Chloe had told him about how she had felt guilt-tripped into telling Maria about seeing Tom at the hotel that day, but Tom was still none the wiser about it, and they had to admit it was entertaining watching him fuss over them when it was blatantly obvious he still loathed them.

Grant reflected for a moment on the things people did for love and decided that if someone as arrogant as Tom could pretend to adore cats to please his wife, then Chloe could surely do the same for him and make an effort with Crystal. He knew Tom wasn't perfect, but he also knew that deep down he loved Maria and even if their marriage didn't work out he would be able to say he had tried which was more than could be said for Chloe right now.

CHLOE

Chloe was busy in the kitchen getting things ready for a dinner party with Imogen and Quentin. Much to her dismay her daughter was completely besotted with the man and had been pleading with her for months to give him a chance so with a bit of encouragement from Grant she'd finally relented. She smiled as she emptied an extra tin of tomatoes into the meat mixture which she planned to turn in to one of her signature lasagne dishes. She felt a tiny bit guilty because Imogen had been so happy when she agreed to cook for him and had seen it as a sign of acceptance, but Chloe still had her reservations, and she wasn't about to give him the green light to continue taking advantage of her daughter any time soon. Imogen had, of course, reminded her about the tomatoes, but as far as Chloe was concerned no lasagne would be complete without them. She had deliberately declined any help in the kitchen and told Grant to pop over later once he'd got rid of Crystal at her grandparents. In all fairness cooking for Quentin was the lesser of two evils because if it hadn't been for the dinner party which Grant had actively encouraged, she would have been forced to spend the day with him and Crystal at the zoo. She had pretended to be sorry about missing it and promised to go with them the next time but one way or another she intended to put it off for as long as possible. Grant turned up just after 7 pm by which time the lasagne was bubbling away nicely in the oven with the offending tomatoes disguised by a layer of pasta and a generous helping of thick cheese sauce. He mumbled his approval as the spicy aroma stimulated his taste buds, and as he folded his arms around her small waist, she caught a hint of the new aftershave she'd recently bought him. She turned to kiss him gently on the lips before playfully burying her face in his neck to take full advantage of the fragrance which evoked strong memories of a lost love. For a brief moment, she closed her eyes, and she could see Mel standing in front of her. She whispered his name and gently caressed his soft skin before opening them again only to be confronted by a very confused looking Grant.

When Mel left, it was the only thing she had left to remember him by which was why she refused to wash his pillowcases for months afterwards. She had cried into them night after night until her tears eventually washed the smell away, forcing her to go out and buy another bottle just so she could spill a few precious drops back on to them. She hadn't been ready to let him go, and the powerful aroma helped her to sleep at night but before long she was addicted to the stuff, and she found herself needing more and more of it to help keep his memory alive. It was costing her a fortune, and the medicinal benefits were short-lived because after a while she started to wake up with thumping headaches, and eventually she forced herself to make the decision to stop buying any more replacement bottles.

The silence was deafening, and although it was probably no more than a few moments, it seemed like an eternity before Grant finally spoke. She was worried she might have given the game away after all the only person who knew about Mel was Maria, and she couldn't be sure how much Maria had told Grant about her past. He was talking to her, but she was too busy worrying about what excuse she could make to hear what he was saying and without thinking she blurted out how much she liked the smell putting an unnecessary emphasis on the word smell because smell had 'Mel' in it and if he thought she had said something else he was obviously mistaken. As it turned out she had nothing to worry about because Grant was merely pointing out that he thought it was time to put the garlic bread in the oven because Imogen and Quentin were due to arrive at any time.

The table was set with a huge salad bowl in the centre which contained a generous helping of cherry tomatoes to accompany the lettuce, onions and grated carrot. The four placemats were individually designed in memory of her late boxer dog Norman who had passed away peacefully at the age of seven years after suffering complications from colitis. Norman had been her soulmate, and his loyalty and devotion had helped her through some difficult times, and the placemats were a tribute to a dog that was truly unique. When she was younger, Imogen would cry whenever she got the mats out, but these days she traced her hand lovingly over his face and stopped to give his velvety ears a gentle rub because he used to love having his ears rubbed. She planned to get another dog when the time was right and was waiting on a call from a rescue organisation for a suitable match to be found. She had passed the home check, but apparently, they still had some concerns about the amount of time the dog would be left alone because of her job, especially now the children weren't around so much. She had argued that she only worked part-time, but they were adamant that she would have to be patient and wait for the right dog to come along.

Although Imogen still had a key to the house, she still chose to ring the doorbell because she insisted it was only polite given that she didn't officially live there anymore. Chloe had refused to take the key back because she secretly hoped that one day she would come to her senses and move back in or at least find a man closer to her own age to shack up with. Imogen said age shouldn't be a barrier to love, and although Chloe knew that was true, she would have been happier if it had been someone else's daughter she was talking about. As she walked to the door, she mentally prepared herself to meet Quentin, the man she had heard so much about. She was quietly intrigued, but she hoped she didn't like him because if she did it would make it that much harder to convince her daughter that there were plenty more fish in the sea to choose from.

As she opened the door, Imogen greeted her enthusiastically with an excited shriek which Chloe thought sounded a bit like a child let loose in a toy shop for the first time. Quentin, on the other hand, stood next to her looking awkward with a bunch of red roses in one hand and a bottle of bubbly in the other which he handed over quickly to avoid the need for formal introductions of any kind. As they walked through to the kitchen together, he held Imogen's hand and only let go briefly when Imogen introduced her to Grant, so they could get the formalities out of the way and shake hands. Chloe pretended to look busy by taking longer than necessary to arrange the roses in a vase before checking the progress of the dinner in the oven. So far Quentin had said very little, and he appeared nervous which she knew she could use to her advantage, especially after a glass or two of wine. Usually, she would have a glass while she was preparing the food, but she hadn't eaten much today, and she knew the bubbles would go straight to her head if she did and tonight she was determined to avoid getting drunk until after dinner.

As they sat down to eat Imogen instinctively reached out to stroke Norman's face on her placemat and Quentin placed his hand over hers and gave it a gentle squeeze to silently acknowledge he understood. He was more of a cat person, but his respect for all living creatures came from his love of God and his devotion to his church. He was used to saying grace and giving thanks before dinner, but he knew Imogen hadn't been brought up that way, and like a true Christian he loved her for who she was, and he had no desire to force his own personal values, attitudes, and beliefs on to her or her family.

Chloe gave both the men an extra-large helping of lasagne and told everyone to help themselves to garlic bread and salad and then sat back and watched as Quentin pushed his dinner awkwardly around his plate with his fork. It reminded her of Imogen as a girl retching on every mouthful of peas that Pete forced her to swallow yet somehow, he managed to separate the majority of the tinned tomatoes from the meat and sauce mixture and by the end of the meal there was a neat pile of tomatoes left in the corner of his plate for which he apologised for not eating. Imogen threw her a knowing look which she pretended not to see choosing instead to refill their empty wine glasses and join in the conversation which up until now had been slow. Grant had somehow managed to steer the conversation around to Quentin's daughter, and miraculously he had opened up and was now talking almost to the point of verbal diarrhoea. He explained how he had turned to god for help when his marriage to her mother started to break down and that it was God who had got him through some of the most difficult times in his life, but Chloe remained sceptical. She was still licking her wounds from her own painful experiences of third-party involvement in a relationship firstly with her ex-husband Pete and later with Mel, and it simply didn't work and although she wasn't in any way religious she though God of all people should know better than to go poking his nose into other people's affairs, especially affairs of the heart.

As the evening wore on Chloe didn't warm to him, and even though she hadn't wanted to like him, she was beginning to feel guilty about not liking him because Imogen was clearly smitten and by the way she was talking it seemed like a wedding might be on the cards. She couldn't imagine him being her son in law, after all, he was only ten years younger than she was, but she consoled herself by the fact that Imogen wasn't wearing a ring yet. She was also feeling a little bit hurt that her eldest daughter hadn't confided in her about her wedding plans even though deep down she knew it was probably her own fault for not embracing their relationship sooner and for a brief moment she stopped to think about Grant's daughter Crystal. She would be six next birthday, and Grant had been pestering her to meet her for months now, but she always found an excuse to get out of it and now she wondered if she might end up pushing him away because of it. She vowed to try harder, but she wasn't good at keeping promises, so her goodwill gesture came with no guarantees, but it was a start.

MARIA

Maria was beginning to bitterly regret her decision to allow Tom to pressurise her into getting Chloe and Grant together. Grant was a kind and gentle man and although Chloe was someone, she now loosely classed as a friend she knew that given the opportunity she could easily take advantage of his good nature and frankly he deserved better. It was Tom's fault for hounding her but against her better judgement, she had given in to him, and that was part of the problem because Tom liked to get his own way and until recently, she had allowed him to walk all over her. They had just started dating again, and although they were still only taking little steps, she thought they were making steady progress.

For the time being, she was still staying with Thelma, but Thelma's ground rules were beginning to turn in to a full-length novel, and she wasn't sure she could keep up with her finicky sister's unreasonable expectations any longer. She knew Thelma could be neurotic at times, but her obsessive behaviour seemed to be escalating, and her latest demand was that all the tins in the food cupboard must be stacked in alphabetical order which was unnerving because Tom insisted on doing exactly the same thing with his collection of CD's. She had been the one to insist Tom went for counselling, but now she was beginning to wonder if her sister should be going instead or at the very least undergoing some form of cognitive behavioural therapy. Tom seemed to be making good progress with Cain at his counselling sessions which was why she'd agreed to date him again, but she still wanted him to work on his relationship with Grant and be more accepting of his daughter which for some reason was something he was still struggling to come to terms with. She had no idea why he hated Grant's little girl so much, and she was determined to get to the bottom of it before taking him back. He was hiding something, she was certain of it, and whatever it was she hoped that one day they would be able to work through it together.

She had begun popping home at lunchtimes to check on the cats and do a bit of tidying up which was something she would never normally have done and could only attribute to the influence of living with her overly house-proud sister. At the beginning, she had sneaked in without Tom's knowledge, but she had accidentally given the game away one day by picking up the post and leaving it on the side like she used to and although Tom didn't mention it straight away she was secretly pleased she didn't have to pretend anymore.

It had been a long week, but Friday had finally arrived, and she was looking forward to the weekend because she and Tom had a date night planned together at the cinema. She popped home with the sole intention of picking up a nice dress to wear because Thelma insisted she already kept far too many at her house and she didn't want her wardrobes clogged up with any more unnecessary garments.

As she pulled on to the driveway, their regular postie

gave her a friendly wave from across the road. She hadn't bothered to get her post redirected but seeing as most of their post consisted of bills that were registered in joint names, she didn't see much point in forwarding it especially as Tom paid most of the bills. As she stepped inside the front door, she picked up the post as usual and was just about to put it to one side when one particular envelope caught her eye. It had a foreign stamp on it with par Avion written at the top and a French postmark. On closer inspection, she could see it was addressed to Tom, and she could just about make out the word Toulouse which she knew was a city somewhere in France, but to the best of her knowledge, neither of them knew anyone who lived in France. Years ago, she had gone through a stage of having several pen pals, but she'd lost touch with all but one of them who currently lived in Australia, and she'd only stayed in touch with her because she secretly hoped that one day they might be invited to visit but she was still waiting, and that dream holiday was looking increasingly unlikely. She put it to one side and made a mental note to ask Tom about it later in the hope he might tell her it was from a long lost relative that no one knew existed who was writing to inform them they'd inherited a fortune.

Tom

Tom was panicking. Just when it seemed he was finally getting his marriage back on track a bombshell had literally landed on his doorstep and to make things worse, he knew Maria had seen it because the post had been picked up and left on the side.

He had been looking forward to another date night with his wife and tonight he had planned a special surprise for her, but now it looked as if he was going to have to put those plans on hold for the time being at least.

He could have kicked himself for his stupidity, but the damage was already done. There were so many *'what if'* and *'if only'* questions running through his mind and it didn't matter how many times Cain told him they were irrelevant because they seemed to have taken up permanent residence in his brain. A tremendous feeling of guilt had risen to the surface after lying dormant for years, and he could no longer afford to ignore it. Impulsively he clenched his fist and slammed it angrily down on the table. Why now after all these years did his son want to see him and perhaps more importantly what on earth was he going to do about it.

His mind wandered back to when he first met Arielle on the train all those years ago. She was a pretty young French au pair girl who had come to England to learn the language, and he was a bored commuter with too much testosterone who was flattered by her interest. He knew it was wrong, but it was only supposed to be a fling, and she wasn't supposed to get pregnant. It was too late now to regret not wearing a condom although he wasn't entirely sure he did regret not wearing one because if he had worn one, there would be no son, estranged or otherwise. However, he did regret some of the things he had said to Arielle, especially about getting an abortion, and he did regret not having the courage to tell Maria about it. His behaviour had been both irresponsible and unforgivable, and he swept it all under the carpet in the hope no one would ever lift it again and expose the true extent of his deceit.

He had been speaking with Cain at length about his son who he'd nicknamed Pierre simply because it was the only French name he could think of at the time, but now he had the letter he knew his real name was Avellino. He should have realised that someone with a name as beautiful as Arielle would never call her child something as ordinary as Pierre, but he was totally unprepared for what he found out next. He always assumed his son had been adopted, but after reading the letter that was written in surprisingly good English, he realised that Arielle had, in fact, kept him and raised him by herself with minimal support from her family which only served to increase his feelings of guilt. She had since married a Frenchman and gone on to have two more children, both girls and he was relieved to know his childhood had been a happy one. His son's signature at the bottom of the page released a whole host of unforeseen emotions which flooded his confused mind, and he found himself repeating his name out loud time and time again until it sounded pitch perfect. What he found out next stopped him in his tracks, and whether it was deliberate or coincidental he would never know because Arielle had chosen a name for their son that meant *'longed for'* yet he had never actually told her how much he yearned for a child of his own. He wondered if she too had yearned for a child. He knew she was lonely being in a foreign country on her own away from her friends and family, but he didn't think she was like Maria whose only ambition in life was to have a baby. His mind wandered back to Maria, and his heart ached for her knowing how much she had wanted a child of her own and the dignity she had shown when she realised that motherhood was a privilege the good Lord had denied to her. They hadn't talked about it as much as they should have, and he knew he had failed her by not always being supportive but at the time he was hurting to, and he hadn't been strong enough to carry her grief as well as his own.

The letter sent him straight into panic mode, and the only person he could think to call was Cain, but Cain's phone went straight to voicemail, and then he remembered Cain telling him he'd be away for the weekend but would see him at the usual time on Monday. He hadn't seriously expected the counselling to work, but he'd found an unexpected ally in Cain who incidentally was the only person he'd ever been able to talk to about his son. There had been a couple of times when he'd nearly told Grant, but something had stopped him before he could get the words out and Grant being Grant had let it go. Grant was his best mate and these days pretty much his only mate, but he was also a bit of a doormat because he'd allowed him to walk all over him and although he knew it wasn't right it had become a bit of a habit now to mock him at every opportunity and Crystal was an easy target. He didn't really hate Crystal, but he'd pretended to hate her for so long now he didn't know how to backtrack without losing face. He knew it had got out of hand and he didn't know why he made such hurtful remarks, but he found it hard seeing Grant with his daughter when he didn't even know where his own son was and although he would never openly admit it, he was jealous of the bond Grant shared with Crystal.

He picked up the letter and re-read the content just to make sure he'd read it correctly and not missed anything the first time around. The letter was as precious to him as his love for Maria, but at the same time, he knew it could signal the end of their marriage. He wondered if Maria would allow him to have both or whether wanting both was just plain greedy. He loved Maria, but he also loved his son, and he knew if he'd been honest with her at the start, there was a chance, she might have grown to love him too. Obviously, there were no guarantees she would have loved him, but she was a compassionate woman with a soft heart when it came to animals and children, and he had been with her long enough to know she wasn't the type of woman to hold a grudge.

He studied every word memorising the content in detail as if his life depended on it which in a way it did because his son was planning on coming to England to study English and he wanted to meet him.

AVELLINO

As a young boy Avellino always enjoyed hearing stories about his dad and bedtimes were always the best because instead of reading a normal storybook like most other boys of his age, he would beg his mum to tell him stories about his dad and she would smile softly and talk about him until he fell asleep.

Hearing about his dad made him happy, and he thought it made his mum happy to because he could see the warmth in her eyes when she spoke about him. He had only been a boy then, and he had been too young to see the hurt behind her smile, but he could see it now, and it made him curious, and he had questions for his dad that needed answering.

He was only five years old when his mum married Leon, and he was grateful to him for rescuing them and for giving him the happy childhood that all children deserve. He had lived with his mum at his grandparents' home since he was born, but they made it clear from the outset that they didn't approve of the situation and that their stay was only to be temporary. After four years they'd outstayed their welcome, but his mum's bar job didn't earn her enough money to get them a place of their own, and that was when Leon stepped in to help. His mum had met Leon at work; he was a regular customer in the bar where she worked, and he often popped in for a quick pint on a Thursday night before driving back to his home in the south for the weekend. He worked long hours in the city as a stockbroker, and although he had a lovely home, there wasn't anyone waiting for him when he returned. He had been instantly attracted to Arielle, but he was old fashioned and wanted to court her properly instead of just jumping straight into bed with her but despite his best intentions they never had an opportunity to date properly because he knew she needed to be there for her son and from what she had told him her parents weren't exactly supportive of her or the boy. His job meant he often had to take chances and usually his gambles paid off, but he'd never taken a chance on love before and he hoped he was doing the right thing. Avellino could still remember the night his mum came back from work early and scooped him up with a few of his favourite toys and walked out the door without so much as a backward glance. He had been in bed fast asleep and had no idea what was going on, but he could sense his mum's excitement when she told him they were going on an adventure together and when he eventually woke up, he found himself in a place that he thought only existed in his dreams.

Leon's home was everything a young boy could wish for with oodles of land and plenty of space for a dog which was something he always asked Santa for at Christmas, but it seemed Santa always forgot about him because there was never a wagging tail waiting to greet him on Christmas morning. His mum joked that Santa probably had eyesight problems which caused him to go down the wrong chimney so the following year he enclosed a pair of glasses in his letter to Santa pleading with him to wear them, but he still didn't get his dog, and that's when his grandparents told him to stop going on about it and be thankful that Santa had remembered him at all. He'd had a bit of a tantrum after that because his mum had told him that Santa didn't forget about any children and because he'd concentrated hard on being a good boy all year just to make doubly sure Santa didn't forget about him, he didn't know what else he could do to get Santa to notice him.

Avellino truly believed that Leon was some sort of superhero who had been plucked straight from the page of a fairy tale and sent on a mission to rescue a damsel in distress to bring some happiness into her life, and like all fairy tales this one had a happy ending. He knew his mum had been right when she told him he was their knight in shining armour because he had rescued them both from a very dark place and brought sunshine into their lives, and he had proved himself to be a worthy father by willingly raising another man's child as his own and earning the privilege to be called dad.

Arielle had never forced him to call Leon dad, but he could still recall the day when he surprised him by bringing a scruffy looking pooch home in need of some serious TLC and in his excitement, he had just blurted out the word. Initially, everyone fell silent, and he was afraid in case he'd said the wrong thing, but both parents hugged him tight, and after that, he never called Leon by his first name again. Before long calling Leon dad came as naturally as calling Arielle mum and a few years later when his two sisters came along the words mum and dad became everyday language in their happy but hectic household.

He didn't know much about his dad, but he knew he was from England and he knew his name was Tom. His mum hadn't gone into detail about her relationship with him, but now that he was older and hellbent on finding him; she felt obliged to tell him the truth about him being a married man. She looked down at the floor in shame when she told him, but he didn't think any less of her for it, and as he went to hug her, he felt proud to have a mother who was able to confide in him.

He hesitated briefly before posting the letter addressed to the man who he believed to be his father in England and momentarily questioned his judgement. His letter had the power to alter the course of their lives forever, but he had to know one way or another whether his biological father had the potential to be anything more to him than just a sperm donor.

CHLOE

It was Crystal's 6th birthday, and Grant had arranged to take her out for the day while Amberina went stone worshiping at the summer solstice in Stonehenge with a bunch of freaky looking prehistoric druids. The plan was to take Crystal to the zoo and then have dinner somewhere afterwards. It had been planned for months, and Grant was really looking forward to being able to finally introduce Chloe to his daughter.

Chloe felt queasy the instant she woke up, but despite telling Grant she wasn't really feeling up to going out he was insistent some fresh air would do her good, and she'd half-heartedly agreed that maybe it would. There was a nasty sickness bug going around work, and despite her rigorous hand-washing rituals, she suspected it was her turn to catch it, and she consoled herself that Grant would only have himself to blame if he or his precious daughter caught it next.

Chloe hated zoos at the best of times and strongly believed there was something very wrong about keeping wild animals cooped up in cages instead of allowing them to run free in their natural habitat. She wondered if Grant had a season ticket to the zoo and was trying to get his money's worth because it was the only place he ever seemed to go with the child, but she didn't ask in case he thought she was interested which she most certainly was not. She could see he thought she was trying to make excuses to get out of going and she couldn't blame him because that was exactly what she'd been doing for the past two years so reluctantly she pulled on a pair of jeans and an oversized T-shirt and followed him out of the door. Her tummy felt bloated and swollen, and she hoped the T-shirt would be forgiving enough to cover the buttons on her jeans which she'd already had to undo before they exploded on their own accord. She hoped the discomfort wasn't due to trapped wind because letting Polly out of Jail in front of her future stepdaughter would be extremely embarrassing and she didn't want Crystal telling her mother that daddy's new girlfriend was an uncouth slob who couldn't control her own wind problem.

She and Grant had been together for two years, and although he hadn't yet proposed, she was certain it was only a matter of time before he popped the question. She didn't know what was holding him back, but she thought it was probably something to do with the fact she hadn't met Crystal but today that would be rectified and then there would be nothing to stop him from asking her to be his wife.

Although getting married wasn't an immediate priority she wasn't ready to dismiss the idea completely after all Grant was a good-looking guy that most women would be proud to call their husband and with both their jobs they could afford a comfortable lifestyle together. Her thoughts wandered back to Mel, and almost immediately, her heart softened. She hadn't heard from him again, yet that chapter in her life still wasn't fully closed because he had cheated her of the chance to say a proper goodbye and she hadn't been ready to let him go. She pretended she was because under the circumstances it seemed the right thing to do but a few months before that fateful day when he found his wife lying motionless in a pool of blood, she had put a deposit on a wedding dress and was preparing to marry him. Deep down, she knew she was always further ahead with plans than he was, but for him, the timing had been wrong. She glanced at her phone and scrolled down until she reached his last message to her. It wasn't really the type of message she wanted to remember him by, but she had left it there as a reminder to herself to never get involved with a married man again. He had obviously written it after Claire's funeral when the emotions were still very raw, and despite the disparaging remarks, she could sense his guilt because it was he who would have to live with the knowledge that the last person his terminally ill wife ever spoke to was, in fact, his mistress.

It was a twenty-minute car ride to where Crystal lived in a modest end of terrace house with her mother and by the time they arrived Chloe felt almost as green as the rather primitive looking olive-green cloak that Amberina had draped around her generous frame. She had never met Amberina before, but she recognised her from photographs, and rather embarrassingly she was prancing around on the front lawn holding a child's hand with a group of like-minded people wearing equally dubious outfits.

Although she tried hard to remain objective seeing the plump freckle-faced ginger kid jumping excitedly up and down in front of Grant reminded her of everything Tom had said about her and for a moment she cursed him for influencing her judgement.

As Grant got out of the car, Crystal came running over, and he swept her up and swung her around until she begged him to stop because she said it was making her feel dizzy. Chloe was feeling increasingly dizzy and sick herself and watching all the hysterical antics on the lawn wasn't helping her to feel any better, so she was relieved when Grant finally bundled the excited youngster into the back of the car, so they could be on their way. Amberina waved enthusiastically at Crystal as they pulled away before skipping playfully over to a multicoloured and somewhat wildly decorated Volkswagen camper van that was parked on the other side of the road that Chloe presumed was the group's transport to Stonehenge. Amberina was a free spirit, and a small part of Chloe admired her for her lack of inhibitions. She was also everything that Chloe wasn't and that brought to the surface some nagging doubts, and, on that note, she belched loudly before puking up all over the car.

Grant stopped the car and looked accusingly at the foul-smelling vomit as it dripped unceremoniously from her T-shirt and on to the carpet and into the footwell of the car. Crystal was screaming in the back and trying frantically to open the door that was secured with child locks to get out because by all accounts she had a phobia about sick and Grant was trying unsuccessfully to calm her down. The Volkswagen camper van tooted its horn as it passed them on the road which made Crystal even more hysterical and Grant resigned himself to a day at home valeting the car. Crystal would, of course, have to come with them as apart from his parents there was no one else to care for her, and although he knew they wouldn't mind having her, he didn't want to exhaust his favours by taking unfair advantage of them. As it turned out, Crystal insisted on going to her grandparent's home, and Grant drove Chloe back home in complete silence. He hadn't even had an opportunity to introduce them, and he felt cheated, and now he had ruined Crystal's big day as well. He knew it wasn't really Chloe's fault because she had told him she wasn't feeling well, and it was he who insisted she came out with them, but he thought she was just trying to make excuses to avoid meeting Crystal and now he was looking for someone to blame.

He looked over at Chloe and saw how pale she looked, and for a moment, he felt guilty for thinking about himself. She apologised to him repeatedly, and he could see she was genuinely sorry. He thought she had been looking a bit peaky lately, but he'd put it down to pressures at work. Rather selfishly he hoped Crystal didn't catch whatever it was because if she did, he knew he would never hear the end of it from Amberina whose phobia of sick had rubbed off on their daughter. He kept his fingers crossed, and if it hadn't been a physical impossibility, he would have crossed his toes as well.

MARIA

Despite their differences, Maria and Tom enjoyed a good date night together although she did think he seemed a bit preoccupied at times. She thought he had a romantic meal planned, but instead, they had a quick bite to eat at a burger bar before going to see a film at the cinema. She was surprised because it was a bit of a chick flick and not Tom's usual type of film at all, but he seemed more engrossed with it than she was, and she wondered if he was finally getting in touch with his feminine side. After the film, they had a quick drink at the bar, and then Tom dropped her back at Thelma's which she was a bit disappointed about because she was secretly hoping he might invite her back to share the marital bed with him once more.

She was starting to feel better about herself, and although it had taken a long time, she was finally managing to get on top of her menopause symptoms. Chloe had been nagging her for months to go and see her doctor about it and she was glad now that she had because for once she felt the doctor had really listened to her and she had come away with some new pills that made the physical symptoms more manageable and as a result her emotional wellbeing had improved to. She had even been out and bought herself some sexy new underwear which she hoped would meet with Tom's approval, but so far, he hadn't taken her hints, and she was beginning to wonder whether he still wanted her in that way.

Chloe, on the other hand, was looking dreadful and didn't seem to be recovering very well at all from the recent sickness bug that had struck the staff at the surgery. She looked pale and tired and complained of persistent nausea, which was accompanied by retching at the very sight of food. She even pushed away cups of tea which was unheard of because Chloe never said no to a cup of tea and it wasn't until Maria marched her in to see the senior partner at the surgery that the shocking truth came out. Chloe came out of Dr Dixon's office looking even paler than when she went in, and she was visibly trembling as she handed the little white test strip to Maria which confirmed she was indeed pregnant

The news came as a shock to everyone, especially Chloe, who assumed she was perimenopausal and for Maria, the news was a bitter pill to swallow. She and Tom had yearned for a child of their own, but for some reason or other, the geezer who created the world decided it wasn't to be. She wasn't a greedy person; one baby to love would have been enough, although two would have been nice, and that child would have wanted for nothing. She certainly wouldn't have asked him for five, and she thought it was grossly unfair that someone like Chloe, who wasn't exactly child-friendly, should be given more than her fair share.

She had completely forgotten to ask Tom about the letter, and he hadn't mentioned it, so she assumed it couldn't have been all that important and definitely not a windfall of any kind which in some ways was a pity but like her sister always said , *'what you never have you never miss'*, not that Thelma had ever actually wanted for anything in her entire life.

She wasn't jealous of Thelma, at least she didn't think she was, after all, she had a comfortable life with Tom, or at least she did before she left him, but it wasn't the privileged sort of life her sister had. As a child, Thelma was always the ambitious one, and she knew what she wanted and made damn sure she got it whereas Maria thought she knew what she wanted and didn't get the full package. Tom was her first and only love, and although she still loved him dearly something was missing, and even though they'd discussed adoption once she believed it was too late for them now and even if it wasn't she didn't think it would be fair on the child to have aged parents. She thought back to Grant whose mum had been forty something when he was born and then she thought of Chloe who was also forty-something and pregnant and wondered if she was wrong in thinking it was too late for her and Tom after all. Grant's parents were in their eighties now, but they were still fit and active and in pretty good health, and she wondered if having Crystal around was the secret to their youth. She also wondered how they would take the news that they were going to become grandparents again and for a moment she felt a little bit sad because barring an absolute miracle her parents would never experience the joy of having their own grandchildren to love.

She sometimes wished she hadn't been so stubborn after all if they'd adopted a child there was every chance they would be grandparents themselves by now, instead they were human parents to a menagerie of cats which had temporarily filled the empty void in her life but had only served to anger poor Tom and ultimately driven them apart. She made up her mind there and then that she would go home at lunchtime and prepare a special meal for the two of them and tell Tom that she wanted to come home for good and maybe adopt a teenager too.

Maria was excited about her plan, and as she mulled it all over in her head, the possibilities became more and more real for her. She would, of course, have to go back to Thelma's first to get washed and changed before slipping into the sexy lingerie that she had recently treated herself to. She loved the feeling of soft and silky new underwear on her skin, and she hoped Tom would appreciate her efforts to get things back on track between them in the bedroom department. She had an above knee white faux fur coat that she had bought on impulse a few years previously, but it was still hanging up in the wardrobe somewhere completely unworn. She would grab that at lunchtime too and then turn up at Tom's later that evening wearing the coat with nothing but the lingerie on underneath and she defied him to resist her then.

She was so excited by her plans that lunchtime couldn't come quickly enough but the morning dragged by tediously and at one stage she thought the office clock might actually have stopped working completely. On the stroke of 1 o'clock, she was already in her car and on her way home. She hadn't thought of it as home for a long time, but for some reason today it felt right to do so, and she couldn't resist humming along cheerfully to the songs on the car radio in anticipation of a new beginning.

As she pulled into the drive, she waved at the postie on the other side of the road, and he returned the gesture with a smile. As the front door opened she almost tripped over a pile of what looked like mainly junk mail and she took it inside and dumped it on the sideboard before making her way into the kitchen. As she picked up the kettle to fill with water to make a cup of tea, a letter fell out from underneath the stand, and she realised it was the letter from overseas. If she hadn't touched the kettle, she would never have seen it, and for a brief moment, she wondered if Tom had deliberately tried to hide it from her before reprimanding herself for being so ridiculous because she and Tom never kept secrets from each other. Nevertheless, she was curious because the letter had clearly been opened, and she was tempted to take a quick peek at the contents just to be nosey. As she carefully removed the letter from its envelope she almost stopped and put it straight back without reading it because something didn't feel right. After all, it wasn't her letter to read, and it would be an intrusion of Tom's privacy, but despite knowing it was wrong she knew she had come too far to put it back now.

As it turned out, it was as bad as spying through keyholes. Her mother always told her and Thelma that no good ever came of doing such things not that Thelma would ever do anything remotely naughty anyway because she was a bit of a goody two shoes, but this was worse, much worse than she could ever have imagined, and it deeply saddened her to know that she and Tom had been living a lie for almost half of their married lives together.

She carefully placed the letter back inside the envelope and pondered over what to do next. She could easily have placed it back under the kettle stand, and Tom would be none the wiser, but that would make her as bad as him, and if they still had a future together after this, it had to be a future without any lies. She thought she'd be angry, but she wasn't, but she did feel guilty because that letter confirmed that it was indeed her fault that she and Tom had never been able to have a child of their own. She had long suspected it was her fault although she had no idea why as tests had proved inconclusive, but it was a gut feeling that never went away, and now she knew she was right but being right didn't make it any easier and it wasn't long before she found herself sobbing uncontrollably. As her tears flowed freely they washed away some of the dark clouds and opened her mind to a whole new world that she knew nothing about, yet it was a world that excited her, and she knew instantly what she had to do.

GRANT

Grant was visibly shocked when Chloe broke the news to him about being pregnant after all they had been careful most of the time, and as Chloe was convinced she was perimenopausal, she hadn't worried too much on the few occasions when they'd unashamedly got a bit carried away.

Deep down Grant never thought he would find the right woman to have a child with and although Amberina wasn't his ideal match when Crystal came along it was like a dream come true, and now Chloe was pregnant it was like all his birthdays and Christmases had come at once. He knew Crystal would be thrilled to have a baby brother or sister, and he couldn't wait to break the news to her, but Chloe was adamant he shouldn't tell her until after the pregnancy was confirmed properly by a scan and although he reluctantly agreed he found it hard to hide his disappointment. Over the following weeks, he behaved like an excited kid in a toy shop, and he couldn't resist popping into baby shops at every opportunity, and before long there was a huge pile of Babygro's, vests, tiny white socks and soft toys just waiting for a little person to love them. He knew Amberina probably still had Crystal's baby clothes stashed away in a cupboard somewhere because she had a tendency to be a bit of a hoarder and seeing as Crystal had been a larger than average baby she'd outgrown most of them before she had a chance to get any wear out of them and he didn't like to see things going to waste. At one time he'd cautiously suggested giving them away to a charity shop to free up some room in the house but at the time Amberina had been reluctant to let them go so he wasn't sure why he thought she might be happy to give them away now especially as he was certain Chloe would disapprove of them anyway. Crystal's baby clothes were probably the only normal clothes his daughter had ever worn, and that was only because at the time Babygro's weren't available in flamboyant colours for which he was eternally grateful.

He was hoping Chloe's pregnancy would bring to the surface some of her maternal instincts and encourage her to bond with Crystal, but she seemed more distant than ever, and he was beginning to think it would never happen and while he tried to be understanding his patience was beginning to wear a bit thin. Whenever he mentioned seeing Crystal, she made an excuse about being too tired or feeling sick and although she still looked a bit pale the iron tablets that the doctor had given her had put some colour back into her cheeks, and he joked it wouldn't be long before she was blooming. Chloe didn't seem to appreciate his jokes and raised her eyebrows to show her obvious disapproval, but he loved her 'baby belly' and her plump rounded breasts and although she didn't agree he thought pregnancy suited her.

Chloe was referred for an urgent dating scan because her girth was increasing in size quicker than expected, and her doctor suspected she could be having twins, which was almost enough to make her keel over. She assumed she was about twelve weeks pregnant but couldn't be sure because her monthly cycle had been all over the place of late so when the scan showed she was actually eighteen weeks pregnant with a healthy baby girl she was as surprised as everyone else. When the sonographer handed them the photograph of their precious baby daughter, they both burst into tears, and Grant found himself down on one knee proposing to her and when she said yes everyone around them applauded.

Grant still wasn't entirely sure what it was that had made him propose at that precise moment because there were still unresolved issues with Crystal, but his emotions had got the better of him, and despite everything, he was still quietly confident that they would all come together as a family in time.

There were times when talking to Chloe was like treading on eggshells because she appeared to deliberately misinterpret some of the things he said, and he wondered if she was intentionally trying to start an argument between them. Frustratingly she didn't seem to understand why Crystal or Amberina should know about the wedding or the baby and even when he pointed out that Crystal would soon be her stepdaughter and the baby her half-sister she stormed off like a spoiled child in a huff. Amberina also needed to know out of courtesy if nothing else because she would be the one who would have to deal with the inevitable rollercoaster of emotions and although he knew Crystal would be excited at the news, there was every chance she might feel a bit left out to. She was his first daughter, and he wanted to include her in their plans, but as far as Chloe was concerned she didn't exist, and he was beginning to question his motives for wanting to marry her. He had asked her because it seemed the right thing to do at the time and because he wanted their baby to have two parents who loved each other, but he was no longer sure if love was enough especially if that love didn't extend to Crystal who was equally as important to him. Chloe was jealous of poor little Crystal, he was sure of it, but whenever he voiced his concerns, she would just laugh in his face and make some derisory comment about there being nothing to be jealous about and he knew without a doubt she was referring to her appearance.

Appearance wise Crystal took after her mother, which meant she was 'bigger boned' than some of the other kids her age, but as far as Grant was concerned she was beautiful inside and out. Amberina didn't help matters with her alternative dress sense, and Grant wished she would occasionally think of the child and dress her in something more normal to help her fit in with her peers, even if she didn't quite fit into the same mould as them. Amberina, however, remained adamant that the world was full of people of different shapes and sizes, and she wanted their daughter to grow up to be a confident young woman who wasn't afraid to express herself. Grant wanted that too, but he was afraid Crystal was mimicking her mother's choices and not her own and although he hoped it was just a passing phase he was beginning to wonder if his daughter was, in fact, an exact clone of her mother. He had taken Crystal shopping on a number of occasions to try and buy her some 'normal' clothes, but she was like her mother drawn to gaudy colours and vulgar patterns, and he came to the conclusion she had been well and truly brainwashed.

Unsurprisingly things came to a head following their appointment with the registrar. They'd decided to have a spot of lunch afterwards in a large department store and on their way to the restaurant Grant stopped to browse at some cute little bridesmaid's dresses on the sale rail in the children's department. As he stroked the delicate fabric with his fingers he had visions of Crystal being dressed as a proper little girl in a dress that would complement her vivid auburn hair, but Chloe pulled him away abruptly and announced loudly that she didn't want any bridesmaids at their wedding and the shop assistant who was just about to ask if he wanted any help gave him a sympathetic look before moving on quickly to serve another customer. He was bitterly disappointed because he thought they were making progress given that she had reluctantly agreed they could take Crystal out for her tea at the weekend so they could tell her about the baby and the wedding, but now it seemed they had taken another step backwards with poor Crystal being the innocent victim once more.

Crystal loved weddings and always begged him to stop the car if they passed a church where a wedding was taking place, and he knew it was her dream to be a bridesmaid one day and although their wedding was only going to be a low-key affair he thought it was the perfect opportunity for Crystal to share a piece of the limelight. Chloe, on the other hand, had her own ideas about the wedding and was determined to have her own way, and although he hated himself for doing it, he stood back and said nothing and allowed her to shatter his little girl's dreams once more.

Before long, it was the weekend, and they finally took Crystal out together for the first time as a couple. Chloe's lack of empathy had caused Grant to spend the entire week worrying about it, and he had come close to cancelling on more than one occasion. He had been on tenterhooks waiting for her to cancel because she always managed to find some lame excuse, but surprisingly she went along with it this time without any protest which only served to unsettle him more. Unsurprisingly he was more suspicious of the quiet, amenable version of Chloe than he was of the loud-mouthed opinionated one because being agreeable to anything was completely out of character for her these days. Weddings were supposed to be a time of joy and celebration, yet for some reason, he was filled with angst and trepidation.

Tom was genuinely pleased when he told him about the wedding and even volunteered his services as best man which Grant consented to because he didn't really know anyone else who would be prepared to do it at such short notice. Realistically there wasn't going to be much for him to do but Tom being Tom was insistent on writing a speech and that in itself was enough to fill him with dread because he was fairly certain it would be full of insults about Crystal and Amberina.

Grant hadn't seen much of Tom in recent months because he had been too preoccupied trying to sort out his own shipwreck of a marriage. He also thought Tom might be mellowing because he had suddenly stopped making unfavourable remarks at every opportunity. It was almost as unnerving as Chloe being pleasant, and for a brief moment, Grant wished everyone would go back to behaving like they usually did so he could stop walking on eggshells all the time.

Chloe remained unusually quiet as the three of them sat down for a bite to eat at the quaint little country pub, but Crystal was overcome with excitement. As soon as Chloe stepped out the car, she saw her bump, and she squealed with delight when Grant proudly announced she was soon going to be a big sister. As they sat down at the table, Grant winced when she took off her coat to reveal a bright orange dress with a bold floral design surrounded by an abundance of bright green foliage, but Chloe smiled sweetly and told her she looked pretty, and Crystal was visibly ecstatic to receive such a compliment from her. Grant wasn't convinced and knew she was putting on an act, but he was relieved she knew how to be civil and hoped she'd be able to keep up the performance for the remainder of the day. As Crystal chatted enthusiastically about the wedding and her new baby sister, Chloe became quieter and increasingly withdrawn choosing to listen rather than join in with the conversation. Grant promised Crystal they would go out together to buy her a new dress for the day and Chloe responded by nodding somewhat apathetically which Crystal didn't seem to notice because she was too caught up in the excitement of it all. Grant stuck to the plan and told Crystal she would be attending the wedding with her grandparents and despite her initial protests about her mother not being there with her she eventually agreed the day might be more fun without her. Grant still believed having Amberina at the wedding to take care of Crystal would make life easier all round and take some pressure off his parents, but Chloe wouldn't hear of it and as usual, he gave in to her because he was weak and giving in was the easier option.

As soon as the meal was over Crystal wanted to go home to tell her mum the good news, so they made their way back stopping briefly to buy some flowers from a roadside seller for Crystal to give to her. Being a big sister was the one thing she wanted most in the whole world, and now it was finally going to happen she couldn't wait to tell everyone about it. Grant thought he should be there to help Crystal break the news and Chloe didn't argue with him about it although somewhat childishly she refused to get out the car to meet Amberina. He was glad in some ways that she didn't because he was certain Amberina would have sensed her obvious disapproval and he didn't want Chloe to make her feel bad about herself just because she was different.

Chloe didn't look up as he climbed back into the car and he suspected her cool demeanour suggested she was spoiling for another argument. They'd done nothing but argue lately, and frankly, he was getting a bit sick of it. She didn't ask how Amberina had taken the news, and he didn't bother telling her even though he knew that deep down, she was probably itching to know. Amberina had of course been thrilled and had responded to the news by giving him an impromptu hug. When she pulled away, he thought he saw a tear escape from the corner of her eye, but she quickly brushed it away and made a joke about fresh cut flowers exacerbating her hay fever symptoms. He hoped they were happy tears and not sad ones because he didn't like to think of sad memories running down those chubby cheeks of hers. He had been tempted to brush it away but thought better of it because by the looks of it she was only just holding herself together and he didn't want to embarrass her. Their marriage may not have worked, but they'd had some good times together, and they'd made Crystal and whether Chloe liked it or not Crystal was the bond that would unite them forever.

TOM

Tom was pacing up and down his office floor like an expectant father. The text message from Maria had unsettled him, and he still had one more meeting to attend before he could go home. The text said she needed to speak to him urgently and she said she'd be waiting for him at the house, but she still put two kisses at the end of the message, so he convinced himself it was nothing serious. Urgent to Maria was probably another damned cat needing a home, and he couldn't stop himself from laughing out loud before brushing his initial panic aside. The meeting went on for longer than he anticipated, and he was struggling to concentrate. Eventually, he made his excuses and left on the pretext that he was feeling unwell, and probably going down with the same virus that everyone else in the office seemed to have. He knew it sounded feeble especially as he was senior management now, but he knew if he didn't get out of there soon his head was going to explode. He glanced at his watch and knew if he was quick, he'd be able to catch the 3.15 train which would get him home by 5 at the very latest. As the Train pulled out of the station, he started to relax, and momentarily, he closed his eyes and allowed his thoughts to drift away. He always closed his eyes on the train because it enabled him to leave all the hustle and bustle of London behind, but today he couldn't relax, and within minutes he was wide awake clutching his chest, trying to steady his heart which felt like it was trying to beat its way right out of his rib cage. If he hadn't have known better he would've convinced himself he was having a heart attack, but he knew exactly what the problem was and there was no drug on the planet that could relieve him of the guilt that plagued his tortured mind.

The train was quieter than usual because it wasn't yet rush hour, which meant he had the added bonus of being able to sit down. He refused to pay for a first-class ticket because he thought it an unnecessary extravagance although Maria said she would be more than happy for him to pay a little bit more if it meant he could travel in comfort. Maria's sympathetic approach only served to make him feel more ashamed than ever, so he stuck to his guns and travelled in economy class even though it often meant waiting until the train reached the suburbs before he could find a seat. He argued that he didn't need to sit down after all he spent all day sitting on his backside in the office, but it gave her something to nag him about, and he loved her all the more for it.

As the train raced through the tunnels, the London skyscrapers were soon replaced by fields of bright yellow rapeseed and rolling countryside. He thought about Grant and his forthcoming wedding and made up his mind to catch up with him soon. He knew he owed him an apology for the way he spoke about his family, and he hoped given time his friend would be able to forgive him. He also wanted to tell him about Avellino and ask his advice because up until now, the only person who knew about him was Cain, and unlike Grant, Cain charged for his services.

He always planned to tell Maria about the boy, but there was never a right time, and as the years passed telling her became less important, and he worked on the theory that what she didn't know couldn't hurt her. He could picture her now sitting on the sofa with a cup of tea in her hand, waiting patiently for him to come home. Maria loved her cups of tea, so he knew she must have filled the kettle umpteen times by now, which meant she would almost certainly have found the letter. He didn't know why he had put it under the kettle, and he scolded himself for being so careless , but deep down there was a part of him that wanted her to find it because that letter spoke the words that he was too afraid to say.

Of course, he couldn't be certain that it would spell the end of his marriage, but he knew he needed to pre-pare for all eventualities. Maria always accused him of thinking the worse and most of the time she was right, but he reasoned that it was better to be prepared even if it didn't happen. He had come close to losing Maria once, and it had taken a considerable amount of time and money to get their relationship back on track, and if it hadn't been for Cain, he didn't think they would have come this far. He was sure Cain was sick of him by now because at one stage he had hinted his job was done, but the counselling was addictive, and he was a bit like an alcoholic because deep down he was afraid that if he didn't make contact with him every week there was a risk he might fall off the wagon once more. As it happened after the letter arrived from Avellino Cain retracted his advice and decided there was indeed a lot more work to be done before Tom was ready to make sensible deci-sions on his own and Tom was grateful that he no longer had to make excuses to visit him.

He glanced at his watch, his eyes darting anxiously from his wrist to the rocketing scenery outside the train window. He'd be home early at this rate, and he wasn't sure he was ready to go home and face Maria just yet.

He wished there was a way he could stop the train and as he glanced hopefully at the emergency button, his fingers involuntarily twitched. He knew he would never have the nerve to press it, but he was optimistic a miracle might happen if he stared at it for long enough. In the winter there were always problems with the weather, and in typical British fashion, the tiniest amount of the wrong type of snow on the tracks bought the entire rail network to a complete standstill. He also recalled the time when someone had jumped from a bridge in front of the train and how he had cursed because they had been stuck on the same spot for hours on end and the refreshments trolley ran out of supplies. He had been a different man then and by all accounts not a very nice one but with Cain's help he was slowly becoming a better person, and he was keen to make amends. Nowadays it deeply saddened him to think any person could be driven to the point of being desperate enough to jump in front of a moving train and he couldn't help wondering why they hadn't tried to seek help much earlier.

As the train pulled into the station, he picked up his briefcase ready to disembark, and he knew what he had to do. Life was too short for regrets, and it was time for him to step up to the mark and behave like the father his son deserved, and providing she still wanted him, be a proper husband to Maria as well.

CHLOE

Life seemed to be going from bad to worse for Chloe, and she could see no end to the friction between herself and Grant. Her pregnancy was making her more sulky than usual, although Grant insisted she was just using it as an excuse for her difficult behaviour. He was right of course but he could never know the real reason behind it because even though it had been more than two years now the real reason was still too painful to contemplate and people who said time was a healer were clearly liars because although she thought she could forget about him her heart was heavier than ever.

The wedding was only two weeks away, but as she looked at her plus size dress zipped up in a bag on a hanger, there were no flutters of excitement or anticipation, just a feeling of emptiness. It was the same as she felt when Pete left her, but she had expected it then because it was all part of the bereavement process that had plagued her troubled mind for months after he left. She looked down at her baby bump and stroked it tenderly with her hand, and her baby responded with an almighty kick and even though she was fat and could no longer see her feet she already loved this little human inside her more than she loved life itself.

Once again, her mind wandered back to Mel, and her mood lightened. Despite everything that had happened, she still had a soft spot for him, and she hoped he remembered her with the same degree of fondness. She still had his contact details on her phone, and lately, she had come close to messaging him on more than one occasion, but something had stopped her, and she could only assume it was guilt because texting your ex when you're about to marry someone else simply wasn't right. In the past, she hadn't worried too much about what was right and what was wrong, but now she had a baby to think about to, and she was going to need some stability in her life, and despite their differences, Grant oozed the essential ingredients of family life offering both her and their baby permanence and consistency.

Her kids were, of course, pleased for her although Imogen was a bit peeved that her mum had beaten her to the altar. She was still waiting for Quentin to pop the question and although she pretended to be sympathetic, Chloe was secretly lining up a list of preferred suitors starting with the attractive new registrar at work.

As she zipped up the dress bag, she let out a long sigh. This wasn't the type of wedding she wanted at all, but it was all planned and paid for, and guests were coming so she couldn't possibly back out now anyway. She briefly thought about doing a Shirley Valentine and running away to another country, but Shirley hadn't been pregnant when she had her midlife crisis, and she knew from experience that raising a child alone wasn't easy.

She knew Grant was disappointed that she refused to have Amberina at the wedding, but she didn't think she was being unreasonable after all she didn't know many people who actually wanted their ex at their wedding, and it wasn't like she was planning to have Pete there too. She knew he was only thinking of Crystal, but the child was old enough to be accompanied by her grand-parents, and it wasn't as if they weren't used to looking after her even though they were getting on a bit now.

The three of them had gone out together to buy Crystal a dress for the wedding given that she had nothing suitable to wear at home. They went from shop to shop before finding something she would even agree to try on and then she had a tantrum because it didn't fit her, and the shop didn't stock a larger size. Chloe tried pointing out to Grant that if she was the size of a normal six-year-old, she would have fitted into the dress, but he just dismissed her remark, and they ended up buying a navy-blue dress with a stiff net skirt that was draped on a model in a charity shop window that fitted perfectly. Amberina was thrilled with the dress because it supported her recycling policies, but Chloe thought the overstated larger than life puffed up stiff skirt made her look more like a gypsy girl. She wasn't really bothered what she wore providing she kept out of the way and wasn't in too many of the photographs, but Grant was adamant that if she couldn't be a bridesmaid she should have the privilege of being a flower girl instead and she hadn't been able to come up with a quick enough reason to refuse.

She had tried talking to Maria about her feelings at work, but Maria seemed preoccupied with something else, and she knew she wasn't really listening to her when she brushed her comments aside and told her it was just her hormones talking. She wished it was only the hormones talking because that way she would know everything was going to be okay after the baby was born, but deep down she knew she would never be able to give Grant what he craved because there was no way she was ever going to be able to love his daughter the way he wanted her to. Grant said it didn't matter that she didn't love her because love was something that needed time to grow and she already had a mother who loved her, but as he spoke she could see the tormented look in his eyes, and she knew he was hurting.

On the eve of the wedding, Grant went to stay with Tom, and she found herself at a bit of a loose end with nothing to do. If she hadn't been pregnant, she would have had a glass or two of wine to steady her pre-wedding nerves, but she had to make do with a leftover bottle of alcohol-free beer instead which did nothing apart from leave a bitter vinegary taste in her mouth. There was nothing much to watch on TV either, so she found herself staring at her phone or to be more precise staring at Mel's messages on her phone which she still hadn't had the courage to delete. She managed to convince herself that they should stay there to remind her never to go back to him even if he wanted her to which he clearly didn't given that she hadn't heard a single word from him since that fateful day when he found Claire dead at home and then pretty much accused her of murder just because she had been the last person his wife had spoken to. She knew it was just the emotions talking, but nevertheless, his ludicrous accusations had hurt her deeply, and although she tried telling herself she was better off without him, she knew deep down she was living a lie. She knew it wasn't going to happen, but she wished he would call and tell her he wanted her because that way she wouldn't have to get married to Grant tomorrow, and at this late stage, he was the only person who could stop her from uttering those immortal words 'I do' to the wrong man. Realistically she knew he had probably found someone else, but she didn't want him to love anyone else because their love had been exclusive, or at least it would have been had it not been for Claire.

For some reason, she and Mel had buried their love for each other at the same time as Claire went to her grave, but she knew now they had buried those feelings prematurely because for her at least, those feelings were still very much alive. Claire had taken Mel away from her when she was alive, and somehow she had managed to do it again even though she was dead but dead people couldn't have the best of both worlds unless someone allowed them to and that's where they had gone wrong. One way or another she had to know if he felt the same way before it was too late and there was no time like the present to find out. Her fingers trembled nervously as she began to quickly type out a message and when she finally pressed the send button her heart thumped furiously with anticipation, but after a few seconds, a failed delivery notification appeared on the screen crushing her hopes of a reunion with him once more.

Maria

Maria was trying her hardest to keep busy because after sending the text message to Tom, she started worrying about how she should respond if he became angry with her for opening the letter. He would have every right to be angry of course because it was addressed to him, so it wasn't her business to help herself like that, but its contents were life-changing for her as well as him and if nothing else, she deserved to know the truth. As it was, she spent the entire afternoon sitting on the sofa rehearsing her carefully chosen words over and over again, but she still wasn't sure if they sounded right and Tom's train would probably be in by now which meant he would be home at any moment.

Everything was ready for his homecoming including his favourite cottage pie dinner which was browning nicely in the oven and there was a bottle of prosecco chilling in the fridge which she hoped they might be able to share later. They only ever had prosecco when they had something to celebrate and it had been a while since either of them had anything to be joyful about, but if everything went to plan she hoped they would soon be able to make a joint toast to new beginnings together.

She assumed Tom would want her to know about his love child, but a small part of her was afraid in case he didn't because up until now she thought they had shared everything, and it was a huge shock when she found out that Tom had another life that she knew nothing about.

A few moments later she heard Tom's key in the lock and once again all her doubts came flooding back. Tonight was important and she wanted everything to be perfect, so she ditched the idea of the skimpy undies underneath a faux fur coat in favour of a figure-hugging low-neck dress which she knew was one of Tom's favourites.

Tom could smell the food cooking as he walked through the door, and his mouth watered in anticipation. The journey had made his mouth dry, but the smell of one of Maria's delicious home cooked meals never failed to stimulate his taste buds, and he realised how hungry he actually was. He could hear her in the kitchen, and he stopped briefly just so he could listen to her humming away to herself the way she always used to when they were together, and he wondered if they could ever go back to be that same couple again. He hoped they could because she was a good woman, one of the best according to Grant, and he had loved her since the day she first walked into the classroom at primary school sporting those ridiculous pigtails and a crooked fringe, but his mind was filled with uncertainty because there were things she didn't know about him, things she needed to know, and he hated himself for deceiving her.

He called out to avoid startling her, and she answered with a cheery hello, and when he walked into the kitchen she surprised him with an affectionate peck on the lips, and he couldn't help noticing how beautiful she looked. She had always been beautiful inside and out, but for some reason, it felt as if he was looking at her for the very first time and he wished there was a way of turning back the clock, so they could start over again.

The table was set, but she told him there was enough time for him to shower before dinner and after the sweaty commute through the London smog he appreciated an opportunity to freshen up. As he turned the tap on to full power, the hot water stung his skin, and he stood motionless savouring the frothy warm bubbles from the shower gel until he heard Maria calling him from downstairs.

He hurriedly dried himself off and pulled on a pair of dark causal jeans with a white shirt. Maria always loved the jeans and shirt combination because she said it made him look like one of the male models from the catalogues and although he wasn't convinced he was male model material any more he was secretly thrilled by the compliment.

As he entered the kitchen, Maria handed him a glass of prosecco, and once again, he was overwhelmed by an intense feeling of guilt. He didn't deserve prosecco, and he certainly didn't deserve to have a wife like Maria but when he opened his mouth to protest she gently pressed her finger across his lips and told him to be quiet leaving him feeling more bewildered than ever.

Maria didn't feel in control of the situation, but she thought she was managing to hide her nerves well and so far everything was going to plan. She'd had a couple of extra glasses of wine while Tom was in the shower, but the alcohol must have gone to her head because she was starting to feel a bit dizzy and lightheaded. She hadn't had much to eat, and after rummaging through the cupboards, she managed to find a dried-up scone which although past its sell-by date but was still just about edible enough to eat. As she attempted to swallow the dry crumbs stuck to her throat, causing her to gag, so she quickly took another gulp of wine to help wash it down. A few moments later, her stomach started to gurgle and bloat uncomfortably, and she wished she'd chosen a more loose-fitting dress to conceal the fact that she now looked about six months pregnant. It was a timely reminder that she was supposed to be on a gluten-free trial because after almost fifty years of eating wheat products they had all of a sudden started to disagree with her, and she was glad when they were finally able to sit down at the table, so she could stop holding her belly in and breathe normally again. There was a time when she wouldn't have worried about it after all they had been married long enough to accept each other's flaws, but she wanted tonight to be perfect and more than anything she wanted her husband to desire her again.

Tom was still wondering why he'd been called home urgently. He'd been expecting the worst, but Maria was acting like it was some sort of special occasion and although he wasn't good with dates he knew it wasn't anyone's birthday or anniversary. As he picked up his glass, Maria proposed a toast *'to new beginnings'* and although he wholeheartedly agreed he was also totally bewildered by it all.

They ate their meals together in silence, which gave Maria time to rehearse her speech again. It wasn't the uncomfortable type of silence that stubborn couples tolerated after an argument, they'd had those type of arguments before and they'd had lots of fun making up afterwards, but she could see Tom was puzzled and it was beginning to look like she would have to make the first move. She thought Tom might make things easier for her by asking why he'd been summoned home early and she was a tiny bit disappointed that he hadn't but it wasn't all about Tom anymore, it was about her, and it was about a teenage boy who needed to know where he had come from and she had to know whether her husband was man enough to be able to step up to the mark and be the husband and father they both deserved.

Tom complimented her on the lovely meal, and as their eyes met across the table, she could see the torment behind his smile. His eyes appeared to be searching for answers, but he was clearly too afraid to ask the question, and she knew it was time to put him out of his misery, but as she stood up to clear away the dishes, Tom stopped her and beckoned her to sit back down again. He said he had something important to tell her and even though he knew she hated leaving the dirty dishes he was adamant they could wait and reluctantly she agreed. She was fairly certain she knew what he was about to say to her, but at the same time she was afraid just in case it wasn't what she wanted to hear because despite everything that had happened between them she still couldn't imagine a future without him.

Tom was anxious, but he had waited sixteen years for this moment, and he knew that if he backed out now, chances were he would never find the courage to do it again. His palms were sweating profusely, and he was fidgeting uncomfortably in his chair, but it was a case of now or never, and the latter was no longer a viable option. He had come close to telling her a number of times in the past but had always backed out at the last minute because he feared his motives were nothing more than a purely selfish need to unburden himself. Cain had, of course, warned him about the potential consequences of telling her as well as the implications of not telling her, but he had lived with the guilt of having an affair for far too long, and it wasn't a secret he was prepared to take to his grave with him although he didn't have any plans to meet his maker any time soon. He knew he could never make up for all the lost years he had missed with his son, but he hoped he would have an opportunity to build a relationship with him and although he knew it was a big ask he hoped Maria would be by his side to support him. As Tom went to speak, she could see his eyes glaze over, and for a moment, she thought he was going to cry. Apart from their wedding day she had never seen Tom cry because he always said that crying was for losers, but Cain had taught him that it was okay for men to cry and although he was getting better at expressing his emotions deep down he was still very much a man's man, and he didn't want people thinking he was a wuss.

Tom stood up and picked up the kettle, but the envelope was gone. He was sure that was where he'd left it, but now he was starting to doubt himself, so he started to frantically search all the cupboards in a vain effort to find the missing envelope. He didn't notice Maria slide the envelope out from under her placemat until she gently tapped him on the shoulder and calmly asked if this was the item he was looking for. He looked pale as he slumped back down in his seat with his shoulders hunched and for the first time in their marriage, Maria thought he looked defeated. He looked so vulnerable she wanted to hug him and let him know everything was going to be okay, but she resisted the temptation to do so because still didn't know for sure if they would be okay although for all of their sakes she really hoped they would.

GRANT

It was the night before the wedding, and Grant was over at Tom's for what was meant to be a quiet night in. He was secretly hoping to have a man to man talk with him, and although Tom wasn't exactly a relationship guru he was the only person he had to talk to about his doubts about the wedding, but when he arrived, it seemed Tom had other ideas.

Tom greeted him with a somewhat over-enthusiastic slap between the shoulder blades, which caused him to cough violently and then to his surprise Maria appeared and gave him an enormous bear hug. He hadn't expected her to be there, but he was delighted to see her because she was always so motherly and affectionate towards him and it made him think how wasted she was on a man like Tom. She had so much to give and apart from the menagerie of cats which were currently vying for attention by brushing themselves against his legs she had no one else to give it to and for a brief second he felt guilty for being a parent. At the moment it was just the one child, but very soon there would be two and although he knew he was a very fortunate man he also knew that any child who was lucky enough to have a mother like Maria would be the most privileged child in the world. He had made choices, and he knew they weren't necessarily good ones, but despite her quirky mannerisms Amberina was a good mother, and he believed Crystal had adjusted well.

He wasn't so sure about the woman he was about to marry though. Chloe's kids had grown up to be responsible young adults, but she lacked maternal instinct, especially when it came to Crystal, and he hoped that would change once Phoebe was born. Chloe had chosen the name of their new baby daughter because she said she didn't trust him to choose something sensible after allowing his ex-wife to call a child Crystal. He had been too embarrassed to let on that he hadn't really had much choice in the matter given that Amberina was insistent on following the somewhat bizarre family tradition of naming their offspring after glassware, but he wished now he had put his foot down and had the courage to tell her what he really thought. As it turned out, both of Amberina's parents died within six months of each other not long after Crystal was born, so she was too young to remember them. Her grandad Frank had died of natural causes, but it was believed her grandmother Porcelain died of a broken heart because the post-mortem results were inconclusive and unsurprisingly it took Amberina a long time to come to terms with such a huge double loss. Crystal helped to keep her busy, and eventually, she bounced back with a renewed enthusiasm that surprised everyone. Her zest for life shone through, and instead of moping around she threw her heart and soul into environmental issues and made it her mission to rid the planet of toxic waste and even though it wasn't really his sort of thing he admired her determination and integrity.

When he and Chloe first met, he was certain she was the right woman for him although secretly he thought she was out of his league. She had literally swept him off his feet, and he truly believed that they would have the fairy-tale ending that they were both looking for, but now he wondered if his expectations were unrealistic, after all, how many ex-wives actually got on with their ex-husband's new partner. If only Chloe would let her in he knew Amberina would embrace her with the same level of enthusiasm as she embraced world peace, but Chloe's offhand attitude had rubbed her up the wrong way, and now Amberina treated her in much the same way as she treated other forms of pollution and it had led to a stand-off between the two women. He didn't blame Amberina, after all, she was no different to any other mother, and her priority was to protect the welfare of her daughter especially as it was blatantly obvious that Chloe detested the little girl. Chloe was only weeks away from giving birth and Crystal was excited about having a new sister, but Chloe completely ostracised her, and the final straw came when she threw the new pink teddy bear that Crystal had spent all her pocket money on for the baby in the bin right in front of her. Crystal burst into tears, and Chloe shouted at her and told her not to be such a drama queen, and Grant was forced to take Crystal back home sobbing. When he came back, Chloe made a lame excuse about it being a cheap substandard toy made in Taiwan, which probably didn't conform to British safety standards and therefore posed a danger to their baby. She was being ridiculous of course and throwing it in the bin in front of a small child was unnecessarily cruel but Chloe refused to acknowledge this and said they would have to agree to differ and he had stormed out because he feared he might actually kill her if he didn't, and she wasn't worth going to prison over. He needed time to cool down, and it frightened him to think how close he had come to losing it with her. He had never hit anyone in his life let alone a woman, and it went against all his morals to do so, but she knew exactly which buttons to press, and he was beginning to wonder whether she was deliberately provoking him so as to cause an argument. He wasn't usually the confrontational sort, but after taking Crystal home in such a state, Amberina had told him in no uncertain terms to get it sorted out and although he knew what she meant he didn't know where to start.

As he sat down and made himself comfortable in the lounge on the large corner sofa with an abundance of soft plump cushions a rather fat ginger, tomcat came and settled on his lap. He always thought he was more of a dog person, but there was something comforting about the purring sound vibrating through his body, and for a short moment, he was able to relax and close his eyes. He opened them again somewhat startled when Maria playfully placed a bottle of ice-cold beer on his chest where he had deliberately left a couple of shirt buttons undone and although he tried to smile his face muscles refused to cooperate.

Maria could see he was troubled and it worried her. Chloe was still working, but it wasn't long before she was due to go on maternity leave and as far as Maria was concerned it couldn't come soon enough because she was becoming increasingly difficult to work with. As an older mother she told everyone who was prepared to listen how the pregnancy was taking its toll on her physical health and although she had never been pregnant herself Maria thought she could understand the physical aspect, but she couldn't for the life of her work out how it could have turned her in to such a nasty, manipulative bully. She clearly assumed that she had an ally in Maria in her vendetta against Crystal but that was Tom's speciality and when she made it clear to Chloe that she was in no way of the same opinion as her husband Chloe shunned her before turning to other team members for moral support and to her delight her campaign was gaining momentum. Chloe loved being the centre of attention, and some of the more junior members of staff indulged her by promoting themselves on the popularity stakes. Chloe had a clever knack of making herself look like the victim to win the sympathy vote and an even cleverer knack of making people laugh at some of her hideously insulting comments about Crystal and Amberina, and even though she tried to close her ears to it, because she knew Grant would be mortified if he knew, she felt wholly responsible, because if it hadn't been for her they would never have met. Lately, her husband had taken a surprising U-turn with regards to Crystal, and she finally knew why. They had talked until the early hours of the morning about his affair with Arielle and about his son Avellino and although she knew she wouldn't be able to forgive all the lies and deceit overnight they had made a joint decision to work together as a couple and get some marriage counselling to help them work through their problems. She believed that she and Tom were finally on the right track, but something was telling her that Grant was about to make the biggest mistake of his life. She ummed and ahhed for what seemed like ages wondering whether to tell him before deciding not to. She tried to convince herself that she was doing the right thing by keeping quiet because there were times when ignorance was bliss, and this surely had to be one of them but as hard as she tried the niggling doubts wouldn't go away but before she had the chance to speak Tom came into the room and the moment was lost. She tried hard to convince herself that it was good timing Tom coming into the room when he did because if he hadn't she was certain she would have told him, and Grant was unlikely to appreciate her telling him the night before his wedding to cancel all his plans.

Tom was in high spirits and was keen to start the celebrations. There were bottles of beer all round, and he had several bottles of champagne on ice ready to toast the happy couple and the imminent arrival of Grant's new baby. He was also keen to toast his reunion with Maria, and he was super excited because she had given him her blessing to tell Grant about his son. Up until he told Maria only Cain had known about the boy and he was bursting with pride and ready to shout from the rooftops and tell everyone who was prepared to listen that he was a dad.

Grant was delighted by the couple's news, and even though it was supposed to be his party, he was grateful to Tom for stealing the limelight because for a short while it gave him an excuse to forget about Chloe and the wedding which was now only hours away. He always hoped Tom and Maria would be able to work things out because despite everything they needed each other, and it meant he wouldn't have to listen to Tom moaning anymore about the stigma of being a newly single middle-aged man. Of course, he had never been truly single because they had never got as far as divorce and it wasn't very new either given that Maria had been living on and off with Thelma for the best part of two years, but Tom didn't like the term separated so Grant decided it was easier to just humour him and go along with it.

He wasn't sure why, but he wasn't all that surprised when Tom told him about his son because deep down, he had always known he was hiding something from him. He always assumed Tom would tell him when the time was right, but he hadn't expected to hear it on the eve of his wedding although as it happened, the timing was perfect because it meant he could avoid talking about his own problems. He had come to Tom's tonight specifically to talk about Chloe and all the problems he was having with her because he knew Tom would do what he didn't have the courage to do and talk him out of the wedding, but now all that seemed irrelevant and he wanted to hear more about what was going on in Tom's life because all of a sudden it seemed a whole lot more exciting than his own.

Maria stayed quiet as the two men talked, but he noticed Tom kept hold of her hand and gave it a tight squeeze from time to time to reassure her. The ginger cat seemed to have settled for the night on Grant's lap, and although he was desperate to take a leak, it seemed rude to disturb the sleeping peaceful furball. Tom rarely apologised for anything, but he awkwardly asked Grant to forgive him for his unacceptable attitude towards Crystal and Amberina and for a moment Grant didn't know whether to laugh or cry because having a son with a name like Avellino Tom couldn't exactly afford to be judgemental anymore.

Tom told Grant that Avellino was coming to England to study and that they had already arranged to meet in London in a couple of months' time. Maria had offered to stay behind to give father and son an opportunity to get to know each other first, but Tom wanted her with him, and by all accounts, Avellino was more than happy to meet the two of them together. Grant reflected for a moment on the situation, and he sincerely hoped it was going to work out for them all because he knew Maria would be the best stepmother a child could have and although it might take a bit more practice Tom had the potential to be a great dad too.

Tom's revelations made him think back to his own life with Chloe, and he knew there could never be a happy ever after for the two of them because she was far too selfish to welcome another man's child into her life and he knew Crystal deserved better. She was just a kid, and like all kids, she needed a happy, stable home life, and he was responsible for providing that because he had brought her into the world. He'd spent far too long making excuses for her behaviour, and although he understood the pregnancy hormones were playing havoc with her body, they weren't wholly responsible for her actions.

In a few hours' time, it would be his wedding day, and within weeks he would have another child to consider. He had a lot of thinking to do, but he was fast running out of time, and he desperately wished he had the power to make time stand still so he could have longer to think even though he knew it probably didn't matter how much time he had because nothing short of a miracle was likely to change the outcome.

THE NEXT DAY

It was the morning of the wedding, and Chloe had woken early. She'd had a restless night tossing and turning in bed, and she felt exhausted and even though she wasn't usually able to remember her dreams the vivid fantasies from her disrupted sleep were still very much at the forefront of her mind. Something had woken her with a start in the early hours of the morning. She could see it was still dark outside because there was no light coming in from the small gap in the curtain that had been irritating her for months. The curtains were slightly too small for the window which meant they didn't draw together properly and although it didn't bother Grant it bothered her, and she made up her mind she was going to change them before the baby was born. She glanced over at her illuminated alarm clock on the small cabinet next to her bed and saw it was still only 2 am. The loud rhythmic ticking sound was surprisingly reassuring in the otherwise silent darkness of the room, and she wondered if her nerves were getting the better of her. She had never liked sleeping alone but when Pete left she had to get used to it and after a while she found she actually enjoyed the luxury of having a king size bed all to herself, but the novelty had soon worn off, and it was the loneliness that had lured her into the world of online dating and into the arms of Mel. It hadn't been so bad when her beloved dog Norman was alive because he always made her feel safe and even though she knew he was a dog he thought he was a human and most of the time he was better company than any of the men she had met on the dating sites. He did have some bad habits, of course, like horrendous wind, but at least he had the decency to leave the room when he let one go, and it didn't take him long to work out that everyone would follow him into the garden which meant a game of some sort was on the cards. Norman loved to play, and she still missed him terribly, and although his individuality made him exceptional, she thought it was time to welcome another dog into the family very soon. She and Grant had talked about it, but he was worried it would be too much for her to cope with especially with a new baby to look after but she had argued that it was the perfect time because she would be at home most of the day and it would give her something else to think about apart from the baby. He knew she wasn't the type of mother who would be happy to spend hours at baby groups talking to other mothers about childhood milestones or comparing notes about teething remedies and nappy rash creams, so he agreed to a dog on the proviso that she wait until after the baby was born.

By 6 am, she had given up hope of getting any more sleep, so she decided to get up and make herself a cup of tea. It was her wedding day, and she knew she should be feeling excited, but as she looked at the dress hanging on the back of the door, all she felt was a sense of impending doom. It was more of a tent than a dress given her size, and she wondered whether she would still be able to squeeze into it given that her baby bump had grown even bigger over the past few weeks. She hadn't bothered trying it on again because she no longer cared whether it fitted or not and there was a part of her that hoped it wouldn't because that way she could turn up in her comfy jogging bottoms and people wouldn't have to humour her by telling her what a beautiful bride she was. For a brief moment, she thought about Grant, and her mind was racked with guilt. He had gone to the effort of hiring a stylish suit for the wedding and she had to admit he looked very dapper in it and under normal circumstances she would have taken great pleasure in ripping it off him at the end of the day, but that was that exact behaviour that had got her in to her current predicament, and nowadays he was lucky if he got as much as a peck on the cheek from her.

She climbed back into bed with a huge mug of steaming hot tea. It was big enough to hold about three regular cups of tea, but it saved her getting up to make more although now she was pregnant that amount of fluid played havoc with her bladder. The wedding wasn't until 2 o'clock, so there were still several hours to kill before Imogen came round to help her get ready. Imogen was like an excited schoolgirl about the whole thing, and Chloe hoped her excitement might be contagious and rub off on her although she was still slightly concerned it might put ideas in her head, and she wasn't ready to have Quentin as a son in law just yet. She wasn't sure she would ever be ready, but she was still working on more fitting suitors for her starting with the attractive new registrar at the surgery who unbeknown to Imogen had accepted her invitation to attend the wedding.

She closed her eyes as she sipped her tea and tried to imagine she was somewhere else. In her mind, she was already somewhere else far away, but her body never seemed to catch up with her overactive mind, and she always woke up disappointed. As her mind drifted, her body started to relax a little before a loud beeping sound from her phone jolted her awake, causing her to spill her hot tea all down the front of her dressing gown. She wasn't expecting to hear from anyone, but it was her wedding day after all, and it was likely she would have dozens of messages from well-wishers especially from those people who were unable to attend the celebrations. It was only supposed to be a small gathering with close friends and family, but the list had grown almost as quickly as her bump, and she wished now they had just run away to somewhere like Gretna Green and got married in secret. She grabbed her phone and realised it wasn't a message after all but a delivery notification informing her that her message to Mel had been delivered and read.

Meanwhile, back at Tom's house, the mood was very different. Maria had cooked everyone a full English breakfast, and Grant was taking full advantage of her generous hospitality. Chloe never bothered with breakfast, and it was rare for her to even cook a proper dinner unless they had someone coming round and the only people she ever invited to dinner were Imogen and Quentin, and he was convinced that was only because she enjoyed humiliating the poor chap by serving up another tomato-laden dinner for him to push awkwardly around his plate. Imogen had pointed out crossly on more than one occasion that he was forced to take antihistamine tablets before coming to dinner with them because the reason why he didn't like tomatoes was because they brought him out in hives and Grant often wondered why they still bothered to accept her dinner invitations.

After a good night's sleep, he'd woken up on a more positive note and decided that if Maria and Tom could work out their differences, then he and Chloe should be able to do the same. There was an innocent unborn child involved, and she deserved to have parents who could provide her with a loving and stable upbringing and commit to each other. A marriage was about supporting each other through good times and bad hence the *'for better or worse'* part of the vows and although he assumed most people didn't start their married life together in the *'for worse'* situation he talked himself into believing that things could only get better. He looked at his smart suit hanging up at the door and decided to cast his doubts aside. The radio was playing *'Don't marry her'* by the Beautiful South, and instinctively he started whistling along to the tune. He didn't notice Maria watching him, and he didn't even notice when she joined in with the lyrics even though she made a point of singing them in an outrageously loud voice and didn't stop until Tom yelled at her from the shower to be quiet because she was frightening the cats.

Once he was dressed, he splashed on a generous helping of Chloe's favourite aftershave before heading off to seek Maria's approval. He knew he didn't need her approval, but if Maria thought he looked good then chances were Chloe would think so too, and it was important to him to get it right. He found her in the kitchen with her head in her hands, but she jumped up quickly when she saw him and started fussing unnecessarily over him by pretending to straighten his tie which he knew was perfect because he'd checked it countless times in the mirror already. He laughed and couldn't resist giving her an appreciative hug, but when he let her go, he thought he could see a glazed look in her eyes, and for a moment he thought she was going to cry. She brushed his concerns aside and told him she was just being a bit over sensitive because weddings always made her cry and although he wanted to believe her something didn't seem quite right. He told her not to worry because the day was going to be perfect and she responded with a silent nod of the head because although she tried to speak her throat was too choked up with emotion to utter a single word coherently.

She hoped he was right because according to Tom it was too late to speak out now and she knew he would never forgive her if she were to ruin Grant's special day on what he called a whim. She knew it was more than that, and she had tried talking to him about it, but he had just laughed it off and said Grant was a big boy now who was more than capable of making his own decisions.

To a certain extent Tom was right after all Grant was a fully-grown man who was more than capable of making his own decisions, but it wasn't an informed choice he was making, at least she didn't think it was because if he knew how devious and manipulative Chloe could be surely he wouldn't be foolish enough to go ahead and marry her. In the end, she kept quiet only because Tom was convinced it was the right thing to do, but sooner or later she knew Chloe would break his heart and when she did she knew it would break her heart to.

Tying The Knot

I t was her wedding day, and Chloe was in the back garden pulling up random weeds. The front garden was the part that really needed doing, but she couldn't risk going out there because she knew the neighbours would probably come over and start talking, and she didn't want to talk to them. She didn't want to talk to anyone, she just wanted some time alone to think, but there wasn't enough time, and she was starting to panic. All the bending down was causing the acid reflux to burn her throat, and she knew she should stop but she had to try and keep busy because keeping busy was the only way she could stop herself from thinking about Mel. She had forgotten how bad the pregnancy-related heartburn could be and before long she decided to give up the wedding in favour of a glass of cool milk. Milk was what had got her through this pregnancy and all her previous pregnancies, and she wondered if that was why she looked so bloated all the time. Grant kept telling her she was blooming but as far as she was concerned she was blooming fat, and she couldn't wait for the baby to be born so she could get back to her trim size 10 figure. She longed for the day when she would be able to pull on her tight skinny jeans again instead of the oversized maternity ones with the hideous thick elasticated drawstring waist which she despised because they reminded her of fat people's clothes. As she wandered into the kitchen, the radio was blaring out the tune *'don't marry her,'* and she wondered whether Grant was listening to it too. They always listened to the local radio station when they were at home together, but she had no idea whether Tom listened to the radio at his house. She thought he was probably more of a CD type man because Maria had mentioned something about him having shelves full of them all stacked alphabetically and how he had gone mad when he came home from work one day to find she'd dusted them and put them all back in the wrong order. They'd laughed together about the hours he'd spent putting them all back in the correct order and how she was now too scared to ever touch them again and suddenly she regretted letting their friendship lapse. Although it was her wedding day, it was the first time she'd given Grant a proper thought, and for a brief moment, she felt an unexpected pang of guilt. As the cool milk slid down and soothed her scorched throat the baby suddenly gave an almighty kick as if to remind her that she needed him even if Chloe didn't, and she responded by stroking her swollen belly gently to reassure her tiny baby girl that everything was going to be alright.

Meanwhile, Grant was enjoying a celebratory pre-wedding drink with Tom and Maria. He was confident the generous breakfast Maria had served up would be enough to soak up a few glasses of wine and help to settle his nerves. He wasn't usually the nervous type, but he was anxious for everything to go to plan, and with Chloe's unpredictable mood swings, he couldn't be certain it would. It had felt strange sleeping without her beside him, and at one stage he had thought about texting her to check she was alright, but Tom had warned him it was unlucky to talk to the bride the night before the wedding and even though he thought it was probably some silly superstitious old wives' tale he decided against it just in case there was an element of truth in it.

Chloe was still thinking about the text message to Mel when Imogen arrived and demanded to know why her newly manicured fingernails were embedded with mud. They both ended up laughing hysterically when she finally admitted to doing a spot of weeding and Chloe was relieved when her daughter decided that it had to be the pregnancy hormones affecting her brain because it meant she didn't have to tell her the real reason for getting her hands dirty. She wished she could talk to her about her feelings for Mel but as far as Imogen was concerned Mel was history and she knew her other kids felt the same way about him. Despite constantly checking her phone for messages he still hadn't responded, so there wasn't really anything to say anyway, but it didn't stop her wishing she had someone she could talk to about him. There was a time when she would have confided in Maria, but she'd decided against it because Maria was too close to Grant, and she was afraid she might lose him if it got back to him. It was what her mum would have called keeping her options open, but sadly she was no longer around to talk to either because she had passed away suddenly a few years previously following a short illness aged just seventy-four years. Her death had left a massive void in Chloe's life, and although they hadn't always seen eye to eye, she missed their afternoon get-togethers when they would sit next to each other on her mum's comfy sofa chatting over a cup of tea putting the world to rights. Her mum had left without giving her a chance to say a proper goodbye, and it was this that she struggled to come to terms with the most. It wasn't her mum's fault of course because she didn't know she was going to die, but Mel had left in much the same way except to the best of her knowledge he was still very much alive.

Imogen was too busy clock watching to notice how troubled her mother was and insisted it was time they went upstairs to get ready for the wedding. After a quick shower, Imogen helped to style Chloe's naturally straight hair with heated rollers to give it some bounce as she called it before applying almost an entire bottle of hairspray to keep it in place. By the time she had finished, her hair was as rigid as a cotton bed sheet that had been sprayed with starch and Chloe was convinced there wouldn't be a single hair out of place even in the event of a hurricane. Finally, there was just the dress left to put on, and as Imogen unzipped it, Chloe felt an unexpected pang of emotion. She thought back to the dress that she had impulsively put a deposit on when she believed she was going to marry Mel and suddenly, without any warning she just burst into tears. Imogen responded by giving her a big hug but scolded her at the same time for ruining the eye makeup she'd just applied, and Chloe smiled because she recalled saying exactly the same thing to her own mother after she openly wept on the day she and Pete got married. She assured Chloe they were happy tears, and she had no reason to disbelieve her because she had always been fond of Pete, and Pete was equally fond of her. She had cried again when Pete left because she said it felt like losing the son she never had, and for that reason, Chloe detested him all the more. Chloe knew she would probably cry if Imogen ever got married to Quentin but that would be for very different reasons, and she decided it was preferable to put all thoughts of him as a future son in law aside. She was quietly confident that her plan to set Imogen up with the sexy new registrar from work would succeed and then Quentin would be history after all what woman wouldn't be attracted to a tall, dark and handsome doctor with a reputation for having an excellent bedside manner.

After a lot of huffing and puffing and breathing in Chloe eventually managed to squeeze into the dress but she didn't dare breathe out too deeply in case the zip burst and revealed her enormous pregnant frame to the entire wedding party. It was uncomfortable, and she feared she might faint if she wore it for too long, so she decided to do the sensible thing and pack another dress to change in to for the reception just in case there was a major incident with the original gown. Imogen said she looked beautiful, and she knew Grant would be of the same opinion, but she didn't feel beautiful, and at her age, she didn't appreciate being patronised in that way. Imogen looked visibly hurt when she yelled at her to shut up, and she instantly regretted, opening her mouth. Once again Imogen put it all down to the hormones reaping havoc with her brain, but Chloe knew it had nothing to do it with the hormones, it was Mel making her so snappy because if only he'd taken the time to answer her stupid text message he could have put an end to this farcical wedding once and for all. He was her soul mate, and he was the man who should be waiting at the end of the aisle for her and she needed him now more than ever to take control of the situation and stop her from marrying another man. She had subtly mentioned the name of the registry office in that text and then panicked in case he turned up, but now she was panicking in case he didn't turn up because apart from herself he was the only person capable of putting a stop to the ceremony and she didn't have the courage to do it. She fantasised about him barging into the room at the very last moment openly declaring his undying love for her while the wedding party all stood in stony silence looking around anxiously at each other after the registrar asked the bit about any lawful impediments. He strolled confidently down the aisle with an air of superiority that she admired and scooped her up in his arms before whisking her off in a waiting helicopter, leaving Grant and the entire wedding party completely dumbfounded. It was the type of thing she had only ever seen in films, but it helped to keep her hopes alive and as every minute brought her closer to saying her vows to the wrong man, hope was all she had left right now.

The wedding car had arrived, and the driver was sat outside impatiently, tooting his horn. It wasn't a real wedding car like the ones she had seen at the hotel wedding fayre, it was just a local taxi with a ribbon on it, and it wasn't until they drove away that Chloe realised there was a problem with the silencer. The loud roaring sound on acceleration was more suited to a formula one racetrack than a wedding and Chloe cringed in her seat as the neighbours enthusiastically waved them off. As they drove through the streets towards the register office, people turned around to look to see where the racket was coming from, and Chloe resigned herself to making a memorable entrance.

As they pulled up outside the previous wedding party was just coming out, and Chloe couldn't help thinking it was a bit like a production line. Couples were getting married as quickly as machines were putting labels on baked bean tins, and she wondered if one day divorce would be just as easy. Her divorce from Pete had been especially bitter and acrimonious, and she had promised herself that she would never put herself in that position again. The newlyweds looked radiant as they posed for photographs on the lawn outside and for a moment,

Chloe sat watching their little gestures of affection as they gazed lovingly into each other's eyes. The impatient taxi driver interrupted her thoughts by suddenly throwing open the back door and signalling for them to get out before driving off in a cloud of thick black smoke that billowed shamelessly from the exhaust of the decrepit vehicle which was clearly on its last legs. The wedding guests starting coughing and spluttering, so Imogen grabbed Chloe's hand, and the two of them ran quickly past to avoid their disapproving looks. By the time they got inside, they were giggling at the absurdity of it all, but the stern looking registrar didn't seem to share the joke and by the time Chloe got into the room to confirm her details and the details of the man she was about to marry her mood was more restrained.

Due to her mother's serial wedding habit, Chloe had never got to know a man long enough to consider him a father so as Imogen was her eldest daughter she seemed the most appropriate person to give her away. Imogen had joked that if she gave her away did it mean she didn't have to have her back again and even though she had laughed at the pun it made her realise that she had in fact been something of a liability to her children after the breakup of her marriage to their father.

As they walked arm in arm down the aisle that divided the room to Queen's *another one bites the dust* Chloe barely noticed the guests or the fact they were playing the wrong tune. The staff hurriedly tried to find the correct music, but by the time they had found it, Chloe was already standing next to Grant, and the registrar indicated he was ready to start the service. As he welcomed them and their guests to the venue, Chloe took a quick look around the room. Tom and Maria were sat in the front row next to Grant's parents, and Crystal was sitting in the middle of them. She waived shyly as Chloe caught her eye, but Chloe pretended not to see her and continued to look around the room instead. To her annoyance, Imogen waived at her and pulled a funny face which made the little girl giggle with delight, and she didn't stop until Grant's mother gently placed a finger across her lips and told her it was time to be shush. On the other side of the room were sat some of her work colleagues, including the attractive new registrar. Next to him sat a man that she didn't recognise but she assumed it must be one of Grant's friends or work colleagues that she hadn't yet met. She hadn't met many of Grant's friends out of choice, but she knew she would be expected to meet them after the ceremony, and she owed it to Grant to be civil to them. She knew she had been difficult to live with, and she knew he deserved to be treated far better than she had treated him. The same applied to his daughter Crystal but despite constantly telling herself to try harder, she was struggling to bond with her and seeing her again now simply served to reinforce her lack of interest in the child.

The registrar had just got to the part of asking the wedding party whether anyone knew of any lawful impediment why the two of them could not get married and Chloe found herself staring at the door mentally willing Mel to come and save her but as predicted everyone stayed silent, and the door stayed firmly shut, and five minutes later they had both said their vows and she and Grant were married. Everyone clapped and cheered as they walked back down the aisle together as husband and wife to '*Waiting for a Girl Like You,*' a song by Foreigner obviously chosen by Grant but Chloe felt as '*Cold as Ice*' and couldn't wait for the day to be over.

After the ceremony, they repeatedly posed for photographs to please family and friends before heading to the pub for the reception. The newlyweds went in Tom and Maria's car While Imogen cadged a lift from one of the other guests. Quentin hadn't been able to attend due to work commitments which was ideal as far as Chloe was concerned because it would give her plenty of time to introduce her gorgeous daughter to the surprisingly still single doctor from work. Chloe had hoped she might have been able to scrounge a lift from him, but he was nowhere to be seen after the ceremony because according to Maria his bleep had gone off and he had to make a quick house call before meeting them the pub.

The reception venue was nothing special and certainly nothing like the grand country hotel where she and Grant had inadvertently gate-crashed a wedding fayre. The pub had a function room which her work colleagues had decorated as a surprise, but Chloe frankly didn't care what it looked like, and she couldn't help feeling annoyed that they'd gone ahead and done it without asking her because now she would be expected to say thank you, and she didn't appreciate having to say thank you for something she hadn't even asked for.

The room had a small bar with a few tables and chairs to sit on inside, but the best feature was the French doors which opened out on to a colourful courtyard garden with an array of well-established sweet-smelling flowers planted in cheerful brightly decorated tubs. It was a glorious day, and even the sun decided to put in a guest appearance for the newlyweds. The warmth of the sun helped to lighten Chloe's mood, and before long, she found herself mingling with the guests and joining in with the celebrations. As she was pregnant, she was reluctant to drink any alcohol, but Grant said a tiny glass of Prosecco wouldn't hurt and she quickly gave in to temptation. The bubbles must have gone to her head because the next thing she knew she was strutting her stuff to 'Love Shack' on one of the tables in the centre of the garden and only stopped when party pooper Imogen insisted she sat down in case all the activity caused her waters to break.

Imogen sat her down like a disobedient toddler at a table in a shaded area of the courtyard and gave her strict instructions not to move before going off to find her a soft drink. She hadn't wanted to sit down and to begin with, had made a lot of unnecessary fuss about it, but when she turned around, she realised she was sitting next to Chris, the attractive new registrar from work, and suddenly sitting down didn't seem such a bad idea after all. Next to Chris was the man she hadn't recognised at the ceremony, so she decided to introduce herself on the basis that if she didn't know who he was, then he almost certainly didn't know who she was either. As he stood up to shake hands, he introduced himself as Sebastian, Chris's partner and soon to be husband and for a moment she stood motionless and completely speechless. Feeling rather embarrassed, she realised she was still holding his hand as she waited for the news of what he'd just said to sink in. It had to be some kind of a joke, after all, Chris was far too attractive to be gay, but when she saw Chris smiling longingly at Sebastian, she knew it had to be true. Later that day, she found out that everyone at the medical centre knew that Chris was gay, but no one had thought to tell her. Maria laughed at her naivety and couldn't believe she had missed the not so subtle signs. In hindsight, Chloe knew it was her own fault because she had been far too preoccupied trying to pair him up with her daughter to notice them and she was cross with herself for not being more observant.

Imogen came back with a refreshing cool glass of lemonade for her to drink and she desperately wished she wasn't pregnant, so she could at least add a drop of her favourite coconut rum to it. It was very sobering news indeed, and now she had a dilemma on her hands because there was no one else she could think of to replace the ghastly Quentin with. She reminded herself there was no need to panic after all she still had time to work on it and just because Chris batted for the other side it didn't mean there wasn't a straight guy waiting just around the corner somewhere ready to sweep her lovely daughter off her feet.

Afterwards, the initial introductions there followed an awkward silence, and Chloe was relieved when Grant's parents came over to chat. Crystal was standing in the middle of them both with a tight grasp on each of their hands, and after a bit of gentle prompting by her grandmother, the little girl eventually stepped shyly forward and planted a wet kiss on her left cheek. Chloe resisted the urge to brush the dampness away to avoid offending Grant's parents, after all, she was going to need them to take Crystal off her hands a bit more often once the new baby was born. She had never been happy with Grant's current access arrangements with Amberina and thought it totally unfair that they were expected to entertain the child every weekend while Amberina went out and enjoyed herself. He didn't know it yet, but now that they were married she was determined to have a say in the matter, and she planned to tell Grant it was time to renegotiate the access arrangements because there was no way she was going to agree to continue having the child stay over every weekend. She knew he would argue with her about it, but she already had what she thought was a bulletproof case after all what husband would be able to resist the opportunity of spending some quality time alone with his new wife and baby daughter.

The sound of Tom bashing a beer glass with a metal spoon and everyone around them shouting "*speech, speech* "bought Chloe back to the present. She had been so busy daydreaming about how she was going to get rid of the problem kid that she hadn't noticed Tom getting ready to make his speech. She knew Grant had been dreading it as Tom had a tendency to be outspoken and make thoughtless jokes, so she went over to join him to show some moral support. As she took his hand, he gripped it tightly, and she knew he would always be her rock, although, in her eyes, he would always be more trinket than treasure. Mel was her rough diamond, her precious stone, but Mel didn't want her, and as hard as she tried, she couldn't make him love her again. Her heart still ached for her mother, but she had come to terms with that loss, and even though she still held a grudge she had more or less managed to make peace with the lord for taking her too soon. Her mother had taught her many things in life, but she had never taught her how to grieve the loss of someone who was still alive so one way or another she was going to have to work it out for herself. As she squeezed his hand back, he turned to her and smiled, and she knew she owed it to herself and their unborn baby to make their marriage work.

Tom's speech seemed to go on forever, and as usual, he made it all about himself. Maria stood by proudly by as he rambled on endlessly about the meaning of marriage and the love a child can bring to a couple. Considering they only had cats Chloe had no idea what he was talking about and looked questionably at Grant who whispered softly in her ear to just wait because he would soon let the cat out of the bag. She thought his wording was very apt considering the number of cats they owned but she wasn't prepared for what came next and the last thing she expected to hear on her wedding day was the news that Tom had a son. When he finished, everyone clapped, and Chloe reluctantly joined in. Maria had obviously accepted he had a love child because it gave her the opportunity to be a mother, albeit a stepmother but Chloe didn't approve and couldn't resist taking the opportunity to tell her so. Crystal was stood close by, and Maria responded by taking the little girl's hand and offering it to Chloe and then she went one step further and introduced them to each other as official stepmother and stepdaughter and Crystal giggled awkwardly. Chloe knew she was just a child looking for acceptance, and she knew that Maria had good intentions, and this was her way of encouraging her to put things right. It was only a tiny step, but it was still a step too far, and she simply couldn't do it. For a brief moment, she stopped and stared at them both before unashamedly walking away. Under the circumstances, it was the right thing to do because her mother had always told her never to make promises she couldn't keep.

A Child Is Born

Just two weeks after the wedding, Chloe started having contractions. She had been feeling extremely tired of late, and although she had been having a few pains on and off, she hadn't worried too much about them. All her other children had been born late, and considering the baby wasn't due for another three weeks she assumed they were probably just the practice Braxton Hicks type contractions that she'd had in all her previous pregnancies. It was late one Friday afternoon when her waters broke suddenly only minutes after Grant had left to collect Crystal for the weekend. They had argued because she had told him she was tired and because she had pleaded with him not to go and get her but as usual he had refused to listen to her and instead of being a supportive husband he had become increasingly hostile and accused her of instigating delaying tactics just so that she could make him late and get him in to trouble with Amberina who she knew would no doubt be waiting to join her wacky friends in another protest march of some sort. In all fairness, it was out of character for Grant to lose his temper with her and considering she never made it easy for him to see his daughter she was surprised he had managed to remain calm for as long as he had. It seemed she had been wrong in thinking he was a pushover and she was worried she might have pushed him too far with Crystal because he had responded by making it blatantly clear to her that Crystal would always be his daughter and therefore he expected to be able to include her in all aspects of family life. She had reacted to this statement by childishly hiding his car keys to stop him from going to collect her and he had retaliated by grabbing her keys from her handbag and driving off in a huff in her own precious car which infuriated her all the more because for reasons known only to herself she refused to allow Crystal to travel in her car.

As soon as her waters broke the contractions started, and after only five minutes, she timed them at only one minute apart, which caused her to panic because she already had a strong urge to push. Her body was telling her she needed to get to the hospital quickly, but unless she called an ambulance, she had no means of getting there and calling the paramedics for something as natural as childbirth went against all her principles. If African women could crouch down behind a bush and have their babies then surely she could push one out in the comfort of her own home but that was the problem, she hadn't felt confident enough to have her baby at home in case something went wrong which according to the midwives was more likely because of her age. Up until that moment she hadn't thought of herself as a high-risk geriatric mother and she pretended to be disappointed that she wouldn't be able to have her baby in a blow-up pool filled with warm water in the lounge with whale music playing in the background while Grant crouched down beside her and massaged her back through every painful contraction. She was of course kidding; those sorts of births were for women like Amberina who would have watched every prenatal video on YouTube before setting up her very own *'Baby Bump* 'classes for women who wanted something different. Another painful contraction reminded her the baby was coming, and she wished for a moment that she hadn't been so stubborn when Grant suggested they attend antenatal classes together. It had been more than twenty years since she last had a baby, but she hadn't been alone then, and she had forgotten just how painful labour could be.

As she steadied her breathing her body relaxed a little, so she decided to phone Grant instead of the ambulance, but it went straight to voicemail, and when she tried for a second time there was a message saying the phone was turned off. She knew he was angry with her, but she was pregnant for god's sake, and he had promised to be only a phone call away in the weeks leading up to the birth. Another painful contraction was starting to build up, and out of sheer desperation, she dialled 999 and sobbed with relief when the call handler answered the phone. Despite the pain and all the blubbing, she somehow managed to blurt out that she was having a baby and that she was at home alone. The call handler was very reassuring and told her she would stay on the phone until help arrived and that the only thing she needed to do was stay calm and open the front door so that the ambulance crew could get in. Within minutes she could hear the familiar wail of sirens nearby but her desire to push was stronger than ever, and by the time they arrived, her baby's head was already out.

Grant was enjoying a peaceful cup of tea with Amberina who surprisingly didn't seem to be in any hurry to go out. It was unusual because she rarely made time to talk to him anymore and he had forgotten what good company she could be. He had heard his phone ringing, but he didn't want to hear any more of Chloe's pathetic excuses to get him home and besides he still needed time to calm down. Amberina looked at him accusingly as he turned his phone off, but he didn't want to talk about it, and he was grateful to her for respecting his wishes and not asking any awkward questions. Amberina lived close to the town, so there was always quite a lot of traffic noise, but today there seemed to be more sirens wailing from the nearby ambulance station than usual. He looked at his watch and saw it was already the start of rush hour, so the roads were bound to be busy, so he opted to have another cup of tea with her to allow the worse of the traffic to pass. It was her own fault that he was going to be late home, after all, it was she who had hidden his keys, and although he thought it was highly improbable, he hoped she might have learnt a lesson from it.

Crystal was really excited when she saw the little red car pull up because unlike his car it was sporty looking, and she had never been in a sports car before. He didn't really like driving it because it was what Tom called a hairdresser's car and for once he had to agree with him. He'd told Amberina he was late because his own car had refused to start but judging by the knowing look on her face she didn't buy his story. Thankfully she didn't question it, and he was grateful that he wasn't forced to elaborate any further.

Within minutes of the ambulance crew arriving baby Phoebe had made her entrance into the world, and she made a point of letting everyone know that she'd arrived safely by letting out an ear-splitting scream. Chloe was relieved her lungs were working well, but there was a part of her that hoped she hadn't started out as she meant to go on because if she did she was almost certainly going to have to invest in a pair of earplugs and chances were the neighbours would have to do the same. Although mother and baby were fit and well the ambulance crew insisted on taking them both to hospital for a quick check over and Chloe was happy to oblige. She was physically and emotionally exhausted, but she was also furious with Grant for missing the birth of their baby, and even though the ambulance crew had offered to call him for her she had mumbled some feeble excuse about him being busy at work and told them not to worry because she would call him later. They had given her a rather odd look at the time, but she didn't care because she didn't want to see him because she was still angry with him for prioritising Crystal's needs over her own and more importantly the needs of their new baby daughter. Deep down she knew it wasn't really his fault because he had no way of knowing the baby would be born just minutes after he walked out the door, but it made her feel better having someone other than herself to blame and besides he would find out soon enough because although the ambulance crew had attempted to clear up some of the mess their living room still resembled a crime scene and she knew Crystal would be hysterical if she saw it because she could be a drama queen at the best of times.

Crystal was singing away cheerfully to her new dolly in the back seat of the car as they pulled on to the drive and Grant hoped Chloe wouldn't say anything to spoil her happy mood. Recently she had started to become clingy and wary of visits, and he was afraid she might one day decide she didn't want to come and see him anymore. As he opened the front door, he called out softly that he was home, but he was met with nothing but an eerie silence. Crystal was pestering him for a drink, so they both headed towards the kitchen where she gulped down the remains of a carton of milk. He knew he would have to go out again to buy some more because Chloe drank copious amounts of the stuff to ease the constant heartburn, but as it was getting late he decided it was more important to get Crystal settled in first, so they headed upstairs towards her bedroom, so she could change into her PJ's ready for bed. While Crystal got changed he poked his head around the bedroom fully expecting to find Chloe asleep on the bed but there was no sign of her, so he went back downstairs to the lounge, and that's when he first saw the heart-breaking evidence that his baby had come into the world without him. His hands were shaking uncontrollably as he fumbled awkwardly through his pockets to find his phone, and that's when he remembered he had turned it off. As he waited impatiently for the phone to turn back on, he inwardly scolded himself for ignoring her calls, and although he fully expected to receive an angry voicemail from her there was nothing, and he knew for certain he was in the doghouse. He called her anxiously, desperate to hear her voice and impatient to know they were both okay, but she didn't answer his call which only served to convince him that something terrible must have happened to her or the baby and if it had it would be all his fault. He sprinted back upstairs and told a sleepy Crystal he was very sorry, but he would have to take her home again because Chloe had unexpectedly had her baby and although she begged him to take her with him to see her new baby sister he knew he couldn't because he needed to be sure that everything was okay, and he also knew that Chloe would be furious if Crystal turned up at the hospital with him.

Chloe was sitting up in bed enjoying a well-deserved cuppa when her phone rang, and she couldn't help feeling the tiniest bit guilty for ignoring Grant's call. Her new baby daughter was sleeping soundly in the crib next to her after a hearty feed, and Chloe thought she was simply perfect. She knew Grant would home by now, and she knew he would be worried, but he'd already broken the vows they'd made to each other only a few short weeks ago by not being there for her when she needed him, and she wasn't ready to forgive him for that just yet. She wished her mum was alive because she wanted to share the news of Phoebe's arrival with someone and Imogen wasn't answering her phone, but she knew her mum would be looking down on the two of them from wherever she was, and that helped her to feel better. Impulsively she picked up her phone and text Mel to tell him she'd had a baby girl and that both mother and daughter were doing fine. She didn't know why she chose to text him because it was obvious he didn't care about her anymore, but she was desperate to share her news with someone, and he was the first person she thought of after Imogen and Grant, and they weren't answering their phones. She regretted sending it the moment she received the delivery report, but she knew he was unlikely to respond and if he did she could always pretend it was meant for someone else and say he had received it in error. Her mum always said that new mums could get away with all sorts of mischief because of what she affectionately called 'baby brain' so she decided there and then that if there were any repercussions, she would try blaming it on that. Thoughts of her mum bought raw emotions to the surface and without warning, her eyes filled with tears, and it wasn't long before they rolled down her cheeks, making her unflattering hospital gown all soggy and wet. She was glad the nurse had pulled the curtains around the bed so no one else would notice especially as there were still lots of visitors on the ward. She could hear proud fathers and grandparents cooing over their new offspring and older siblings arguing over whose turn it was to hold the baby next, and it reminded her of when her other children were young. She and Pete had been so happy back then, and she truly believed they would be together forever, and she wondered how many of the couples around her would still be playing happy families in years to come. She willed Grant to hurry up, she thought he would have been at the hospital by now, and she was afraid that something might have happened to him because if it had, she would never be able to forgive herself for making him panic and rush unnecessarily. It didn't bear thinking about, but it would be all her fault if she were to become a widow after only two weeks of marriage and Phoebe had to grow up without a father. She knew she was being melodramatic and probably overthinking the whole thing, but she was alone, and her hormones were causing her to think irrationally, and she just needed him to get there soon so she could introduce Phoebe to her daddy for a much-needed cuddle.

Crystal protested bitterly as Grant hurriedly bundled her back into the tiny back seat of the car and drove off. He hadn't thought to phone Amberina to check whether she was going to be in and Crystal, who was seemingly unaware of the urgency of the situation, was starting to frustrate him by telling him how annoyed mummy was going to be if he took her home. He knew she was acting up because she was disappointed that he wouldn't take her to the hospital with him to meet her new baby sister, but right now he didn't even know for certain if he was welcome there, and he couldn't risk fuelling Chloe's rage for a second time today.

As he turned the car into the road, he was relieved to see there were lights on in the house. His hands trembled as he struggled to release the seat belt that Crystal had somehow managed to wrap around her dolly and he came close to losing his temper with her when she demanded he lift her out of the car and carry her to the house because her legs were tired. By the time they reached the door, Amberina was already waiting and sensing the urgency of the situation she told him to hurry up and be on his way. Crystal was still protesting and clinging to him with her arms wrapped tightly around his neck, and eventually, Amberina had to prise her hands apart and carry the screaming child indoors. As he hurried away from the house he could hear Crystal screaming, and he could hear Amberina yelling at her to be quiet, but he didn't have time to stop and sort it out now because right now Chloe needed him, at least he thought she did.

When he arrived at the hospital, a kindly nurse told him not to panic because both mother and baby were doing fine, and Grant breathed a huge sigh of relief. When he got to the room, Chloe was cradling a wriggling bundle of pink blankets in her arms and when he peeped over a big pair of blue eyes were gazing up at him. Chloe explained she had just been fed and was struggling to bring up her wind, but Grant was certain she was smiling at him, and Chloe could see he was smitten.

For a moment he said nothing, he was completely hypnotized by the tiny bundle of perfection, and when Chloe handed her to him to hold she seemed so fragile, he was afraid she might break even though Chloe assured him she wouldn't. As he stroked her soft fair hair he apologised over and over for not being there for her birth, but she was sleeping peacefully without a care in the world, and Chloe reassured him that it didn't matter so long as he could promise that he would always be there for her in the future and he promised faithfully that he would.

As they sat together quietly cradling their new baby

daughter, there was no mention of Crystal or the argument, and for a short time, their problems were forgotten. The drama surrounding Phoebe's birth had miraculously bought them closer together, but Chloe knew that one day Crystal would drive a wedge between them, and Grant would be forced to make an impossible choice. She still couldn't be sure he would choose her, but she was prepared to fight and do whatever was necessary to make damned sure that he did.

LONDON

Avellino had arrived in London, and the long wait for Tom to meet his son was finally over. Tom and Maria had decided to make a day of it and travel up by train where they had arranged to meet Avellino under the famous Waterloo station clock. Tom thought they would meet by the gates of Buckingham Palace or somewhere equally impressive, but Avellino was insistent they should meet under the clock, and Tom got the feeling it was important to him. He told Tom the idea came from watching the film Hugo because it was one of his favourite films and by sheer coincidence, it was one of Tom's to, and he wondered how many other things they would have in common. They were connected on social media, so he'd seen photos of the boy but every time he looked at them he saw Arielle staring back at him and even though Maria tried hard to convince him they had the same shape nose he knew that appearance wise the lad took after his mother. In some ways, he was glad because Arielle was a beautiful person inside and out, and he hoped the boy had inherited her inner beauty as well as her captivating looks. He spent hours just staring at the photographs studying every detail in the vain hope it would help him get to know the son that had been missing from his life for the past sixteen years. There were photos on there of Arielle to, she had changed very little over the years and if anything, she was more beautiful now than she was back then, and Maria told him she looked like the type of woman a man could easily fall in love with. Under the circumstances, it was a compassionate thing to say, and he instinctively reached out to hug her. She had every right to be jealous, but she remained calm and dignified throughout, and he knew he was lucky to have her as his wife. She was a good woman, and she deserved better, much the same as Arielle had deserved better. She looked happy in the photographs, and that was all down to a man called Leon, who had apparently rescued her from the hands of her controlling parents and bought the boy up as his own. He was the only dad his son had ever known, and although Tom knew Leon had earned the right to be called dad, it hurt him to think he would only ever be known as Tom. He didn't know if he had ever been truly in love with Arielle or whether it was just testosterone fuelled lust that sparked their affair but whatever it was it had left him a legacy in the form of a son, and he was determined not to let him down in the same way he had let his mother down.

As the train hurtled towards London, they both sat deep in thought. Maria was holding a book open, but he noticed she hadn't turned the page in well over half an hour and seemed to be staring vacantly into space. She had been his rock over the years, and he felt deeply ashamed for taking advantage of her good nature.

Maria loved reading, but her mind was elsewhere, and she was having difficulty concentrating on the storyline, and she found herself reading the same page over and over again. It was hardly surprising she couldn't concentrate after all today was a big deal for her as it was the closest she was ever likely to get to becoming a mother. She knew Arielle would always be his real mother, but she hoped eventually Avellino would accept her as a substitute mum while he was in England. She had lots of friends with teenage sons so although she was no expert on the subject she knew a little bit about bringing up boys and in her opinion, the ones who had grown up close to their mothers appeared to have made better life choices than the ones who were influenced by chauvinistic fathers. She thought it was terribly sad that so many estranged parents forced their personal beliefs on their offspring, so she was grateful to Arielle for giving Avellino the opportunity to make up his own mind about Tom. She hoped Tom would take things slowly and not try to push the boy into building a relationship with him, but she knew Tom was an impatient man who liked everything done yesterday, so she wasn't overly optimistic about that. She sighed deeply, so long as Tom's enthusiasm didn't frighten the boy off it would be okay, it had to be.

Tom noticed her sigh, but he said nothing. His mind was filled with ideas and plans for the future, and even though Maria had told him not to get too ahead of himself, he couldn't help it. He had sixteen long years to makeup, and he only had a day to do it, and he wasn't sure it was enough. What if his son didn't like him or what if he didn't like Avellino? As usual, he was worrying about things that hadn't even happened, but they were real to him, and he couldn't rid his mind of all the doubt.

As the train neared London, the rolling countryside was replaced by rows of bleak looking terraced houses with long narrow gardens that bordered the train line. Children waived enthusiastically at the passing trains from the top of slides and climbing frames, and it reminded Tom of his youth. He loved trains as a boy and wished his parents had owned one of these houses instead of the modest semi in the suburbs they were so seemingly so proud of. He still loved trains now although he didn't openly admit it in case people labelled him as a bit of an anorak and despite Maria's objections he never tired of the daily commute to London for his job. If he'd known he had a son he would have made sure he had the biggest train set money could buy, and for a brief moment he felt cheated out of those years. It was partially his own fault of course because he had gone into panic mode when Arielle told him she was pregnant, but he never thought she would actually keep the child, so surely it wasn't right for him to take the all of the blame. Deep down, he knew the answer to that question, but it was still too painful to accept. The past was the past, and if he and his son were ever going to have a relationship he was going to have to put the past behind him, and he hoped Avellino would be able to do the same.

Avellino stood under the historic timepiece and glanced nervously at his watch. He'd arranged to meet Tom and Maria at 11 O clock, but he'd arrived early and had been standing there on his own for a good forty-five minutes already. He liked being early because it gave him time to prepare, and he liked people watching, and there were certainly plenty of people about to indulge his passion. It was hectic with people rushing around in every direction, some were hard-working businessmen dressed in swelteringly hot smart suits carrying designer leather briefcases, but there was also a large proportion of excited tourists gazing dubiously at maps trying to work out where exactly they should go next. His mum had often talked about London to him when he was a young boy, and he loved hearing her stories as she stroked his silky hair while waiting for him to drift off to sleep. He tried to picture each and every place as she described them to him, and even before she told him about Tom, he always knew that one day he would come to London and see it for himself. She seemed happy when she talked about London, so he always pictured it as a happy place. There was never any malice when she spoke about Tom either, but sometimes she sounded sad when he asked her questions about him, so he tried not to ask her too much in case he made her cry. She had cried in front of him many times before, but she always said they were happy tears because he reminded her so much of Tom and he liked that. She told him she thought she was in love with Tom at the time but that it was complicated and there were reasons why he couldn't commit to her. He didn't understand what she meant by that at the time, but he now realised that the complications she talked about were, in fact, a person, Tom's wife, and his new stepmother, Maria.

From where he was standing, he had a good view of platform eleven, and he waited eagerly for the train to appear. He still hadn't decided exactly what he was going to say to Tom, but Arielle had told him it didn't matter what he said so long as he remembered to always be kind. She had brought him up to see the good in people, so he never had reason to believe that Tom was anything other than a good man. The only bad man he could vaguely remember was his grandfather, and despite everything, Arielle had chosen to forgive him, and she tried hard to get him to do the same. He hadn't seen his grandparents since the day Leon whisked them off to a new home and a new life, but he didn't miss them. Arielle had tried hard to protect him from their malicious words when he was a small boy, but he could still hear the raised voices and their obvious disgust echoing in his ears, and he couldn't forgive them for treating his mother like that. They sent birthday cards and money for him, but he always sent them back unopened because he didn't want their money and he definitely didn't need their charity. Arielle said he'd inherited Tom's stubborn streak but as far as he was concerned they'd had their chance and blown it and they didn't deserve to be his grandparents. His mum had told him their health was failing and she had gently suggested it might be time to build bridges with them, but he wasn't Arielle, and he couldn't just forgive and forget although there were times when he wished he could if only to please her. He loved his mum dearly and although he'd only been in England a few days he was already missing her. Although she had told him to phone whenever he wanted, he used any excuse to call and hear her voice. She joked it was her mouth-wateringly delicious home cooked meals that he missed the most and while he had to agree he was fond of her home cooking it was she that he missed the most because she made him feel safe and secure and right now he was venturing into unknown territory, and he couldn't be certain that Tom knew how to be a parent.

As the train pulled slowly into platform eleven at Waterloo station, Tom gazed impatiently at the huge clock. It was 10.58, and he was anxious not to be late. The train had been running to time until they reached Guildford where they had sat at the station for a full twenty minutes waiting for debris of some kind to be cleared from the track. Tom thought back to his daily London commute. There was always a delay of some kind which the rail network usually blamed on the weather. Sometimes it was snow, and other times it was heavy winds causing the leaves to bank up on the track, but there was one time when the delay was caused by a jumper, and Tom sincerely hoped that wasn't what had happened today because that would be a very bad omen indeed. When the train finally ground to a halt, Tom grabbed Maria's hand in anticipation, and Maria squeezed it reassuringly. Today was the day they would finally become a proper family, and as far as Maria was concerned, it hadn't come a moment too soon.

AND BABY MAKES FOUR!

To everyone on the outside world, Phoebe was the perfect baby. She rarely cried unless she was hungry, and she only woke once or twice in the night for a feed before going straight back to sleep. Chloe's other children had all been considerably more challenging as babies, but she had been younger then and she'd had more energy to cope with the disrupted sleep pattern and the demands of a new-born. Grant doted on her and did more than his fair share to help look after her when he wasn't at work, but he couldn't do the night feeds because Chloe was stubborn and determined to continue breastfeeding even though the midwife had recommended swapping to a bottle to preserve what little was left of her battered nipples. She'd had mastitis in the past which quickly cleared up with a course of antibiotics, but this was different. Phoebe's grip was so strong her nipples were permanently cracked and bleeding, and no amount of cabbage leaves stuffed into her oversized front fastening nursing bra seemed to help. It didn't help that the bra was always sopping wet. They could be out in a supermarket somewhere with Phoebe fast asleep in her carrier, and her breasts would immediately react to the sound of another baby crying even if the infant was at the other end of the shop. The appearance of two wet patches on her clothing indicated that her breasts were full and ready to feed any number of hungry babies and Chloe had no choice but to accept the fact that she would have to walk round smelling like a stale milk carton until she decided to stop breastfeeding. One of the midwives on the ward had joked about her having enough milk to feed the entire ward while other new mums were struggling to produce enough to satisfy their offspring. She hoped it would settle down once she was home and relaxed, but if anything, it had got worse, and her breasts continued to produce enough milk to feed triplets. Unsurprisingly Phoebe was thriving and managed to gain over a pound in weight during her first week unlike most other babies of her age who took several weeks just to regain their birth weight. Chloe was proud of what she called her 'gold top' milk. She called it that after the milk that was delivered to the house by the milkman when she was a child. Gold top milk was her favourite because it was a thick creamy milk that came from either Jersey or Guernsey cows, but the birds also liked it, and if she didn't get there quick enough it wasn't unusual for her to find a hole pecked in the gold foil top from a peckish bird that had already helped itself to the rich and creamy topping.

Phoebe was two weeks old when Grant mentioned Crystal again. They hadn't spoken about her since Phoebe's birth, and Chloe would have preferred for it to remain that way because she liked their cosy threesome but having Crystal in the background was like having an elephant in the room, and Chloe knew it was inevitable that the conversation would eventually steer back to her. She was, of course, expecting Grant to mention her and although she had mentally prepared an entire list of feeble excuses as to why Crystal shouldn't meet Phoebe, she found herself unusually tongue-tied when it came to communicate them to Grant. Grant, on the other hand, had raised the subject fully expecting to do battle and was pleasantly surprised when his wife made no comment. He had his own list of reasons why Crystal should meet her sister and chose to ignore Chloe's tactless half-sister remark when she rudely interrupted him. He was secretly hoping Chloe's maternal instincts would kick in after she had Phoebe and that she might at least be a bit more tolerant of Crystal. Well-meaning work colleagues had tried to warn him that leopards don't change their spots, but he was a glass half full type of bloke who liked to stay positive even when the odds seemed stacked against him. Somewhere along the line, his mate Tom had managed to change from a selfish, arrogant man into a man with strong family values, so he hoped in time Chloe would be able to do the same. It had taken him a long time to realise how similar the two of them were, but it gave him the confidence to believe Chloe could change, but the question was how long he should give her before she damaged his emotionally fragile daughter forever.

CRYSTAL

Crystal was testing Amberina's patience to the limit at home with daily tantrums and a constant stream of questions about her new baby sister. She had of course seen photos of the baby courtesy of her Grant sending photos to Amberina's smartphone, but it wasn't enough for Crystal, she wanted to meet her, and she made up her mind to repeatedly pester both of her parents until they gave in to her demands.

Amberina couldn't help feeling sad. The photos of the new baby reminded her of happier times and what could have been, but she was thankful that she and Grant had a good relationship now which enabled them to parent their strong-willed daughter together despite living apart. Up until he met Chloe Crystal had seen her father regularly every weekend, so it was hardly surprising, she had turned into a bit of a rebel now. Grant was the first to admit that he had spoiled her, especially in the early days, and because of that, she had come to expect a significant amount of one to one attention that he could no longer commit to. It was obvious she missed the regular contact with him but deep down Amberina was worried and secretly feared for her young daughter's welfare because although Grant had never said as much, her instinct told her something wasn't quite right, and Chloe was at the root of it. It was obvious to Amberina that Chloe looked down on her because she was what Grant liked to call 'alternative' but just because she dared to be different it didn't give anyone the right to judge her. She had to admit Chloe was good on the eye and by all accounts, it looked like Grant had bagged himself a bit of a trophy wife, but Grant always said beauty was on the inside and from what she had witnessed so far Chloe was rotten to the core.

It was obvious Grant had been stalling for time, and she didn't want to be the one to force the issue, but Crystal clearly wasn't going to give up, and Amberina reasoned with Grant that the only way to appease her would be to allow a short visit, so she could meet the baby. She was pleasantly surprised when he agreed without making too much fuss. She had been expecting all sorts of feeble excuses about why she couldn't go just yet, and for a brief moment, she dared to hope that things might actually get a bit better for Crystal.

Crystal was counting down the number of sleeps until the day finally came when she was scheduled to meet her baby sister. She only usually got this excited at Christmas time when her mum gave her a special homemade advent calendar for her to open. She loved having an artistic mum because her mum always created unique gifts for her to open on Christmas day and her advent calendar was always so different to the ones that the other kids got at school that contained boring things like sweets or chocolates. Recently she had been out shopping with her mum in a local supermarket when she spotted an advent calendar containing gin. Her mum hadn't stopped laughing when she crossly pointed out that gin shouldn't be given to children and she still didn't get it when Amberina told her that certain advent calendars were for adults only. Crystal was adamant that advent calendars were unique to children and continued to argue about it until they got to the checkout where the portly cashier confirmed a gin advent calendar was indeed an essential coping strategy for stressed-out parents during the run-up to Christmas. Her mum had joked with the cashier that her daughter had an old head on young shoulders and although she wasn't entirely sure what that meant she thought it must be something complimentary other-wise her mother wouldn't have said it.

Crystal sat at the table carefully, adding the finishing touches to the card she had proudly made for her new sister. It had been her own idea to make a card, and while Amberina actively encouraged her to express herself, she hadn't inherited her mother's artistic talent, and it was fair to say that some of her efforts could only be truly appreciated by a doting parent. Although she was quite good at English there wasn't yet one particular subject that Crystal shined at, but she was still very young and as her teacher said she still had plenty of time to develop. Amberina knew Crystal was far from stupid, but Chloe had unreasonably high expectations that her daugh-ter struggled to meet and Amberina feared that Crystal would never be good enough for someone as perfect as Chloe. Of course, Chloe wasn't perfect, but she thought she was and people like Amberina and Crystal didn't fit neatly into her box. As it happened Amberina didn't care about fitting into boxes or impressing people with trendy smart clothes or up to date gadgets, and that was just as well because her flamboyant dress sense wasn't to everyone's taste. Grant wasn't unduly concerned about how she dressed when they were together, and he didn't seem to mind now either despite being married to the snooty impeccably turned out Chloe who she suspected had never willingly ventured into a charity shop in her life. Despite their difference, they'd had fun when they were together, and she wondered if he still had fun times now he was with Chloe or whether success and vanity had taken priority and cast an ugly shadow over their lives.

Crystal stood eagerly at the window, waiting for her dad to come and get her. She hadn't seen him for a few weeks, and she couldn't wait to tell him about the school trip she was going on. She knew her mum struggled to afford school trips, but this was a day trip to France, and they were going on the Eurostar, and her mum had saved hard for it, so she didn't miss out. She had never been abroad before, so her mum had been helping her to learn some basic French words because she said it was important for the Brits to make an effort to speak the lingo even though most French people spoke very good English. She had been practising hard and could already count to ten as well as say please and thank you and her mum said that was a good start because having good manners was far more important than knowing lots of words.

Amberina stood quietly by the kitchen door as her daughter counted her numbers over and over again until she had them exactly right. She was a bit of a perfectionist, and she wanted to show her daddy just how good she was, and Amberina hoped he hadn't forgotten how to praise her. She was proud of their little girl, and she hoped he was too. She opened her phone and studied the photos of baby Phoebe again. She hadn't looked at them properly until now, but she could see for herself that she was indeed a delicate little soul with exquisite soft features and flawless skin, unlike Crystal who someone said resembled a wrinkled overcooked turkey as a new-born. Those obviously weren't her words because as far as she was concerned Crystal was simply perfect, but they were the words of Tom, Grant's so-called best friend at the time and although she had tried hard not to show it his words had cut deeper than any knife. Naturally, she expected Grant to stand up and defend their defenceless daughter, but he chose to ignore the remark along with all the subsequent disparaging remarks giving Tom the green light to make her the laughingstock in any social situation. She knew she wasn't pretty like Chloe , and she knew Crystal was unlikely to win any beauty contests any time soon, but that didn't give Tom the right to use them as punch lines for his inappropriate party jokes. Grant simply let everything go over his head, but she knew now it was because he was weak. He was afraid to stand up to Tom, and he was afraid to stand up to Chloe, and it was already blatantly clear that it was she that wore the trousers in that household now.

An excited squeal from the living room brought her back to the present, and for a moment she wondered why Crystal was hopping around the room trying to get her shoes on like a child possessed. When a familiar car drew up outside in the road, Crystal ran to the door, and Amberina followed. She stood there shyly for a few minutes not knowing what to say while Crystal danced around him frantically waving the card she'd made. It was a special father-daughter moment, and she felt like an intruder as she waved the excited little girl off to see her other family, the family that she would never really be a part of and the family where she feared neither of them would ever be truly welcome.

HOMEWARD BOUND

As the train pulled slowly out of the station to head back towards the south coast, Tom was deep in thought. They had cut it a bit fine and had to run to catch the last train home after saying goodbye to Avellino at the student house where he was staying. Tom had been reluctant to leave him there, after all, he was still only a boy, and this was a foreign country to him, but Avellino was insistent he would be okay, and by the time Maria finally managed to coax him away, they only had minutes to spare before the train was due to depart. Fortunately, the student accommodation was close to the station, but neither Tom or Maria were as fit as they used to be and by the time they arrived at the station they were both completely out of breath and Maria had managed to get her shoe stuck in a crack in the pavement taking the heel clean off. The London lights masked the gloom outside, but the illuminated silhouette of the city soon gave way to the darkness of the suburbs, and before long there was nothing left to see apart from the occasional lights of a car waiting at a crossing for the train to pass.

Maria closed her eyes, it had been a busy day, and she was dog tired, but her brain was still buzzing and refused to let her rest. Meeting Tom's son for the first time had gone better than either of them could have ever wished for, and she knew Tom was already counting down the days until he could see him again. They had already made provisional arrangements for the boy to come and stay with them at their home during the half term break instead of going back to France, but Avellino said he would have to check his mum didn't have any plans for the holidays before making any concrete arrangements. She knew Tom desperately wanted him to come and stay with them, and she did too, but Tom was still a stranger to the boy, and she knew it was important not to try and influence him to do something that could be interpreted as trying to come between him and his mother who had been this boy's rock for his entire life.

Tom continued to stare blankly out of the window. He was an impatient man, but he knew Maria was right when she said he had to take little steps to gain the boy's trust. He had stuck his size eleven feet in where they weren't wanted before and had almost lost his best mate over it, and he couldn't afford to do that again. He thought about Grant and wondered how he was coping with the demands of a new baby, and his eyes unexpectedly filled with tears. He was happy for Grant, of course he was, after all Grant had the privilege of being a father to both of his children from the day they were born, and for a brief moment, he resented Arielle for denying him that honour. Of course, she had done what she thought was best and at the time it was probably the right thing for Tom at least because he didn't think Maria would be able to forgive such a blatant indiscretion and he hadn't been prepared to lose her. He wondered now if he would have felt differently about things if he had known about his son and he was thankful that Arielle had spared him the heartache of having to make a choice because he wouldn't have known how to choose between his wife and his son. It was his own fault of course, after all, he had been busy enjoying the best of both worlds, but he hadn't been prepared for the consequences, and as a result, he had to live with the regret of not seeing his only child grow up. Now he'd met the boy he felt ashamed of himself for telling Arielle to have an abortion, and he hoped Avellino would never find out that his dad didn't want him because nothing could have been further from the truth. It was true he had panicked when Arielle told him she was pregnant because it was the type of news he had been dreaming of hearing from Maria but after years of unprotected sex with his wife they were never blessed with a child of their own. Somewhere along the line, they had stopped talking about having a family, it wasn't deliberate, at least he didn't think it was, but it was less painful that way for both of them although it was hard to ignore Maria's frustrated wails every month when her period started. He hated to admit it now but there was a brief moment when he thought about ditching Maria and running off with Arielle so they could bring up their baby together but he wasn't sure it was ever really an option because deep down he loved Maria, she was his childhood sweet-heart after all, whereas Arielle was nothing more than his attractive mistress who was good for flattering his ego. Knowing how desperate Maria was for a baby of her own he was certain it would have crucified her had she had found out he had got another woman pregnant, and it would also have confirmed what he suspected she already knew, that she was the reason why they couldn't have a baby together and that was something she hadn't been ready to accept back then. Of course, if they had sought treatment early on she might have been able to become pregnant with the help of a test tube and a few suitably placed porn magazines, but Maria didn't want any sort of medical intervention at the time, and he had respected her choice. He wished now he had been more insistent because if they'd had a child of their own he might not have gone looking for attention elsewhere and they might not have ended up with so many cats, but hindsight was a wonderful thing and it was too late for regrets now.

Maria had been watching her husband for some time, but he seemed lost in a world of deep thought, and it seemed rude to intrude on such a private moment. She could see the emotion in his eyes, and as much as she wanted to reach out to him, she decided against it because she knew he wouldn't thank her if she made him cry in public. Tom wasn't the type of man who appreciated public displays of affection, so he certainly wouldn't appreciate her turning him into a blubbering wreck on a train full of high-spirited theatregoers. She closed her eyes again in the vain hope her brain would finally switch off and allow her to sleep for the remainder of the journey and she reached for his hand just to show him she was still there for him. He remained silent but rewarded her loyalty by giving it a tight squeeze, and she knew then there was no need for any words.

CHLOE

Phoebe was sleeping peacefully after a good feed and Chloe was tempted to have a nap herself, but she couldn't relax knowing that any moment Grant would walk in with that other child of his. She regretted now not putting up more of a fight when he mentioned bringing Crystal over to meet the baby, but she had been too tired to argue, and now it was too late. Just before he left, she hadn't been able to resist making a comment which he had conveniently ignored. To be fair, it was probably just as well he had ignored it because otherwise it would have led to a full-scale row and that wouldn't be good for the baby. She had read somewhere that tension between parents could adversely affect a child's behaviour and development and she didn't want Phoebe getting labelled as having some sort of behavioural disorder just because she and Grant couldn't get on. She looked at her watch and yawned. It was only 10 am, but she already felt like she had worked a twelve-hour night shift on a geriatric ward. Night shifts were tedious at the best of times on any ward, but as much as she loved the *'golden oldies'* as she affectionately liked to call them, they had a nasty habit of turning in to deranged psychopaths overnight. As a student nurse she'd lost count of the amount of times she was forced to do battle with many a confused pensioner on a cold floor in the middle of the night while trying to empty a bulging catheter bag. Turning the tap on the bag while holding a plastic jug steady was an art in itself in the dark, but when a confused old biddy starts bashing you over the head at the same time and screaming " thief, thief, call the police" it became a fight for survival. Of course, by the time the morning staff came back on shift at 7 am they were back to their normal selves, sitting up in bed smiling sweetly in their winceyette pyjamas, enjoying a cup of tea, and no one would believe she had just endured the night shift from hell.

She looked around the house despairingly. There was another huge pile of washing waiting to put through the machine, and the dirty dishes were still in the sink following last night's meal because she hadn't had the energy or motivation to unload the dishwasher before falling into bed. She wondered how one such tiny baby could have the ability to create so much work, and she was thankful she hadn't had twins. Before giving birth to Phoebe, she liked to think she was a relatively well organised person, but in recent weeks she had become an expert in the art of procrastination and was struggling to regain her mojo. When Imogen made a seemingly harmless light-hearted comment about the baby blues she blew it all out of proportion and even though she knew she was being more prickly than usual, she knew the reasons why and it had nothing whatsoever to do with her new baby daughter who she adored more than anything else in the world.

Her phone beeped to indicate a new message, and she hoped it might be Grant texting to say he had broken down or something equally as inconvenient because that would give her a bit more time to herself and delay the arrival of her stepdaughter. Crystal would never be anything more to her than a stepdaughter as far as Chloe was concerned the same as Phoebe would never be anything more than her half-sister, and she insisted Grant emphasised this so the child would understand even though her own kids all referred to Phoebe as their little sister. Imogen had already irritated her by pointing out that she wasn't being fair, and that she couldn't have one rule for one child and another rule for the rest, but Chloe answered that life wasn't always fair and the girl would simply have to get used to it.

Amberina's home wasn't in the best of areas, and she hoped some little thug might have done her a favour by letting his tyres down. Grant often accused her of being a snob, and she had to agree to a certain extent, but when she asked him how many successful entrepreneurs were raised on a council estate, he just shook his head in disbelief. Of course, she had no idea whether any true business tycoons had grown up in social housing and she was somewhat mortified when Dr Google told her that someone as prolific as Sir Alan Sugar was indeed the product of a London council estate.

She picked up her phone fully expecting it to be Grant updating her on his estimated time of arrival. She had told him before that he wasn't driving an Uber taxi, so she didn't need to follow his journey from A to B all the time, but he said he didn't want her to worry and she didn't like to tell him she rarely worried about him when he was driving or at any other time for that matter.

Before she had time to read the message, her phone started to ring, but it wasn't Grant, it was Mel, and her hands started to tremble uncontrollably.

MEL

Mel stood in his kitchen, openly chastising himself for not responding to Chloe's message sooner. He feared he may have left it too late, but he had to put things right between them for his own peace of mind. He hated the way they had parted, and he regretted his words especially the way he'd blamed her for Claire's death, but he'd been in deep shock when he said them, and he hadn't been thinking clearly. Nowadays, he blamed himself for her untimely death even though his counsellor told him he shouldn't. He'd met Cain not long after Claire died following an online enquiry Cain had made to get some building work done in his home. Mel answered the message, and Cain invited him over to give a quote, and somehow they'd got to talking and the rest was history. They'd become good friends, and he truly believed Cain was his saviour because after losing both of the women in his life within such a short space of time he didn't know how he would have coped without him. He hadn't really coped in the true sense of the word, but he had coped in his own way, and he was ashamed to admit he'd gone off the rails for a while by prostituting himself to any girl that showed the slightest interest in him. When he said *'girl,'* he meant girl because some were probably young enough to be his daughter and for that reason alone he was glad he only had sons because he knew how worried he would be if any teenage daughter of his displayed such promiscuous behaviour.

He'd read her message about getting married, but he didn't know what she expected him to do about it. He thought it was odd because she'd written down both the time and the place of the wedding and he wondered whether it was some sort of last-minute informal invitation to attend but he wasn't the tough 'Milk Tray' man preparing to rescue his damsel in distress, he was damaged goods, and he was still far too busy licking his own wounds to save anyone else. Reading between the lines it didn't seem like she really loved the guy and in a funny way he felt a bit sorry for him, but she was having his baby, and it sounded like she was either getting cold feet, or she was panicking because she felt trapped. Either way, he had more than enough of his own demons to deal with and at the time and it was easier to ignore her message than get involved. He regretted it now because he had loved her once and he thought he could probably love her again if she were to give him another chance. If he was totally honest with himself, he didn't think he had ever stopped loving her, but he had tried to because he thought that's what she wanted him to do. He was just starting to get his head straight again when she messaged him, and he had to admit it threw his brain cells into complete and utter turmoil. Not knowing who to turn to he confided in Cain about it and Cain said that life was too short for regrets, so he should just go for it if that's what he wanted to do, although he made it blatantly clear that he didn't approve of anyone coming between a husband and wife like that. He assumed Cain wasn't implying he should pull on a trademark black polo neck jumper and land a helicopter on the registry office roof before seizing a desperate Chloe from the grips of a stern-looking registrar before she had time to utter the immortal words '*I do*' to her unsuspecting husband to be. He had done some impulsive things in his time, but the thought of doing such a foolish thing made him chuckle. One of the things that had attracted him to Chloe was her spontaneity, but at eight months pregnant, he thought she would be unlikely to be impressed by such a reckless act. He couldn't help wondering what would have happened if he had shown up. Would he have sat quietly at the back of the room waiting for the registrar to do the legal bit before standing up and declaring that she couldn't possibly marry whoever he was because she was in love with someone else, or would he have taken the cowards way out and sat back and allowed her to marry another man. The former sounded fun providing there was a fast getaway car waiting outside for them but in reality, he knew he would have said nothing because he was a coward, he had always been a coward and that was how he'd managed to lose her in the first place.

He sent the text quickly before he had a chance to change his mind, but after reading it back to himself, he wasn't happy, and he knew he had to hear her voice again. He knew he was taking a big risk by ringing her, after all, she was a married woman now, and if her husband was around, it was likely to put her in a very difficult situation. When they were together previously he was the one that was still married, but now the tables had turned, and it was she who was married while he was a lonely widower. In the early days he didn't like telling people he was a widower because they automatically felt sorry for him and under the circumstances, he didn't think he deserved their sympathy, but it became easier as time went on ,and Cain said it was because he had reached the acceptance stage of the grieving process.

When he was with Chloe, he was happy, and he wanted to be happy again more than anything else in the world. Cain said he deserved to find happiness after everything he'd been through and even his boys were starting to come around to the idea of him finding love again with someone new. They had never really accepted Chloe before, but that was hardly surprising given that she was their mother's love rival at the time. They blamed her for wrecking their parent's marriage, and he hadn't defended her the way he should have because at the time it was easier to let someone else take the blame for his shambles of a marriage. The problem was Chloe wasn't someone new, and he was afraid his boys would jump to the wrong conclusions about her again. After Claire died it had taken a long time to get his relationship with them back on track, and he was reluctant to do anything that could jeopardise it, but Cain said he should start prioritising himself because whether they liked it or not they were old enough to make their own way in the world now. His hands were becoming progressively clammier, and his heart was now thumping so loudly he was certain she would be able to hear it if she ever picked up her damned phone. It had only rung a few times, but he was mentally willing her to answer it because he didn't think he would ever have the courage to put himself through such torment again. He took some slow deep breaths through his mouth to steady his breathing and counted to ten. He didn't know what the counting was supposed to do, but Cain said it helped some people to relax and right now he was more wired than an electric fence. He knew he was getting ahead of himself, after all, she was a newlywed with a baby, so she came as a package much the same as he had come as a package when Claire was alive. A baby was different though because it signalled a new life and a new beginning, and unlike Claire, it drank breast milk instead of vodka. If things had been different, it could have been their baby, and he thought maybe it still could be if Chloe and the baby's father weren't compatible. He could adopt it, and they could bring it up together, he'd always wanted a daughter, and he was certain Chloe had said it was a little girl. The idea excited him, and his breathing quickened again, and then when a familiar soft voice answered the phone, his heart began to race a little bit more.

GRANT

Grant decided to take the long route home in the vain hope it might give Crystal a bit of time to calm down. She was understandably excited about meeting her little sister, but right now she was completely over the top, and he wondered if she'd had one too many glasses of the bottle of bright orange squash he'd seen sitting on Amberina's kitchen worktop that was clearly overloaded with E numbers. Crystal tended to be a bit over-excitable at the best of times, but her behaviour was noticeably worse after eating certain foods, especially brightly coloured sweet things. He didn't want to dictate to Amberina what she should and shouldn't feed their child, but he did try to tactfully suggest she use the main culprits sparingly for the sake of her health and wellbeing. Although he didn't say it, he meant for his health and wellbeing to because an overexcited Crystal caused Chloe to become angry and the combination of the two resulted in one big headache. He didn't want Crystal to miss out completely but Amberina's understanding of the word moderation differed from his, and he sighed as he realised he would have to talk to her about it again. He knew Amberina shopped on a tight budget and it wasn't his place anymore to tell her what she should and shouldn't buy especially as the healthier options were usually considerably more expensive, but Crystal needed boundaries, and he wasn't happy that Amberina allowed her to go to the kitchen and help herself to the contents of the fridge whenever she wanted. It was a habit she had only recently got in to, and he was keen to nip it in the bud quickly because he knew Chloe would go berserk if she attempted to do it while she was staying with them. She had also started to get fussy and had begun dictating to Amberina what foods to cook, and because Amberina was afraid she would go hungry she gave in to her, and as a result, she was starting to look undeniably chubby. She had never been a thin child, and Amberina always used the excuse about her being big boned and taking after her side of the family. Up until now Grant had shrugged it off and hoped it might just be a bit of baby fat that would disappear as she grew taller, but instead of growing taller she seemed to grow wider, and it clearly wasn't doing her any favours. It also gave Chloe more ammunition to hurl insults about the girl, and he knew if something wasn't done, she would become the victim of bullies at school too. He knew from personal experience just how cruel other kids could be if you were the slightest bit different, but Amberina was the kind of mother who actively encouraged self-expression and individualism because she said she wanted Crystal to grow up to be a confident adult. He wanted that for her too, but at the same time he was worried for her because she was still only a little girl, his little girl, and conforming to normal social standards and fitting into a clearly defined box would be a much easier option for her right now. She would have plenty of time when she was older to step outside of the box and spread her wings if she wanted to but for now, she needed guidance from both of her parents to make the right life choices, and in his opinion, Amberina was a bit out of her depth. If he trod carefully he was certain he could bring Amberina around to his way of thinking, after all, as the girl's mother she would want what was best for her, and as Crystal currently spent 99% of her time with her, she would be the key influence. To be fair, he knew she spent too much time with Amberina these days, but under the circumstances, it had been the easy option to take, and ,he put his hands up to the fact he had unashamedly taken full advantage of Amberina's generous nature in order to make his own life more bearable. He made up his mind to see more of her now Phoebe was born, and this time he was adamant he was not going to allow Chloe to sabotage his access arrangements. He knew Chloe wouldn't like it, but if he used the right words and emphasised how he thought she might be a good role model for the child, it would help to make her feel important. For a short while, he thought she might have mellowed towards Crystal, but the snide remark she had made just before he walked out the door left him feeling dejected, and it saddened him knowing how much his wife hated his eldest daughter. He hadn't responded because that would have caused another row between them and then everyone's day would have been spoiled, and he was anxious not to spoil the short time he was permitted to spend with Crystal. He had hoped she might be able to stay overnight, but Chloe was insistent he take her home after her tea because the night feeds would disturb her. He knew it was just another excuse to get rid of her at the earliest opportunity, but the night feeds wouldn't be forever, and once Phoebe started to sleep through he planned to re-negotiate the terms and conditions to suit Crystal's needs and not the needs of his selfish wife.

When he watched Chloe with Phoebe, she was a natural, and despite being an older mother, he truly believed motherhood suited her. She was also a career woman, and he knew she was keen to make her way up the nursing career ladder as quickly as possible. Getting pregnant had put a temporary stop to her promotion dreams, but she had already made plans to go back to work as soon as her maternity pay ended. They hadn't managed to come up with any childcare arrangements yet that Chloe was happy with, but Chloe said she was looking into various options, and he was more than happy to leave her to it, because he knew he could trust her to make the right choice as far as his youngest daughter was concerned at least'

They were close to home now, and Crystal was still finding it difficult to contain her excitement. He had tried talking to her about Phoebe, putting an emphasis on the importance of being gentle as she was still only tiny, but she was more interested in the card she had made with the word 'SISTER' written in big capital letters, and he hoped Chloe wouldn't spoil it for her by pointing out she was biologically only her half-sister. Crystal was still too young to understand the concept of being a half-sister and he was certain that when the girls grew up they would be happy to be known as 'sisters', because having a brother or sister from a different mother or father was not exactly unusual anymore.

As he turned the car into the driveway of their home, he could see Chloe sitting on the sofa through the living room window. She was smiling and it was clear she hadn't noticed the car draw up outside. He hadn't seen her smile much of late, and he hoped it might be a positive sign. When he got out the car he tapped gently on the window and made a silly face against the cold glass, and Crystal joined in the fun by making funny faces to. He hadn't meant to startle her, but when she jumped up and dropped the phone he pulled a sad face and mouthed the word sorry, while waving a tatty white tissue from his pocket to indicate that he came in peace. She didn't respond to his well-meaning gesture and he could tell she was annoyed because she quickly grabbed the phone and ended the call. He wasn't certain if it was the sunlight reflecting on the smeared glass, but he thought she looked flushed, and he hoped she wasn't sickening for something. If she was, he would go in and offer to take Phoebe out for a walk in her pram so that she could rest. A walk would do them both good and Crystal needed the exercise, but when they went in Chloe said she was feeling fine. He suggested taking her for a walk anyway and Crystal was overjoyed when she didn't object. Chloe watched from the window as Crystal pushed the pram down the road while Grant helped out with the steering. She felt an unexpected pang of jealousy as she watched the two of them giggling together, but she decided not to dwell on it. She had other more important things to worry about right now, and that phone call was just the beginning of them'

AMBERINA

Amberina stood in the road outside her home long after Grant had gone. It was chilly outside, but she liked to wave Crystal off until the car was out of sight. She always found it difficult to say goodbye to Crystal but today she felt empty for some reason, and it wasn't until a well-meaning neighbour tooted their horn that she realised she was standing waving at an empty road. She pulled her cardigan tightly across her chest before hurrying back indoors to get warm and treated herself to a steaming cup of her favourite hot chocolate complete with marshmallows and whipped cream on top. She loved chocolate, and her frequent overindulgence was beginning to take its toll on her figure. She knew she was comfort eating and each day she promised herself it would be just one more treat before starting her diet, but she had never been any good at sticking to diets, and the thought of doing any exercise horrified her. It wasn't because she disliked exercise because there was a time when she used to swim regularly, but she couldn't possibly let unsuspecting members of the public see her in a swimsuit. The unflattering phrase *'beached whale* 'sprang to mind when she caught sight of herself in the mirror wearing a swimsuit. Crystal became all excited when she put it on because she thought they were going to the pool together and she couldn't help feeling guilty after seeing her face crumple with disappointment when she told her she was only trying it on for size. Like all her other clothes nowadays it was far too small for her, but after twisting and bending her ample frame into a whole host of unnatural positions, she finally managed to squeeze into it. The mirror didn't lie, and after seeing the rippling cellulite on her thighs and the unflattering spillage from the reinforced breast cups, she threw it in the bin in disgust before dissolving into tears. It was her own fault of course for seeking solace in comfort foods, and she knew Crystal was doing the same thing but the problem wasn't going to go away by feeling sorry for herself so she made up her mind she had to do something about it, not only for herself but for Crystal to because although she had been trying hard to ignore it Crystal was overweight for a child of her age and she didn't want her developing type 2 diabetes because of it. She already felt like an unfit mother because she couldn't afford to buy her the toys that other parents bought for their kids and food had become an easy substitute because Crystal had a sweet tooth. When star charts failed to control her temper tantrums, she got into the habit of using tasty treats as a reward for good behaviour, and it wasn't long before Crystal learned how to manipulate the situation and use it to her advantage. She'd thought about talking to Grant and asking for his help, but she was worried Grant had enough on his plate to worry about with Chloe and the new baby, and she didn't want him thinking she couldn't care for their child. She had been a vegetarian when they were together, but Crystal wasn't keen on vegetables, and after a while, it seemed easier to eat the same foods as her daughter to avoid cooking separate meals. Obviously, it went against all her principles, but she had to admit the smell of crispy bacon frying in a pan was more appealing to the taste buds than bubbling broccoli and carrots. She had never been thin, not even as a vegetarian, but she knew that was because she had a passion for adding rich cheese sauces to the pasta and vegetables. Grant used to comment that the spoon stood up in her sauces, and he was right, but she enjoyed her food, and she couldn't see the point in making a weak and wishy-washy tasteless sauce just because it contained fewer calories.

She looked at her watch and realised they would probably be home by now and she pictured Crystal sitting on the sofa next to Grant fondly cradling her new baby sister. Crystal had always wanted a baby brother or sister although she said she would prefer a sister and without fail she put one on her Christmas list every year in the hope Santa might oblige. Of course he always bought a new dolly of some kind for her to play with and that was enough to keep her happy for a while but then she said that maybe Santa didn't know how to read properly and could mummy teach him so that next year he could get it right and she didn't quite know how to answer her because quite frankly she had run out of excuses for the neglectful Santa. Fortunately, she didn't have to worry about it anymore because as far as Crystal was concerned her daddy was a true superhero and had saved the day by bringing a real baby home which he joked was a late Christmas present from Santa.

The warm chocolate bought comfort to her troubled mind, but the relief was only temporary, and it wasn't long before her brain started thinking of other things to worry about instead. She knew the constant worry wasn't doing her any good, and she wondered how she managed to help other people solve their problems when she couldn't even manage to solve her own. Her counselling course had been a real eye-opener, and she had come out of it ready to take on the problems of the world, but it hadn't taught her how to look after herself, and her lack of self-esteem was beginning to show. She knew she had let herself go since Grant left, but it didn't seem worth her while making an effort when there was no one to impress although she knew that wasn't entirely true. She'd had her eye on someone for some time now, and they'd become good friends, but she was pretty certain he didn't see her in a romantic way, and she didn't want to spoil their friendship by overstepping the boundaries. They'd met at a local counselling event and hit it off straight away. She'd surprised herself because she was usually shy around men, but Cain had been so easy to talk to, and he had made her laugh too. They'd gone for a coffee afterwards and chatted some more, but then he left to see a client who he said was actually more of a friend than a client and she wondered if it was actually a girlfriend and he was looking for an excuse to get away. He had texted her a few days later and asked if she would like to meet up for a coffee again, but she'd made up some silly excuse not to go because she thought he was only asking because he felt sorry for her. She regretted making such a hasty decision almost immediately as she seldom got an opportunity to spend quality time with an attractive man anymore, but it was too late to go back on her words without looking silly and besides she thought she had probably done him a favour by turning him down.

As she walked back to the kitchen to refill her mug, she caught sight of herself in the full-length mirror in the hallway. As a general rule, she avoided mirrors because denial was easier to tolerate than the truth, but today she lingered and confronted the stark reality staring back at her. Her plus-size figure definitely needed some work, but with the right motivation and a huge helping of willpower, it was all very doable, especially as she'd read somewhere that men preferred curves to stick insects. That same magazine would probably have described her as curvy, but she was a realist, and she didn't need anyone to paper over the cracks by using words like 'curvy.' She knew she was fat, morbidly obese even according to the body mass index calculator, which she quickly switched off following the discovery that the first number started with a three. She wasn't entirely sure what it was supposed to be, but she was pretty certain to be healthy it was supposed to start with a two, and she didn't need that kind of negativity in her life right now. She was ready to change, and that was all that mattered, and there was no time like the present to get started.

CAIN

Cain was confused. He thought he was making progress with the vibrant Amberina from the counselling service, but she'd unexpectedly binned him off leaving a massive dent in his ego. He wasn't confident with women at the best of times, but he found her easy to talk to, and he hoped she would give him another opportunity to find out more about her. It was unfortunate that he had to leave early to meet Mel on the day they had coffee together but when Mel phoned he sounded anxious, and he felt obliged to offer a listening ear. As it turned out all he wanted was to talk about this Chloe woman again and he couldn't help feeling a little bit annoyed that Mel's so-called crisis had cheated him out of spending more time with Amberina. He had never met Chloe, but it wasn't exactly an unusual name, so he presumed it was entirely coincidental that two of his clients had links with someone of that name. Amberina had also mentioned a Chloe, and she seemed troubled by her, but she hadn't elaborated, and he had to leave before he had the chance to find out more.

He had never had much luck with women on a personal level, but professionally he never had any problems with them which was just as well because restricting his clientele to men only would not only be financially crippling but might also give people the wrong idea about his sexuality.

He had come close to proposing once when he was just seventeen years old although he was glad now that he hadn't gone ahead with it because as it turned out it, he would almost certainly have made a complete fool of himself. Her name was Grace, and she literally was the girl next door until she moved away to go to university that was, and she never came back again. After finishing her law degree, he found out that she had moved to America where she became a Pro bono lawyer before going on to marry one of her clients, a woman who she had successfully defended in court against allegations of murder made by the family of her abusive ex-husband who she claimed to have killed accidentally in self-defence. To be fair, they had a point because beating him with a cricket bat until his brains spilled out on to the floor did seem a bit extreme, but the court had ruled in her favour, and the two of them had run off together to live their happily ever after. A few months later Grace came crawling back home with her tail between her legs after the woman showed her true colours and attempted to murder her to but the double jeopardy clause in US law prevented her from being tried again for the death of her ex-husband and Grace felt so traumatised by the whole thing she fled back to England to take refuge at her parents' home. Their parents had become good friends with each other over the years, and it was assumed that he and Grace would eventually become an item, so it was fair to say her mum and dad were extremely embarrassed by her shenanigans as they liked to call it and his own parents joked he'd had a lucky escape.

They'd only gone out a few times to the cinema together, but she was his first love, and he had been totally smitten with her although it soon became obvious that his feelings for her went a lot deeper than hers did for him. He spent a long time licking his wounds when she left, and despite everyone telling him that someone else would come along and sweep him off his feet, he was still waiting patiently for that day to come. His parents kept telling him that he had to get himself out into the big wide world if he wanted to find his Mrs. Right because it was unlikely she would come knocking on his door to find him but Amberina had found him, and he was certain it was fate. They'd got chatting at one of their local meetings after she sat down next to him and boldly introduced herself and he was intrigued by her name which for some reason sounded strangely familiar although he was certain he would have remembered her if they had met before. She seemed so confident as she openly held out her hand, and he admired that level of poise in a woman. To be fair, she wasn't the sort of woman he'd usually go for, but life had taught him that people come in all shapes and sizes and it wasn't all about looks. She was a big girl, but she had striking long red hair which fell to her shoulders with wispy curls that outlined what he thought was a kind face. She wasn't the sort of girl the likes of Mel or Tom would look at twice because they were both too shallow to see the inner beauty of someone like Amberina although he was pleased to report that Tom's attitude towards women had improved considerably in recent months. He didn't see much of Tom now that he'd got his marriage back on track, but he still sent him occasional updates, and he was glad that things had worked out so well for him because there was a time when he thought Tom was far too arrogant to change. If nothing else it proved a point that leopards could change their spots if they wanted to and he knew Tom had worked hard to become a better man. He had come close to losing everything, but it seemed that was the wakeup call he needed to change, and he was lucky to have a wife like Maria who loved him enough to give him another chance. Cain knew that if he were in her situation, he wouldn't have taken him back because he couldn't abide infidelity but in his job he had to try and appear impartial even though there had been plenty of occasions when he was sorely tempted to grab someone by the throat and throttle them. He had felt like doing that to Tom in the early days, especially when Tom made obscene remarks about some poor woman with a weird name that he was struggling to remember and her young daughter too, but as Tom mellowed so did he and they had managed to part amicably as friends.

Mel, on the hand, was a weak man who was still struggling to come to terms with events surrounding the tragic death of his wife but at the same time, he was completely hung up on some woman called Chloe who by all accounts had only just got married and had a baby. It had all become very complicated now, and after exhausting all of his ideas, Cain said he could offer nothing more than lending a listening ear, a kind gesture which Mel happily took full advantage of.

Cain's life was simple, and he was happy to keep it that way, but there were times when the solitude became tedious and deep down he longed to find someone special to share his life with. He rarely spoke about himself because his clients were always far too busy talking about their own self-inflicted turmoil-filled lives to ask about his and he was paid to listen to them. He doubted they would be interested in him anyway, after all, he was the original 40-year-old virgin, and his lack of progress in the lady's department led him to believe he was destined to remain that way forever.

As he made his way to the kitchen to make his favourite hot chocolate drink, he let out a big sigh. He would have to change his ways if he wanted to bag himself a lady because most women wanted more from a man than a cup of hot chocolate and an evening spent watching the soaps on TV. He liked watching the soaps because their intricate storylines reminded him of the lives of some of his clients and there were times when he became so engrossed in the storyline he actually started to problem solve on their behalf. More often than not, the solution was blatantly obvious to him, which made it all the more frustrating when the producers dragged a storyline on unnecessarily for weeks. He wished for a moment he had something in common with his namesake, the rugged Cain in TV's Emmerdale because he never seemed short of female attention but at the same time he was the kind of man that lived his life in the fast lane, a life tarnished by crime and corruption and he knew he was far too humble a man to ever live that kind of life.

CHLOE

Even though Grant and Crystal were well out of sight, Chloe was still standing at the window, staring blankly into an empty space. It was a cloudy day outside, and rain was forecast, so she hoped Grant had wrapped their little daughter up in plenty of blankets before taking her out. Under normal circumstances, she would have been there to make sure Phoebe was properly dressed to go out, but Mel's unexpected call had flustered her, and she was keen to get Grant out of the house quickly before he noticed something was wrong. She could feel her face burning when he was stood outside, making silly faces at the window, and a quick glimpse in the mirror confirmed her cheeks were still a little bit rosy now. Grant assumed she was sickening for something and it had been easier to go along with it than admit to such a blatant betrayal of his trust. He didn't know it of course, but he had caught her red-handed sexting her former lover, and when he turned up with Crystal, she could feel the guilt written all over her face. She wasn't sure if she felt guilty because she'd been caught or whether it was because she knew she was cheating on a good man, but her heart was pounding so hard it was starting to make her feel giddy, and she decided she should probably go and have a lie down until they got back. It was she who had started the sexting because Mel asked her to send a recent photo of herself for him to keep as the screensaver on his phone and she had rather mischievously sent him an explicit photo that Grant had taken of her before she became pregnant which left very little to the imagination. Grant had kept it as the screensaver on his phone for a while but had since changed it to one that was more suitable after Crystal picked up his phone to play a game and started asking awkward questions about it. She still didn't know exactly what he'd said to Crystal to try and explain it, and frankly, she didn't really care, but he had a bad habit of leaving his phone lying around, and she started to wonder how many of Grant's work colleagues had seen her stark naked too. She had planned to delete the photo, but it served as a visual reminder of how good her body looked before she became pregnant and it was an incentive to get the baby weight off and get back in to shape again. She wasn't doing too bad and had recently joined a local group of *'buggy runners,'* a fitness session where baby comes too. It had been hard work to start with, but now she was starting to see results she was beginning to enjoy it a bit more. As she closed her eyes she tried to convince herself that what he didn't know couldn't hurt him, but the guilt still plagued her, and she began to think it would have been easier if he had actually caught them having sex on the sofa right in front of him. At least that way he would know, and she wouldn't have to hide it from him anymore, but he would never understand if she told him about Mel and she couldn't possibly expect him to.

Mel knew exactly what it was like to have three people in a marriage after all Chloe had been the other woman in his marriage and now he was the other man in her marriage. She'd told him her marriage to Grant was as good as over, which was much the same thing he'd told her when he was married to Claire, but deep down she knew she was still keeping her options open. Grant was a good man, but Mel satisfied her need for excitement and right now excitement was in short supply. When Claire died ,she told him she was going to let him go and at the time, she truly believed she was doing the right thing for them both, but she had since realised that it hadn't been right for either of them and her hasty decision had caused more pain and suffering than was absolutely necessary. She was angry with herself because she knew that if she had just backed off gently instead of binning him off completely, they could have worked things out between them, and baby Phoebe might have been his baby instead of Grants. They had talked about having a baby when they were together, but they had talked about a lot of things, including marriage and Mel had got her hopes up about that on more than one occasion, but things had never progressed from the initial planning stage, and given that Mel already had three boys baby Phoebe would almost certainly have been born a boy. She knew deep down Mel would have loved to have had a daughter although he claimed it was Claire and not he who was overwhelmed by their testosterone-fuelled household. She knew she was lucky to have had two of each before Phoebe came along although apart from Imogen she saw very little of the other three. She knew they were busy leading their own lives, but she thought they might have come around to see her a bit more now Phoebe was born although she knew they were probably terrified in case she decided to ask one or the other of them to babysit. To make things worse, Imogen was still with the ghastly Quentin, and she had reached the stage where she thought she might have no choice but to accept him as her future son in law. He and Imogen were engaged, and she had recently started to drop hints about them going wedding dress shopping together. She had dreamed of going wedding dress shopping with her daughters since the day they were born, and she knew that if she didn't swallow her pride and accept Quentin into the family soon, Imogen would never forgive her.

She must have dropped off to sleep because she woke to find Grant standing over her holding out a cup of tea, causing her to sit bolt upright with a start. Crystal was stood shyly behind him, but before she had the chance to speak, he put his hand gently on to her shoulder and said she had no need to get up just yet because Phoebe was still sleeping soundly downstairs in her pram. She relaxed again briefly and gratefully accepted the tea. Her mouth was dry, and she had a foul taste at the back of her throat, which she knew was probably due to dehydration. She had been so engrossed in her thoughts about Mel she hadn't thought about keeping her fluid intake up although by the looks of her sopping wet jumper her milk supply hadn't suffered too much as a result. She hoped Phoebe would wake soon for a feed, so she could relieve her painful engorged breasts, and a few moments later Phoebe obliged by letting out a huge cry which sent her overflowing breasts into a complete frenzy. Grant hurried downstairs to fetch the baby and Crystal giggled as she sat trying to stuff wads of tissue into her ugly nursing bra in a vain attempt to protect her clothes. She had no idea why Crystal thought it was funny because she most certainly didn't, and more than anything she was sick of constantly smelling like a stale yoghurt maker and having enough washing to run her own Chinese laundry.

As she struggled to free her swollen breasts from

the front fastening bra to allow the impatient Phoebe to latch on she caught her flesh in the zip causing her to yelp out loud which for some reason made Crystal cry and made Phoebe scream even louder. She had no idea why Crystal was crying, and it irritated her even more when Grant rushed to comfort her instead of trying to soothe their frustrated baby. The last time he prioritised Crystal's needs over the needs of her own he lived to regret it because he missed the birth of their precious baby as a result, and if he didn't step up soon and behave the way she wanted him to she would make damned sure he lived to regret it again. She didn't actually need him now Mel was back in her life because Mel had already promised to look after both her and her baby, but she knew her hormones were still all over the place and although her heart was convinced she wanted Mel she knew it wasn't a good time to let her heart rule her head.

Eventually, Phoebe settled down and latched on to her breast, but the milk flowed so fast into her tiny mouth she coughed and spluttered before hunger and frustration got the better of her. It took a full five minutes of her wriggling and squirming and screaming before she calmed down enough to feed properly by which time she had worn herself out, and she fell back to sleep again after only five minutes on the breast. Chloe knew she would wake again if she tried to prise her off again and she wasn't ready to face another battle with her angry new-born just yet. It was also a good excuse for her to just stay in bed cuddling her baby and she encouraged Grant to leave them alone for a bit and go downstairs and spend some quality time with his daughter because as she pointed out, it wouldn't be long before it was time to take her back home again. Grant looked at his watch feeling a bit puzzled. It was only just 2 O clock, and he'd told Amberina he would bring her home after her tea around 6 O clock and for a moment he wondered if Chloe had forgotten about the arrangements they had made. He had hoped that Chloe would agree to let her stay overnight especially as he hadn't seen Crystal for a while but as usual, she came up with a whole host of excuses about why she couldn't possibly stay over, and he was either too weak or too emotionally drained to argue with her about it. Whichever one it was he knew Chloe was probably relying on him postponing the conversation but it was a battle he was going to have to fight soon because Crystal was growing up fast and he didn't want to miss out on her precious younger years because he knew with a blink of an eye they'd be gone and one day he would wake up to find she had grown in to a fully-fledged gobby teenager. Chloe must have been reading his mind because she glanced at her own watch before declaring that she had no idea it was still so early, but he could see from the expression on her face that she wished it was much later.

Chloe really did wish it was later, but she hoped if she gave her an early tea Grant might take her home a bit sooner. Realistically she knew she couldn't get away with feeding her much before 4 O clock, but she already had a homemade shepherd's pie defrosting in the fridge which wasn't going to need much more than half an hour in the oven and hey presto tea would be ready. She liked quick and easy meals, and luckily she still had plenty of them stored in the freezer left over from the baking frenzy she had unexpectedly embarked on a few weeks before Phoebe was born. In hindsight, she should have realised she would go into labour early because the books mentioned something about a 'nesting' period a few weeks prior to giving birth where the mother makes preparation for the arrival of her young. At the time she thought it sounded more like something the likes of David Attenborough would talk about in a wildlife documentary on TV but in the weeks leading up to Phoebe's birth she found herself doing all sorts of things she wouldn't usually do, and she realised that must have been why.

She watched as Crystal timidly followed Grant out of the door. She was clinging tightly to his hand almost as if she were afraid to let go, and for a brief moment, she felt an unexpected pang of guilt. She was only a child, but she was his other child, so she was always going to be a threat to her and Phoebe, and despite Grant's assurances that he had more than enough love to go round all three of them he would soon learn that a one third share was never going to be enough for a woman like her.

MEL

Mel had a noticeable spring in his step and whistled cheerfully to himself as he walked along the road. He hadn't felt this positive about anything for a long time, and he couldn't wait to phone Cain and tell him his good news.

He knew he had taken a big risk by phoning Chloe, and he didn't know what her reaction was going to be, but he had tried hard not to get his hopes up just in case she turned him down. He had nothing left to lose, at least he didn't think he did, apart from his sanity that was, because a life without Chloe was completely unthinkable now. She always told him not to have expectations because that way he wouldn't be disappointed if things didn't go to plan, but he couldn't help having a certain level of expectation, and her response to his spur-of-the-moment phone call had exceeded his wildest dreams. She sounded pleased to hear from him, which was a good start, but she told him she didn't want to rush into anything, and he understood that because she had only just had a baby after all. He wasn't too worried about the baby although it was inevitable it was going to make things more complicated for them, but he was confident that one way or another they would be able to work things out, they would have to.

He stared lovingly at the photo she had sent to him, and he wished he could be with her now. When he cheekily asked for a picture he thought the best he would get was a head and shoulders shot but the photo she sent reminded him of what he was missing, and he was more determined than ever to win her back whatever the cost.

He was disappointed when Cain sounded disinterested on the phone. He relied heavily on him for support, and he couldn't afford for him to back out now at this, the most crucial of times. Cain had been his rock, and he had a lot to thank him for. If it wasn't for Cain, he would never have had the courage to make that call so at the very least he assumed he would show some interest in the outcome of it all. He assumed Cain didn't have a woman on the go because he never spoke about any women in his life and his home, although neat and tidy, definitely lacked a female touch. They were supposed to be mates, but he had always been too busy talking about himself to ask Cain about his life, and he wondered whether now was a good time to ask. He knew Cain was a very private person and he didn't want to offend him by asking him about things he might not want to talk about but if he were to take him out for a few pints one night he might be willing to open up to him, and they could have a laugh and compare notes at the same time. Luckily Cain was up for a night out, but something gave him the feeling he was eager to end the call, and he hoped he hadn't agreed to it just because he wanted to get rid of him. He put it to the back of his mind, he was overthinking things as usual, and he knew Cain wouldn't be impressed if he started blowing everything out of proportion again. It had taken Cain a long time to get him back on track again, and he didn't want to let him down. Claire always complained about how he made such a big deal about everything but the majority of the time she was too wasted to notice their world was falling apart. There was a time when he was tempted to join her in one of her vodka induced comas just so he could get away from it all and experience for himself the oblivion she enjoyed on a regular basis, but he had their boys to think about and if he wasn't there to look after them he dreaded to think what might happen. He had come close to losing them once when the youngest started acting up at school, and Claire showed up completely rat-arsed to confront the teacher who she claimed wasn't doing his job properly. Luckily he had arrived on time to drag Claire away and diffuse the situation, but the poor teacher was visibly shaken after his encounter with Claire and looked like he could do with a stiff drink himself. After that he fully expected the social services to come knocking on the door to take the boys away to a place of safety and in some ways he wished they had because then he wouldn't have had to worry about them anymore. He knew it was selfish of him to think that way, but the truth was he was struggling to be both mum and dad to them and keep an eye on Claire at the same time, and realistically he knew they would probably have been better off elsewhere. They would have objected of course because they adored their mother, but she was dragging them down in much the same way as she'd dragged him down and they deserved better especially as there were so many people in the world that were unable to have children of their own. After everything that had happened with Claire, he knew he was blessed to still have them in his life, and he wouldn't have blamed them if they'd walked away from him. They were still very close to Claire's ex-work colleague Angela, and he knew she could be relied upon to step in and help during times of crisis. She had stepped in a lot when Claire was alive, and she had been a tower of strength to them all in the dark days following Claire's untimely death. The boys often stayed with her, and he used that time as some well-earned respite for himself because when they weren't with him, he didn't have to think or talk about Claire. Cain said it was not only healthy but also completely normal for the boys to want to talk about their mother as much as possible and it was also an important part of the healing process for them, but it hadn't been easy for him because keeping Claire's memory alive for them only served to bury the memories of his beloved Chloe even deeper. Now they were older they didn't need him as much, apart from when they needed money that was, but by what he could gather from the people around him funding your kids into adulthood was pretty much the norm these days and seeing as Jack had opted to join Lewis at university he knew he would have to dig deep into his pockets for a good few years to come. Joel's ambition was to become a PE teacher, so he was at a local college studying sports sciences and came only came home when he was hungry. In a strange sort of way, he missed feeling needed by them. Claire had stopped needing him a long time before she died, and it didn't make him feel good about himself, knowing she had traded him in for booze. Whenever she ran out of money she used some cheap and nasty mouthwash instead but at the time he had no idea that mouthwash could be used as an effective substitute for alcohol, but it did explain why she got through such a lot of it. In the early days, he blamed himself for her death because after she lost her job, it was he who provided the money to fund her addiction. As the sole wage earner in the family there were times when he found it difficult to earn enough money to pay all the bills let alone meet her constant selfish demands for more booze, but he hated confrontation, and he wanted an easy life, and he knew that if he didn't give it to her she would make his life hell. It had taken a long time, but Cain had eventually managed to convince him that Claire was what he called a ticking time bomb and that nothing short of a straitjacket and a padded cell would have been enough to stop her from drinking herself to death. It was comforting to know that he wasn't entirely to blame, but he knew the likes of Angela thought he should have done more, and she was right, he should definitely have done more.

He had arranged with Chloe that she would ring him again as soon as she could, but he was impatient to get the ball rolling as soon as possible. She didn't want him to ring her for obvious reasons, and he accepted her cautionary slap on the wrist without making too much protest. It felt good to feel wanted again, and he was certain that she wanted him as much as he wanted her, so it was a win-win situation for both of them. He made up his mind he would have to talk to Cain about it because now she was married it had all become rather complicated and he couldn't afford to make a silly mistake and risk losing her again. Cain would be able to tell him what to do because Cain always knew what to do, but there was a little voice at the back of his head warning him not to rely on Cain lending him his full support this time. Cain was a man with morals, and although he tried hard to remain non-judgemental, Mel knew he didn't believe in coming between a husband and wife unless someone's life was at risk. He didn't expect Cain to understand, but Cain had never had to walk in his shoes before, so he couldn't possibly understand the emotional rollercoaster his brain was going through. Nevertheless, Cain's blessing was important to him, and he hoped that at the very least, they could agree to disagree.

GRANT

Having sensed the growing tension upstairs between his wife and his eldest daughter Grant took Crystal back downstairs to play. He was disappointed that Chloe hadn't made more of an effort to make her feel welcome but, at the same time, he wasn't all that surprised because Chloe had never made an effort to get to know his daughter. If nothing else her behaviour was consistent, but it was consistently vile, and as much as he hated to admit it, he was ashamed to call her his wife. It had got to a point where he was fast running out of excuses, and he knew he couldn't pull the wool over Amberina's eyes for much longer. When he told her he was having a few difficulties at home, she had raised her eyebrows at him, and although Chloe thought otherwise, he knew his ex-wife was no fool. The strain was beginning to take its toll on all of them and with Crystal acting up things could only get worse. It was obvious to him why Crystal's behaviour had suddenly changed, and he felt wholly responsible for it. Tom told him it was probably just an adjustment period for her, and she was still testing boundaries, but he knew that if he hadn't brought a wicked stepmother into her life things would have been very different.

It made him laugh to think how the once obnoxious Tom was now apparently a so-called expert in child psychology, but he wasn't complaining too much because he much preferred the new child-friendly version of Tom to the completely insensitive and tactless unedited edition. He was happy that things had worked out so well for his friend because it was not often that stories involving infidelity had such happy endings. Chloe nevertheless remained sceptical about it and said it was typical for someone like Tom to wade knee deep in muck and still come up smelling of roses, and she hadn't been impressed when he replied that it was hardly surprising because muck, as she so aptly called it, was a fertilizer which his parents used on their allotment all the time to help the vegetables grow. She wasn't even happy for Tom's long-suffering wife Maria who had positively blossomed since Avellino had come into their lives. It had been a difficult time for them both, but somehow she had managed to proudly stand up and face the world and show everyone what a loving and sincere woman she was who had not only forgiven her husband's not so minor indiscretion but had also accepted his son as her own. Of course, as far as Chloe was concerned, Maria would never be what she called a 'proper mother,' and she had no qualms about telling her either. In Chloe's petty-minded world a woman wasn't a proper mother as she called it unless she had given birth to a child of her own and seeing as Maria had been denied that privilege Chloe claimed she wasn't entitled to use the title in any shape or form. Poor Maria, who clearly didn't need reminding about her childlessness, remained calm and dignified when she replied that she had no intention of replacing Avellino's mother because she was fully aware that he already had a wonderful biological mother in

France, but she would always be there to provide motherly support for him during his real mother's absence. As it turned out, Chloe was left feeling foolish, and her words came back to haunt her because Maria and Avellino grew surprisingly close and formed a bond that was comparable with that of any biological mother and son and the next thing they all knew Avellino was calling Maria his charming English mother.

Grant was happy for them both, but he was especially happy for Maria because life had knocked her down so many times, and she had emerged stronger than ever. Tom, on the other hand, was just a lucky sod who, despite doing the dirty on his wife, had fallen on his feet and he sincerely hoped their good fortune would continue. His life though was falling apart, and he wasn't sure that he, or anyone else, would be able to do anything about it.

Crystal was pestering him to play, but he wasn't in the mood to play, and luckily she seemed happy enough to watch a film on TV instead. He placed the card that she had made on the shelf above the television with all the other cards, and she was thrilled because hers was at the front. She said it was because hers was the most important card and he smiled at her natural innocence. As they settled on the sofa together, he could hear laughing coming from upstairs, and he realised Chloe was on the phone again. He was glad whoever it was had managed to lighten her mood, but it also saddened him to know that he wasn't the one to make her smile anymore. In the early days they'd laughed and cried together all the time, but these days it was nothing, but tears and ferocious arguments followed by a frosty silence and it wasn't doing any of them any good, especially little Crystal. As she snuggled up close to him on the sofa he wondered why Chloe hated her so much after all, she was only a little girl looking for love, and like all children, she deserved to grow up knowing she was loved by her parents. Maria had once told him that children should be treasured because they were a gift more precious than any other jewel. She also said they needed to be handled with care because if you broke them, they couldn't just be repaired or replaced with an alternative from the shop shelf. They were wise words from a wise woman who knew from experience what it was like to feel broken and he hoped he hadn't left it too late to save Crystal.

MARIA AND TOM

L ife was truly on the up for Maria and Tom. Avel-lino, now more affectionately known as '*Avvy*' by his English family and friends had been in England a whole year now, and his English was already almost as good as theirs. Maria said he put them both to shame and before he had a chance to stop her, she had purchased the entire volume of some self-study language course, so they could learn French together. During long car journeys, they no longer sang out loud to the songs on the radio instead they listened intently to some French tutor teaching them how to say ridiculous phrases like "*avez vous pas de glacons pour le vin* 'which translated into English as don't you have any ice cubes for the wine. Tom thought he was making a valid point when he pointed out that no one in their right mind would ever put ice cubes in their wine, but Maria said he was just being picky for the sake of it. Avvy rolled about laughing when Tom tried speaking a few words using his best French accent and luckily he didn't take it to heart when he and Maria agreed between them that French wasn't going to be Tom's forte.

They had been to see Chloe and Grant out of duty more than anything else a few weeks after Phoebe was born. Maria hadn't wanted to go, and she tagged along reluctantly only because Tom said Grant was having a difficult time and needed their support. She had no time for Chloe these days, but she still had a soft spot for Grant although she couldn't help thinking his injuries were self-inflicted. They weren't physical injuries, of course, but the mental scars were blatantly visible to those that were close to him, and she was shocked to see how tired and drawn he was looking. She had tried to warn him about Chloe long before he pushed the no return button by actually marrying the woman, but Tom insisted they should keep out of it and now she was beginning to regret letting him talk her out of it. Chloe, on the other hand, looked radiant, and Maria had to admit that motherhood suited her. Her skin was glowing, and although her figure was a little fuller than it was before the extra weight suited her shape. She had been too skinny before, at least Maria thought she was, but Tom said she was just jealous because Chloe could fit into a size ten pair of jeans whereas she still struggled to squeeze her shapely curves into a generous size fourteen. She was itching to hold the baby, but as they were no longer friends, it seemed rude to ask, so she sat back and waited politely for Chloe to offer and a few moments later Chloe gently placed the wriggling pink bundle in her arms. It was almost as if she had read her mind, and for a brief moment, she was so overcome with emotion she felt too choked to talk. A tiny face with big blue eyes peeked out at her from underneath the blankets, and Maria thought she was simply perfect. She was still only a few weeks old, but it was already obvious she'd inherited her fine bone structure and exquisite, delicate features from her mother and when Tom leaned over to take a peek he told her that one day she was going to be a heartbreaker. Maria was certain she smiled at him although Chloe was adamant it could only be wind or a reflex smile because evidently, babies don't smile before they are six weeks old and Maria couldn't resist raising her eyebrows at what was clearly nothing more than a textbook description of a baby. Grant interrupted and said he was certain Crystal had smiled when she was about the same age and Maria watched as Chloe scowled at the mere mention of the poor child's name. She had been sorely tempted to say something along the lines of it being in the genes seeing as they were sisters, but Tom gave her a sharp nudge, and she thought better of it. He wasn't usually the diplomat in such situations, but he knew how fiercely protective Maria was of Grant and he had an uncanny knack of knowing exactly when she was going to say something that could cause trouble and by the looks of things Grant was in enough trouble already. He looked world-weary, and Maria's heart went out to him but as Tom rightly said he was a fully-grown man and as hard as it was to sit back and say nothing he was going to have to learn to fight his own battles.

Grant said no more. He had seen for himself how Chloe raised her eyebrows at the mention of Crystal's name, and it wasn't worth the aggro to continue the conversation. He knew there would be repercussions because there always were whenever Crystal's name was mentioned, but this time, she had surpassed herself by successfully managing to stop the conversation without even opening her mouth. It was true he was a coward when it came to standing up to Chloe, and he hated himself for it but having Phoebe brought back happy memories of Crystal's birth and whether his wife liked it or not the two little girls would always be sisters. He knew exactly what Tom meant when he said Phoebe was going to be a heartbreaker, but he hoped she wouldn't break a man's heart in the same way as Chloe was breaking his because if she grew up to be anything like her mother he knew his heart would break all over again.

Two cups of tea and numerous awkward silences later Tom and Maria made their excuses and left. Grant lingered unnecessarily at the door and seemed reluctant to release Maria from the extra-long bear hug that he had initiated. It wasn't unusual for Grant to embrace her, but she couldn't help noticing the haunted look in his eyes before Chloe intervened by firmly closing the door behind them. She had muttered something about the baby getting cold because he was letting all the warm air out but seeing as the house was like a sauna Maria thought it unlikely that anyone was going to freeze to death anytime soon. It was also exceptionally mild outside for the time of year, and Maria was glad to escape the stifling heat in favour of some much-needed fresh air. They left sporting artificial smiles on their faces, and as they waved goodbye to a solitary Grant standing motionless at the window, Tom shouted out they would be back to visit again soon. It was just words of course because neither of them wanted to go back to that hell hole that Grant was forced to call home, but Maria knew they would go back if only to keep a check on Grant whose life was unmistakeably spiralling out of control.

CHLOE

Time was flying, and Chloe couldn't believe little Phoebe would soon be one year old. It also signalled the end of her maternity leave, and very soon she would be going back to work. The thought of leaving her baby with a complete stranger horrified her, but she was fortunate to have found a local day nursery with glowing recommendations and an outstanding Ofsted report. She knew that this particular nursery had long waiting lists, so she had decided to get in early and book a place while she was still pregnant, and she was glad now that she had because they were now so busy their waiting list was currently closed. Phoebe had been going to the nursery for two half days a week since she was six months old for a one to one session with her key worker Beth who she clearly adored, and this should have made the whole returning to work process a whole lot easier for Chloe. She thought time was supposed to be a healer, but if anything, handing over her precious daughter was becoming harder than ever and instead of making good use of her child-free time she found herself sitting at home clock watching and wishing the time away. She was always one of the first mums waiting outside at the end of the session and she was beginning to become paranoid that Phoebe preferred being with her key worker to her because whenever she went to collect her she would cling to Beth like a child possessed and then proceed to humiliate her even more by screaming hysterically as she forcibly tried to prise her from her arms. She and Beth always made a joke about it, but she wanted her little girl to respond like all the other kids did when they saw their parents if only to stop her from feeling like a sadistic child abuser. Grant said it was just a phase Phoebe was going through and that she shouldn't take it to heart so much, but she couldn't help it, and it annoyed her knowing how blasé he was about the whole thing. Fortunately, she didn't have to rely on him to understand anymore because Mel understood, and he was more than happy to listen to her going on about it for hours at a time. She knew once she was back at work, it would get easier because she wouldn't have so much time on her hands to mull over so many ridiculous thoughts in her head, but it would also give her less time with Mel, and she knew that was going to be a high price to pay. She hoped having less contact with him would help her to make a decision because he was pushing for more commitment from her, but she was in no hurry to rush into anything all the time she still had the best of both worlds. Grant was steady and reliable, and he brought in enough money to enable her to live comfortably, and he had even told her that she didn't have to go back to work at all if she didn't want to but being a kept woman wasn't her style, and she certainly didn't want him thinking he had done her a favour because that might mean she owed him something and she couldn't stomach debt in any shape or form. Mel, on the other hand, was exciting and spontaneous and definitely better in the bedroom department, but for some reason it had been a lot more exciting when she couldn't have him, and she couldn't help wondering whether the novelty of a bit on the side as her mother would have called it was wearing off. It was certainly exhausting keeping two men on the go at once, and there were a couple of occasions where Grant had come close to catching them, but the near misses added a bit of spice to an otherwise dull and rather bland existence, and as a self-confessed thrill seeker she was starting to enjoy living life on the edge.

Against her better judgement, she'd agreed to Grant's idea of holding a small birthday party for Phoebe at the weekend, but she was already beginning to regret her decision because Grant wrongly assumed it would be okay to change his weekend access arrangements without asking her so that Crystal could come to. He claimed it was nothing but a simple oversight and that he had been meaning to tell her, but Chloe knew it was deliberate because he knew if asked she would have said no, and he would have been right. As it was, she had already managed to convince him to reduce her visits down to just one weekend a month now even though it meant her staying over on both Friday and Saturday nights, but she was working on a plan to change that too. She protested of course by telling Grant it wasn't a proper party and that Crystal would probably be bored because it would be mainly adults there, but he said it didn't matter who was there because Crystal would enjoy celebrating her little sister's first birthday with her. She visibly cringed when he mentioned the word sister, but before she had a chance to object, he walked away, leaving her exasperated. She liked to have the last word in an argument but these days he had a habit of walking away, so she had no choice but to follow him from room to room if she wanted to continue the fight and it was physically more tiring especially if she happened to be carrying Phoebe too. As a result of this, they had fewer arguments, but the awkward silences dragged on for much longer, and sometimes they would go days without speaking a single word to each another. It didn't bother her too much because she still had Mel to talk to and just like a loyal dog, he didn't stray far from his mistress. She didn't think his phone had ever rung more than twice before he answered it even when he was supposed to be at work, and she often wondered how he managed to get away with it. She knew he was the boss, but his job was much like hers, and it involved spending a lot of time talking to clients, and she knew there was no way she would ever get away with answering her phone during a consultation with a patient unless it was an absolute emergency. The tables had well and truly turned, and this time, she was the one in control, and she was loving every second of it. The situation was so absurd she couldn't stop herself from laughing out loud, but her hysterical laughter startled poor Phoebe and made her cry. As she picked her up to soothe her, she whispered in her ear that everything was going to be alright and she was delighted when the little girl responded with a beaming smile.

Whoever said you couldn't have your cake and eat it clearly had no idea what they were talking about because she knew otherwise, but that was a secret she shared only with Phoebe who luckily was still far too young to know what she was going on about. She knew once her little girl started to talk properly, she would have to be extra vigilant because children didn't understand secrets in the same way as adults did and she was already starting to call Mel 'dada' at times. Mel thought it was great of course, but she didn't want to encourage it but calling him uncle Mel didn't seem right either. When she was growing up her own mother actively encouraged her to call her numerous male admirers *'uncle'* then when she married them they became known as *'staddy'* instead, a name her mother made up by using letters from the words step and daddy. She clearly thought she was being clever and had no idea how much it confused her, and she didn't want Phoebe growing up feeling confused to. She still didn't know what name Phoebe should call Mel, but it wasn't worth losing sleep over because she wasn't sure if she wanted him to become a permanent fixture in her life. He came with a whole heap of excess baggage, including three emotionally traumatised kids, and she was already struggling to be a stepparent to just one. That wasn't entirely true, of course, because she wasn't exactly struggling, but kids like Crystal took a great deal of effort, and her resources were already drained from worrying about her own children.

As she lovingly stroked Phoebe's soft curls, she knew she must do what was right for her, if only she knew what that was.

MEL

As expected, Cain hadn't been all that enthusiastic about the *'Chloe situation'* as he liked to call it, but his disapproval wasn't enough to deter Mel. It would have been nice to have his approval of course but it wasn't essential, and the good thing was they had managed to remain friends on the proviso he didn't talk about her when they were together. As they drank their beers, the silence was deafening as Mel struggled to find something they could talk about, and it soon dawned on him that he rarely thought about anything apart from Chloe these days. It wasn't healthy he knew that already and prior to Cain imposing a ban on the *'Chloe situation'* he told him quite bluntly that he thought his behaviour was bordering on obsessional.

The truth was he was frustrated with his lack of progress with Chloe, and he was even more frustrated that Cain had forbidden him to talk about it. He knew they just went round and round in circles when they did talk about her and Cain said there was no point in going on because he clearly wasn't ready to listen. It was true he hadn't been ready to listen then, but he thought he might be now, but Cain was having none of it and seemed more than happy to sit with him in complete silence rather than address the huge elephant in the room. To be fair on Cain, he knew he had taken advantage of his good nature because he had never paid him for his counselling services on the basis that he had never seen him in an official capacity before. He thought about offering him money now because that way Cain would have no choice but to agree to let him talk about Chloe, but in the end, he decided it would be better to keep him as a friend and find himself another counsellor instead. While checking through the list of names in the local directory, he came across someone called Amberina who didn't live all that far from Cain. It was an unusual name, and it sounded vaguely familiar to him, but he had no idea why. Anyway, he'd gone ahead and booked an appointment with her because she told him she had some late availability because her daughter was going to a party and because her prices were low compared with some of the others on the list. His dilemma now was whether or not he should tell Cain about the appointment because even though he knew it was probably the right thing to do he didn't want to offend him although he thought it was probably a bit too late to start worrying about that now. If he was going to offend Cain, he knew he had probably already managed to do it so in the end he just blurted it out because saying something was better than sitting there in a deathly silence with him. For a moment Cain said nothing, and he was worried in case he really had offended him, but then Cain smiled and told him that Amberina was a kind and colourful lady with a big heart and he was sure he had made the right choice. Mel was initially slightly taken aback by this revelation because he hadn't stopped to consider that Cain might actually know her, but no harm was done and if nothing else it served as a stark reminder of what a small world they all lived in.

He decided it was purely coincidental that Chloe was hosting a party on the same day as his new counsellor's daughter was attending one after all kids of that age went to parties all the time. They'd had a few cross words about it though because Saturday was supposed to be their time together and even if it was only for a few hours that time was precious, at least it was for him. Sometimes she had Phoebe with her, and they would go to a park somewhere far enough away not to get recognised, but when she was alone, he would whisk her off to a hotel room for hours of uninhibited sexual adventure. They had always been good together in the bedroom, but he was looking for something more than that now, and he thought she was too. The physical side wasn't a problem, and most of the time she couldn't get enough of him, but afterwards, she could be cold and distant, and he was beginning to think she was just using him as a temporary escape from her unhappy marriage.

He didn't know much about her husband Grant, but a little part of him actually felt sorry for him. He knew he had been married before, and he knew he had a daughter that Chloe hated, but that was the full extent of his knowledge. He was the first to admit there were times when he struggled to understand her intense hatred of her husband's seven-year-old daughter, but she painted such terrible images of the child he was haunted by shocking visions of evil and sheer wickedness. He was glad in a way that he never had the opportunity to introduce her to his boys when Claire was alive just in case she tarred them with the same brush as this poor little girl who he knew realistically was probably confused and only looking for acceptance and love.

He wasn't sure whether to tell Chloe about his counselling appointment, but in the end, he decided against it. She didn't need to know how desperate he was for her to leave her husband, so they could run away and get married and do all the things they were going to do before Claire died especially as it was his fault it hadn't happened back then. At the time he had been too busy enjoying the best of both worlds, and he couldn't bring himself to choose between her and Claire, but he had paid the ultimate price for his philandering lifestyle because one way or another he had eventually lost them both.

If worse came to worse he knew he still had his trump card to play but once it was gone it was gone, and it felt reassuring to know he still had a safety net of sorts up his sleeve. Ideally, he wanted her to come back to him because she wanted him and not just because of the dog he was willing to buy for her, but he knew how desperate she was to have another dog and according to her Grant was refusing to let her have one. He didn't know how true that was because he was fast learning that Chloe would say anything to get the sympathy vote from him but they always planned to buy a dog together and they had even gone as far as choosing a name for her but then it dawned on him that they would have to find a different name now because Chloe had already used the name for someone else, and it would be totally impractical to have a puppy and a toddler called Phoebe living together in the same household.

THE BIRTHDAY PARTY

The day of the party had finally arrived, and Chloe was dreading it. She wasn't in the mood for celebrating or for being nice to people, especially strangers but Grant was insistent they invite Tom and Maria along with 'Avvy' and Maria's sister Thelma who he apparently knew from school. She had never met her, but she seemed to remember Maria going to stay with her for a time when she and Tom split up, and she was certain Maria said she was a pain to live with because she had OCD. She took a quick look around the house and saw it was a complete mess with piles of laundry everywhere and she wondered if she dropped enough hints whether Thelma might fancy doing a bit of clearing up for her. Next, there would be 'Avvy.' She hadn't met him either, and a small part of her was intrigued enough to want to meet him, but the prospect of watching Tom and Maria playing happy families all afternoon was utterly nauseating.

For Phoebe today was the same as every other day except when she woke up her mummy and daddy had given her some new toys to play with. She wasn't interested in the toys of course because there were boxes to chew on and the rigid cardboard was so much better at helping to cut those beastly back teeth of hers. She had a temper tantrum when Chloe tried to take the soggy cardboard away, and as a result, she was now back in bed because she had worn herself out screaming. Phoebe had no idea that it was her birthday, she didn't even know what day of the week it was for god's sake which is why Chloe hadn't wanted to make a big deal of it. She had tried telling Grant that there would be plenty of time for proper parties later on when she was old enough to understand, but he was adamant it was just a bit of harmless fun that would give him the opportunity to show his girls off together.

She bit her lip to avoid saying something she shouldn't, and she knew by the acrid metallic taste in her mouth she had made it bleed. Grant took a tissue and leaned over to wipe the blood away from her mouth, but she grabbed it angrily from his hand telling him she was perfectly capable of looking after herself and he wisely backed away from her.

This was Phoebe's special day, and she didn't want Crystal stealing the limelight from her, so she made it clear to Grant she didn't want her at the house before midday because she would only get in the way. He agreed he would pick her up around eleven because Amberina had a new client coming at twelve and apparently she needed time to prepare the paperwork. She had always been a bit sceptical about this so-called counselling qualification of Amberina's, and she'd told Grant on a number of occasions that she thought his ex-wife looked more like a dominatrix than a counsellor. Most of the time, he ignored such comments, but one day, he asked her what she thought a dominatrix was supposed to look like, and she felt her cheeks burn with shame. Of course, she'd never gone quite as far as dressing up as Miss Whiplash or anything sleazy like that but she and Mel often enjoyed a bit of adult fun in the bedroom, and she knew without a doubt that her naughty nurse outfit drove him wild with desire.

Once her lip finally stopped bleeding, she set about preparing the party food in the kitchen. Grant offered to help, so she gave him the peeler to prepare the vegetables for the dip. She detested peeling vegetables but little Phoebe, who was cutting more teeth, was more than happy to munch on hard carrots for hours on end. An hour later, a huge pile of sandwiches and finger foods filled the kitchen worktops, and Grant commented that she'd made enough to feed an army. As she opened the box containing the birthday cake, she thought back to all the parties her other kids had enjoyed when they were little. In those days, buying a cake was considered an unnecessary extravagance, so she and her mum always baked a cake together for their birthdays. More often than not it turned out looking like a complete shipwreck, but the kids didn't mind because it tasted okay and as her mum pointed out it didn't matter what it looked like because it all went down the same hole. They'd had fun making those cakes together, and she wished her dear mum was still around now to help her make cakes for Phoebe who she knew she would have adored. She hoped when Imogen eventually had a child of her own they might be able to continue the tradition of mother and daughter baking, but Imogen was the kind of girl impressed by the finer details and lots of fancy packaging, and unless you were a pro those sort of cakes were only found on the supermarket shelves.

Grant looked at his watch. It was already 10.45am, and he said it was time for him to go and collect Crystal. He hesitated for a moment as if he were expecting a response, before picking up his keys and going out the door. There was a time when she would have hidden his keys as a delaying tactic, but the last time she did that things didn't quite go to plan and these days she knew it was a pointless exercise because she was only delaying the inevitable.

Phoebe was still sleeping soundly after her ridiculous temper tantrum, and Chloe found herself with some unexpected time on her hands. There were things to do around the house, but they would still be there tomorrow unless of course, the pernickety Thelma was feeling generous. She thought about phoning Mel after all this was meant to be their day together, but he had tried to make her feel guilty for hosting her own daughter's birthday party, and she still hadn't forgiven him. She couldn't believe he had actually tried to make her choose between him and her own daughter and she had told him in no uncertain words that he was playing a dangerous game because if he was going to turn it into a contest, her daughter would always win. After that, he backed off, and then he mentioned something about having an appointment somewhere that day anyway, and she was left wondering what all the fuss had been about because surely if he was busy, he would have been the one letting her down had it not been Phoebe's birthday. As it was he was beginning to become a little bit too needy for her liking and she was starting to question whether a man who couldn't cope without seeing her for just one day was actually the right man for her and after a few moments of soul searching she sat down with a cup of tea instead. Her mum used to think a cup of tea was the answer to everything because whenever someone had a problem she automatically went to the kitchen to put the kettle on but, as refreshing as it was, Chloe knew no amount of hot tea was going to help solve her current dilemma, and she was glad when Phoebe finally woke up, so she didn't have to think about it anymore.

Fortunately, she had woken up in a better mood, and by the time Chloe got to her room, she was standing up in her cot impatiently banging at the sides to get out. She greeted Chloe with one of heart-melting smiles, and Chloe didn't think she could love her more if she tried. She truly was the one good thing that had come out of her and Grant's relationship, and she made a mental note to try harder if only for the sake of their beautiful daughter. Thankfully now she'd had a good sleep she was happy to play with her new toys on the floor while Chloe finished her tea and mentally prepared herself for the afternoon ahead.

Grant came back with Crystal on the dot of twelve, and she suspected her rigid rules had forced him to drive the car around until he felt it was safe enough to come home. Crystal rushed straight over to play with Phoebe who proudly presented her with one of her dribble covered wooden blocks, and both girls giggled as Crystal took the sticky brick from her hand. It was obvious that Phoebe loved having Crystal around and for a brief moment, Chloe's heart softened towards her stepdaughter, and she could see Grant visibly relax as the tension between them eased.

By 12.30 everyone except Imogen and Quentin had arrived, and Phoebe who was now bored of playing with her toys was screaming loudly and demanding to be fed. Quentin had asked rather nervously if it would be okay to bring his daughter Eva to the party because it was his access weekend and for some inexplicable reason she had agreed although she was already starting to regret her decision. With Phoebe in one arm and a pile of plates in the other, she attempted to navigate her way around the narrow galley kitchen while Grant chatted to Tom and

Avvy. Phoebe instantly stopped screaming at the sight of all the food and immediately pointed to the chocolate fingers, but when Chloe shook her head, she had one of her temper tantrums, and Chloe was relieved when Maria unexpectedly came to her rescue. She hadn't seen Maria since Phoebe was just a few weeks old, but Grant had been out with Tom a couple of times to *'wet the baby's head'* as he put it. As Maria held out her arms to take the little girl, Chloe wondered whether she would kick up a fuss but much to her annoyance she took to Maria straightaway reinforcing her deep insecurities and her belief that Phoebe preferred to be with anyone but her.

The food was almost ready by the time Imogen and Quentin arrived, and Imogen seemed unusually flustered when she joined her mother in the kitchen to help prepare the last of the food. Apparently, Quentin's daughter wasn't ready when they arrived to pick her up, so Quentin had kicked off at his ex and she had retaliated by saying he couldn't have her only to change her mind when he got back into the car to drive away. Chloe made all the right noises, of course throwing in a comment about how selfish ex-wives could be, but at the same time, she thought how wonderful life would be if Amberina were to make similar threats.

A few moments later, the buffet was ready, and in true British style, everyone formed an orderly queue for the food. Maria suggested letting the children go first and she offered to help feed Phoebe who had already spotted the chocolate biscuits again and was now protesting by angrily hurling her carrots onto the floor. Crystal was standing holding a rather terrified looking Eva's hand, and for a moment, Chloe thought she was going to cry. She had enough drama coping with Crystal, so she certainly didn't need another emotionally challenged child to deal with, especially not today.

Fortunately, Eva cheered up at the sight of the food, and as she and Crystal filled their plates to the brim, Chloe couldn't resist casting a critical look at Grant. As it happened, he was too busy catching up with Thelma to notice, and she felt a sudden unexpected pang of jealousy at the sight of her husband talking to this other, undeniably attractive single woman. She assumed Thelma would be a bit of a plain Jane like her sister, but with her tall, slender frame and colourful trendy specs, she was surprisingly good on the eye. Everyone seemed to be talking among themselves, and suddenly she felt very alone, and she wished now she hadn't made an enemy out of Maria because life was definitely better when they were friends. She had said some terrible things to her which she bitterly regretted, and although she couldn't turn the clock back, she hoped that one day Maria might be able to forgive her.

The room fell silent as everyone eagerly tucked into their food, and she was glad to find something to finally divert Grant's attention away from Thelma. Phoebe was merrily sucking on an object which looked suspiciously like a chocolate finger, and she couldn't help smiling as she watched Maria desperately trying to wipe the evidence off her face with a packet of baby wipes. As soon as she walked over to help Phoebe proudly held the soggy biscuit up to her face and she pretended to take a bite which made the little girl giggle and to her delight it made Maria smile to, and she hoped this moment between them might turn out to be the icebreaker they so desperately needed.

A few moments later Avvy joined their little group and added to the fun by blowing raspberries and playing her favourite peekaboo game with her and Chloe immediately warmed to the charming young Frenchman. Crystal and Eva were busy undressing their dollies in the far corner of the room, and Chloe secretly hoped they would stay there but her wish was short-lived because Crystal, who clearly thought she was missing out on something, startled poor Phoebe by joining in and shouting boo in such a ridiculously loud voice it made her cry. She wasn't aware she was doing it, but she must have scowled at Crystal because Maria immediately sprang to the child's defence, and when she looked around the room she was shocked to find people were staring at her like she was some kind of monster.

She tried to brush it off, but she felt humiliated, and that's when it dawned on her that she didn't want people thinking she was a bad person. When Pete left she spent years building barriers and creating a tough outer shell, so everyone automatically assumed she was a 'tough cookie' but she wasn't as tough as she made herself out to be and as she carried the teddy bear cake with the single pink candle through from the kitchen she struggled to hold back the tears as everyone began to sing "happy birthday" to her rather bemused one-year-old daughter.

THE APPOINTMENT

Mel arrived early for his appointment with Amberina, so he thought it best to wait outside in the car for a while. He watched as a rather weary looking man went into the house and then came out again some time later holding the hand of a young red-headed little girl before getting into a car and driving off. A rather plump woman stood at the door waving them off, and he couldn't help noticing how she lingered at the window long after the car was out of sight. He assumed the woman was Amberina, and he thought she looked sad, but he hoped she wasn't because he was paying good money for this service and he was relying on her to help him make an important decision today. He had a lot on his mind, and he wanted to offload as much of it as possible in one session to keep the costs down. He knew from Cain that counsellors usually preferred to take things slowly and build a rapport with their clients over several weeks, but he didn't have enough time for that, so he was keeping everything crossed for a miracle. Keeping things crossed had never worked for him in the past so he wasn't all that hopeful it would work this time, but he did know that if Chloe had kept her legs crossed they wouldn't be in this predicament now. A baby had certainly complicated matters for them, and he couldn't help feeling a little bit resentful because if it wasn't for Phoebe, he was certain she would have left Grant a long time ago. His late wife Claire always said Chloe was nothing but a trollop and he was beginning to think she may have been right, but towards the end of her life her brain was so addled by all the booze she had no idea what she was saying, and he had stopped listening anyway.

At ten to twelve, he decided to go in. He hated being late for appointments, but at the same time, he didn't want her thinking he was too keen by showing up ridiculously early. They had never met before so she wouldn't know he had been sitting outside in the car for the last hour but it had given him some much needed thinking time and consequently he had a whole wad of scribbled notes in his hand because he was afraid that if he didn't write it down he might forget to say something important.

Amberina was watching from the window. She had spotted the unfamiliar car with a man sitting in the driver's seat parked up in the road long before Grant arrived, and she had made a note of the registration number just in case there was a sudden rise in the number of house burglaries in the area. She was an active member of the local neighbourhood watch scheme, and everyone's vigilance was beginning to pay off with the police reporting a significant drop in crime levels as a result. There was no denying the fact that living alone made her feel nervous, but she was anxious not to let Crystal pick up on it because otherwise she would become nervous too and she didn't want her growing up believing she needed a man in order to feel safe. Like all mothers, she dreamed of her daughter's wedding day, but she wanted Crystal to grow up strong and independent, and it was her mission to give her the confidence to do exactly that.

She watched as Mel got out of the car and walked towards the front door. He had a confident stride about him, and she thought he must be either an expert at disguise or just plain arrogant. On the phone, he sounded desperate which was why she had fitted him in at such short notice, but he looked almost cocky, and she hoped he didn't turn out to be another one of those blokes with a bizarre foot fetish. She was inexperienced with men, she knew that, and she wasn't good at picking up signals from them either. Her lack of confidence around them meant she often avoided them, and as a result, most of her clients were women. As a general rule, she found women easier to talk to and in her profession, it was vital for her to have some sort of emotional connection with her clients in order to do her job properly. Mel was her first male client in a while, and she hoped her naivety and inexperience with men wouldn't end up letting her down.

As she opened the door to him, he smiled and held out his hand and immediately introduced himself to her as Mel. She wasn't sure whether Mel was short for something like Melvin or whether he might actually have been born a Melanie, but if it did transpire, he was born a woman she decided it would be an added bonus because it was probably going to make her job a whole lot easier. His handshake was firm and business-like, but his skin felt rough, and she couldn't help noticing the fragments of dirt underneath his fingernails which suggested to her that it was extremely unlikely he had ever actually been a woman. He must have caught her studying his hands because he quickly pulled them away and apologised for the state of them at the same time making a light-hearted joke about running out of moisturiser.

She took his coat before leading him to the small

room that she used as her therapy room. The confined space was barely bigger than a large cupboard, so it was far from ideal, but she had done her best to make it feel warm and cosy, and she sincerely hoped he didn't suffer from claustrophobia. She had dreams of one day being able to buy a bigger house where she could have a decent size proper workroom, but unless she won the lottery chances were it would remain nothing but a pipe-dream.

It wasn't what Mel had been expecting, but he was pleasantly surprised by the tiny room with the two over-sized bean bags on the floor and soft colourful scatter cushions. There was a shelf on the wall with a small jug of iced water and a vase containing fresh flowers and a pot of sweet-smelling Pot Pourri which was a bit overpowering given the size of the room. As he slumped his tall, lean frame into one of the bean bags, Amberina handed him a glass of water and he couldn't resist mischievously asking her if she had a wee drop of whiskey to go with it. He had only said it in jest of course as an icebreaker, and he certainly didn't expect her to take him seriously yet judging by the startled look on her face he'd managed to fluster her, and he was already starting to regret his decision to choose her as his therapist. Good old reliable Cain had endorsed his choice so he thought he would be getting the equivalent of a five star hotel but Claire always said, '*you only get what you pay for*' and even though that reference was made to a cheap bottle of vodka he once had the audacity to bring home, he knew exactly what she meant by it. He fidgeted around on the bean-bag until the beans were more evenly distributed inside the bag in a futile effort to make himself feel more comfortable. He reassured himself it was only for an hour and after that, he would never have to come back again if he didn't want to and as much as he wanted to give her the benefit of the doubt he already knew it was going to be his first and last visit there.

He screwed up the paper in his hand and quickly put it back into his pocket before Amberina had a chance to notice it. The agenda he had planned in his head had gone skewwhiff, and now he just wanted the whole thing over and done with as quickly as possible. Without thinking he started babbling on and in just a few short breaths he somehow managed to tell her the whole sorry story about him and Chloe and about her husband Grant and how she wouldn't leave him because she had a baby and then he told her about Claire, and that's when he had started to cry.

Amberina gently handed him a box of tissues but she didn't speak, and when he eventually stopped snivelling, he looked up, and he was shocked to see she had been crying too. She tried to disguise it of course but her eyes were red and teary, and he knew he must have unintentionally said something to deeply disturb her. She slowly got up and left the room and came back just a few moments later with a photograph. She pointed to a little girl dressed in a pretty blue dress, and she said she was her daughter Crystal. Behind her stood his very own Chloe with a man who looked identical to the man he had seen walk into the house earlier who she said was her ex-husband Grant and he knew their time together was over.

He collected his coat and left without saying another word. He had already said more than enough for one day, and he knew he'd opened a huge can of worms as a result. He had no idea what would happen next and he no longer really cared because Amberina had unexpectedly given him an answer to his question. The only thing he knew for certain was that none of their lives would ever be the same again, and for that, he was grateful.

AND FINALLY

It was several weeks later when Mel received a rather blunt text message from Chloe to say he must never try contacting her again. He assumed that meant he was dumped and as tempting as it was to tell her that it was he that had actually dumped her Cain advised him not to respond.

After his disastrous but somewhat enlightening therapy session with Amberina, he went into panic mode and drove straight round to see Cain for advice. Cain's initial concern was for Amberina, so he ended up jumping into Cain's car with him, and the two of them drove straight back there. When they first arrived, Amberina appeared confused, but Cain sat her down, and between the three of them they managed to piece everything together. Amberina was distraught and uncertain whether to tell Grant, but the decision was made for her because Grant brought Crystal back early from the party and found the three of them huddled together. Amberina made some basic introductions, and it wasn't long before Grant realised that this was the very same Cain that Tom spoke so fondly about. He had no idea of course who Mel was and wrongly assumed he was probably Amberina's boyfriend and Mel hung his head in shame when the truth finally came out. To be fair to him, he took the news better than anyone expected, but Cain said he was probably in shock and the extent of the emotional damage wouldn't be apparent until later on when he'd had enough time for it all to sink in. As he walked away he looked like a man carrying the weight of the world on his shoulders and Mel was mortified for the damage he had caused to this good man. Crystal had gone upstairs to play but she must have been earwigging because moments after Grant left she ran sobbing in to the room and threw herself at Amberina demanding to know why her daddy had gone without saying goodbye to her and Cain, who wasn't keen on hysterical children, took that as the cue for them to leave. Before they left he gave Amberina a hug and told her he would be in touch very soon, and she nodded appreciatively. Right now, it was a sorry situation, but he had the feeling something good would eventually come of it providing he was patient with her and luckily for him he had all the time in the world.

Chloe felt both horrified and humiliated when Grant found out what had been going on from the wretched Amberina of all people and she couldn't believe how Mel could have been stupid enough to drop her in it like that. When she didn't hear from him, she assumed he was probably lying low licking his wounds somewhere, but she didn't care where he was because she didn't need a man who needed therapy to manage something as simple as a relationship.

Grant, on the other hand, felt numb. There was a time when he thought he loved Chloe, but now he wasn't sure if he was just in love with the idea of being in love or whether any of it had ever been real. He was still at the marital home because Chloe had literally begged him to stay all the time blaming Mel for the affair by claiming he took unfair advantage of an emotionally challenged hormonal woman. He knew that wasn't entirely true, and he knew that nothing would ever change because Chloe was incapable of taking responsibility for her own actions. He had given her numerous opportunities to fess up in the vain hope that she might eventually admit to her part in the whole sordid affair, but she was adamant that Mel had done all the running and after that, he lost what little respect he had left for his wife.

It was getting late, and Phoebe was clearly over-tired, but he struggled to settle her down for the night in Chloe's absence, and he was annoyed because she still wasn't home from work. She had only recently gone back following her maternity leave, so he knew she probably still had a lot of catching up to do but she wasn't even answering her phone, and he was pretty certain she was already back to her old tricks. She had, of course, made all sorts of promises to stop him from leaving her, and she promised him faithfully that she would make more of an effort with Crystal and rather foolishly he decided to give her the benefit of the doubt. Much like all her other promises it hadn't lasted long, and it didn't take an expert to work out why on the last Friday of every month she didn't come home.

He stood pacing at the window trying in vain to settle his increasingly fretful youngest daughter. Crystal was close by and although she too was tired she refused to go to bed until Phoebe went to bed and he didn't have enough energy left to argue with her about it. Finally, a pair of headlights shone into the road, and a familiar red car pulled on to the drive, and he heaved a sigh of relief. He had something important to tell her, and he needed to say it before he lost his nerve.

He glanced at the big pile of bags stacked up at the

bottom of the stairs and briefly wondered what kind of things life would throw at him next. Crystal had been worried when she first saw the bags but when he told her they were going on an adventure together, she struggled to contain her excitement. She had asked somewhat anxiously if Phoebe was coming on the adventure to and he had answered her as truthfully as he could. He was confident that once things settled down, Phoebe would be able to join them on adventures at least every other weekend but probably not this time because Chloe was going to want her to stay around to keep her company. She then asked if Chloe would be coming, and when he shook his head, the little girl smiled, and he knew without a doubt, he had made the right decision.

Chloe wouldn't be coming this time or any other time for that matter because they were going to stay with Maria's sister Thelma. He and Thelma had grown surprisingly close since Phoebe's birthday party, and in recent weeks she had become much more to him than just a shoulder to cry on. He hadn't planned to fall in love with her, but somehow it had happened, and he had to admit he hadn't put up much of a struggle. When she finally confessed that she had secretly been in love with him for years, he didn't know whether to laugh or cry, and Tom couldn't resist remarking that he never had been much good at spotting the obvious. For once Tom was right, but Grant had the last laugh when he told him that one day, they might become brothers in law. Obviously, that day was a long way off, but unlike Chloe, Thelma was a woman with integrity, and he knew without a doubt that his search for love was finally over.

But he kept his fingers crossed just in case.......

CPSIA information can be obtained
at www.ICGtesting.com
Printed in the USA
BVHW030844140220
572397BV00001B/105